Pair-a-Dimes

Pair-a-Dimes

Tom Tynan

To order additional copies of this book, contact:
Xlibris
1-888-795-4274
www.Xlibris.com
Orders@Xlibris.com
726088

To Donald E. Tynan who showed me how to work...and how to keep going...no matter what happens.

Thanks Dad

In Memory of:

Shirley Jean Tynan   1933-1978
Beloved Mother

Sheryl Ann Tynan   1962-2010
Beloved Sister

PROLOGUE

Pain shot up through his face and chest. Cold. Alone. Afraid. Agonized. In despair. His digestive system relieved, he stood up, chilled, his groin throbbing. The kidney stent was supposed to prevent the blockage of two large acidic stones. He shuddered. Urinating felt like he was expelling one-inch finishing nails, leaving behind crimson toilet water. It was two or three o' clock in the morning and the room felt as dark as the inside of a sarcophagus. The only sound was his labored breathing. His lungs burned.

He hobbled two short steps and gazed into the light, then down the dark hallway and into his past, shattered like a crystal goblet smashed by a bullet. Should he change? Could he change? He still had hope. Hope he would survive this gut-wrenching ordeal. Hope is the thing we all hang onto when reality gives us the shaft. Piercing blue eyes bored into him, clinical and cool, like a scientist studying a rat in a maze, a screwdriver gripped in the man's hand like a knife.

"I cannot have you walking around here knowing my plans. Now I told you I would pay you one millions dollars; if you do not want to help, that is alright. Ah, I will have you, your wife and your little boy killed. Do we have a deal?"

CHAPTER 1

Horrified and delirious, the Russian executive slid in and out of consciousness. He sensed he was close to death. Neurons misfiring across synaptic gaps generated bright flashes of light, creating bedlam in his brain. Compounding his confusion, he could not understand how the Burmese python had slithered up and wrapped itself, coil upon coil, around his frame, causing him to writhe in blistering pain and his heart to race. In a moment of vague lucidity, he whimpered softly, "Sonya, I'm sorry. I love you."

Fedor's eyes were so raw that each time he blinked his eyelids chafed the veins in his eyes, until the capillaries felt like little creeks of sand. His torso was bound tightly to a bar chair bolted to the floor, both arms pinioned by nylon cords, an intravenous line in his right hand, allowing copious amounts of a saline solution to infiltrate his bloodstream. Each time his delirium surged, his head would sag, and rivulets of saliva would stream down his chin. Before his head slumped again, his nose was wracked with an amalgam of pungent urine and a sweet, lavish fragrance. It must be her. The she-viper must be near. He saw the silhouette of a large man, and heard the footsteps of another approaching. His mind pleaded: Send the money, send the money, before his white-stubbled chin settled onto his chest.

"Is he dead?" Iouri asked in Russian as he entered the room. "No, I don't think so," Nikki replied, with his maniacal grin and demonic eyes. "I was just having fun with my toy." He compressed the plunger on the hypodermic syringe in his hand and clear fluid arced through the air. He grabbed the victim's wrist, searching for a pulse. Iouri was annoyed. "We do not have time for your antics," he snapped. "He is in arrhythmia," Nikki barked back at him.

Fedor's misadventure began two weeks ago when he stopped at an eatery in Thousand Oaks, California. Stanley's was usually flushed with beautiful women, and the local clientele knew the wizened, silver-haired businessman was harmless, titillating his libido with fantasies of sexual liaisons, while innocently flirting with patrons. Although arduously faithful to his wife, the CEO of Radio International shivered when he thought how hurt his lovely Sonya would be if she knew about his occasional lustful escapades.

He noticed a luscious blonde with sensual blue eyes at the bar, sandwiched between two men, like a diamond between two lumps of coal. She winked at him as she walked outside. Removing her cell phone from her Louis Vuitton handbag, she punched in a number.

"Is he there?" the voice asked.

"Da," Alejandra said, ended the call, then strutted back inside. Fedor watched, mesmerized, as she returned to her place at the bar.

"She is something," he murmured to himself, then reached out to prevent her stumbling.

"Are you alright?" he asked, as his eyes met hers. Her crystal blue eyes were so clear he saw a reflection of himself. "Be careful," said his inner voice; but he was too blinded to hear. He was smitten. She felt nothing.

"Yes, I'm fine, just turned my ankle." She seemed flustered as she massaged her boot. Her smile sparkled, her scent intoxicating, so rich and supple he could almost taste it.

"Hi, my name is Nadia," she purred.

Trying to come up with something debonair, he fantasized a James Bond moment, wanted to say, "Andreev, Fedor Andreev;" but, maintaining a modicum of chivalry, he extended his manicured hand and replied, "My name is Fedor Andreev."

"Leaving so soon?" she asked demurely.

"Well, I guess I could stay for one more."

"Marie, I'll have a water with a slice of lemon," he said to a passing server.

"I'll have the same. I've already had two drinks and that's my limit."

"So Nadia, what do you do?"

Alejandra told him she was a performer trying to break into acting or modeling in Hollywood. There was an aura of innocent vulnerability about her.

. After fighting with himself for a moment, he remembered that he was married and had two children, and he too had immigrated to the United States. "I love my wife," he recited silently three times, lost in her seductive eyes. She realized she would have to change her strategy.

"Nadia, I saw you leave to answer your phone, and when you returned you looked upset, is everything alright?" Alejandra knew just what to say:

"It was my mother calling from Armenia; she is very concerned about me. She thinks I should give up my dreams of becoming a star and return home. I'm confused and don't know what to do. What do you think?"

"It's a treacherous and deceitful business you're trying to break into," he replied, with an avuncular tone. "I know. I'm the CEO of a major communications company and I meet Hollywood types all the time."

She knew that already. She knew that not only was he the CEO of Radio International and a Russian recreant, he was also on the board of directors at the U.S. Title Company in Los Angeles. She knew everything about him.

"Without the proper agent, you'll grow old fast and never get the necessary breaks. But I could make a few calls and set up a meeting for you if you would like?"

"Really?" she said, as her cheeks blushed. "I would be glad to." He reached to the inside of his suit jacket and produced a card. Handing it to her, he said, "Call me in a few days; it will give me the chance to rouse the right contacts, and introduce you to the people you've been pursuing."

"I can't thank you enough," she said, but wondered, why he used the word, pursuing. What does he know?

"It will be my pleasure," Fedor said, bidding her goodbye. She flashed her patented smile, put the card in her purse and strolled toward the door.

"Looks like the lady's ankle healed up quite nicely," Fedor said to himself, a little suspicious as he watched her amble steadily out of Stanley's.

He entered his Mercedes Benz, drove toward the mall, remembering it was less than a month until Christmas. Fedor delighted in assisting disenfranchised, budding starlets, helping the little birds fly on their own. He would make her his new pet project. Yes, Nadia will do just fine.

Three days later, his assistant announced on the intercom, "Sir, Nadia on line five."

"Nadia, I'm glad you called."

"I wasn't sure if I should. I feel like I'm imposing," she said, trying to exude the innocence she lost so many years ago.

"Don't knock on a teapot!"

"What on earth does that mean?" she asked.

"It's a Yiddish expression that means 'nonsense', so, no, you're not imposing." They chatted for a few minutes, Fedor allowing her to become more comfortable.

"Would you like to meet those people I was referring to the other day?"

"Right now!?"

"No." In about ten days. That should give you enough time to prepare. Should I pick you up?"

"Uh, I don't want to put you out. I mean, you're doing so much for me already," she said, piercing him with her hook like a carp.

"It's no bother. Where do you live?"

"Glendale."

Alejandra gave him an address, an area Fedor was familiar with and knew housed a plentiful cross-section of Russian and Lebanese inhabitants. "If you have any problems finding me, don't be too proud to call me." She solicited this, knowing he would never find the address.

"Okay, Nadia. I'll pick you up at 4:00."

"Goodbye," she replied, no longer sounding seductive. Perhaps it was her way of warning him; or perhaps it was to alleviate the guilt she would feel later, but she definitely drifted out of character for a moment and revealed herself to him. Defiance seemed to have briefly overtaken her. She was mad that it was interfering with her assignment.

Two weekends passed. Fedor left his office at 3:00 p.m. Navigating the streets of Glendale, he was baffled. That's strange. There is no such address. He drove to the Galleria, dialed his cell phone. Alejandra answered on the first ring.

"Hello?"

"Nadia, I can't find your home."

"Where are you?".

"In Glendale, at the address you gave me." His voice had changed.

"Fedor, I'm so sorry. I was so nervous when I spoke to you that I gave you my old address. I used to live in Glendale."

"That's fine; I'm at the Galleria in the parking structure near the Nordstrom entrance."

"Stay right there, I know exactly where it is," she said rapidly, not allowing him to reply, then snapped her phone closed.

Fedor was uneasy, thinking her voice sounded strange. Fifteen minutes later, Alejandra maneuvered her BMW next to his Mercedes. He had assumed it was her when he flashed his headlights. They simultaneously lowered their tinted windows. "Fedor, I'm so sorry for the mix-up," she said, back in character.

He was distracted by her scintillating, Castilian red lips. "That's fine. We need to get going, though, and I don't want to be late. Just follow me."

"Oh, shoot," she said, looking at her purse.

"What's wrong?"

"I forgot my insulin; I left in such a hurry."

"You're a diabetic? I would never have known. I mean, you're in such good shape."

"Can you just follow me?"

"Sure, but we'll have to go fast."

She rattled off an address. Wondering if James Bond ever had days like these Fedor followed her as she raced ahead of him. I told her I don't want to be late, but I don't want a ticket either, he thought. It was a mistake to tell her to go fast.

Alejandra laughed girlishly as she drove. Who's pursuing who? she wondered. When they arrived at the Woodland Hills residence, Alejandra sped into the three car garage, spotting Fedor in her rearview mirror as he pulled around front. She scrambled inside, met by an anxious Iouri.

"Is that him?"

"Yes. So far so good," she said, slowing her pace to greet Fedor at the front door.

"Good job," he said coolly. She is so professional, but difficult to figure out sometimes. And she sure has been acting strange lately; more defiant, and moodier than usual. Actresses! He strolled upstairs. "We must be quiet," he warned the others. "He is here."

Fedor was standing next to his car, tapping his foot, when Alejandra opened the door.

"Come on in, Fedor," she said, cheerfully. "By the way, I love your suit."

"Thank you," he answered as he went inside.

"Would you like something, a drink, or a snack?" she asked.

"Something light to drink would be fine," he said, scanning his watch. She returned quickly with his refreshment. Almost too quickly. Fedor was fixated on her rosy complexion, inhaled her heavenly fragrance. He was distracted, too, by her succulent lips. Those lips. I've never seen anything like them. Alright, Fedor, behave yourself, you're a happily married man, he thought, as impure carnal thoughts polluted his mind.

"Allow me to freshen up," she cooed. The house was as silent as a monastery. He watched as she went upstairs. Unaware of her anxiety, he glanced at the immaculate furnishings. Nadia was definitely not falling through America's cracks as he first suspected. How does a struggling actress afford such a place; she must be renting.

Pacing through the living room looking at a Raphael, he was captivated by the artwork. These must be replicas, because if they were authentic, they would be worth one or two million dollars. This place looks like it was decorated by Marie Antoinette, he said to himself. A line of worry crept between his eyebrows. Most homes have a unique odor; this place has no scent at all. Very clinical. Very sterile. Very strange.

Fedor ignored all the warning signs. He was having trouble concentrating. Impatiently, he glared at his watch. I do not like to be kept waiting. A singular painting caught his eye. It was a painting of Napoleon Sacking Moscow.

Why would a Russian have such a painting? He was perplexed, but exalted when suddenly he saw a thousand green-tinged images of the painting, as if he was looking through the compound eyes of a fly. A fog engulfed his mind, his vision blurred completely and the parlor spun around 360 degrees. Something was wrong. Very wrong.

His knees buckled and he slumped like a slow-leaking balloon. The crystal glass shattered against the stone hearth. He slammed into the armrest of a chaise lounge, then bounced off the hardwood floor before coming to rest in a very unnatural position.

Alejandra peeked through the partially-open, bathroom door. "He's down," she whispered, opening the door. The three men jogged past her. She hurried down the stairs, knelt down avoiding the glass splinters and, with a moist washcloth, dabbed at the blood running down his forehead. At least he isn't as hurt as our last victim, she thought. She whispered in his ear, "An ambulance is on the way," hoping the others would not hear her. She was decompressing, racing downhill toward despair. She feared her internal turmoil was an embryonic conscience, or perhaps the original one resurfacing. Ethics had been losing the war for many years, but it looked like the tide was turning.

Iouri began snapping orders like a Medieval lord. This was his fiefdom and they were his serfs; they all knew the drill. "Petrov, check his phone and check out his latest calls. Alejandra, clean up this glass, please," he said, remembering she loathed being

commanded by him. Petrov retrieved Fedor's phone, scrolled
through the numbers.

"Last call at 3:29; must have been his call to Alejandra. Another
at 12:15, probably when he was at lunch." Petrov switched off the
phone, removed its back and disconnected the circuitry to the
GPS transponder. He waved a wand-like detector over the body,
searching for radio signals.

"He's clear," he announced.

"Nikki, shoot him!"

"Gladly," Nikki said. He tore open Fedor's sleeve, wrapped
a tourniquet around his forearm and clicked open a small case
containing twelve ampoules in foam pockets. Gripping the syringe,
he drew up 6 ccs of sodium pentothal and 9 ccs of scopolamine
and injected Fedor.

"Now you can tell us all your Jew-boy secrets!" he wisecracked.

"Get him upstairs," Iouri snapped; he found Nikki's vulgarities
tiresome.

"Alejandra, did he tell you where you were going?"

"Yes, to a restaurant on the first floor of an office building
close to Paramount Studios, across the way from the Forest Lawn
Cemetery."

"Good. You two know what to do," Iouri said referring to
Alejandra and Petrov. Donning a paper jumpsuit that he shimmied
on over his clothes, and a pair of booties, Petrov signaled Alejandra.
"Let's go," he said.

Petrov drove the Mercedes to the meeting place, followed by
Alejandra. If the car were to be dusted for identification, it would
appear to be a missing person's case, with no evidence of foul play.
No kidnapping alert would be broadcast; just another executive
enduring a mid-life crisis, fleeing for greener pastures. Or blonder
pastures.

CHAPTER 2

"That will be two millions dollars," repeated the synthesized voice, a distorted, inhuman voice. In the back room, euphemistically dubbed, Command Central, utilizing a voice scrambler attached to a stolen cell phone, Iouri waited for a response. "You've heard Fedor's voice."

Silence. The person at the other end was absorbing the gravity of the situation; he was becoming nauseated. Iouri was a brilliant negotiator and knew that he who talks most, often loses. The ominous silence was leverage, leverage that usually triggered the other party to concede. But if not, the gifted dealmaker always has an ace or two. "I know about your personal numbered account in Zurich," Iouri said. Although disguised, Iouri's speech had an Ivy League pedigree.

More silence. "I also know you're planning to use the money in Switzerland to abandon your wife and run off with your mistress."

Reluctantly, Fedor's partner murmured, "All right." He leaned over and vomited into the brass wastepaper basket next to his desk.

Iouri gave him his account information for the Kasikorn Bank in Thailand. When the money was received, Iouri would divert the deposit piecemeal to twelve other global banks; leaving only a small balance, making the funds virtually untraceable.

"We are monitoring your every move. You cannot go to the bathroom without us knowing about it," Iouri warned him. "Now get going. The clock is ticking." Iouri terminated the call. Fedor's partner threw down the phone; it seemed soiled after the conversation. He needed a shower.

Petrov offered a congratulatory high-five, but Iouri interrupted him, saying, "Wait until the money arrives."

With today's masquerade over, Alejandra removed her wig, allowing her shimmering brunette hair to cascade down. Her own hair was so shiny, it seemed to have a light of its own. "Who says blondes have more fun?" she murmured. She brushed her hair, smiling, enjoying a little narcissism, when suddenly she froze. An apparition loomed in the mirror, causing her hands to tremble. Her heart raced. She became lightheaded. She *thought* she recognized the vision.

Is this an epiphany? An oracle? Maybe some kind of omen? If it was, she did not wish to figure it out, nor dwell on its meaning.

She felt like a character in a Stephen King book. Her mind scrambled. She twisted away from the mirror. She bent over, rested her clammy palms on her knees. Her heart calmed. She had been suffering frequent anxiety attacks lately. She remained there, hunched over, panting, begrudgingly accepting what had happened.

Her conscience asked the familiar questions: Who are you? What are you? What have you become? Then, the killer - he does not love you. Alejandra knew she had to atone, make a transformation; and she would begin now.

The other back room, a sanctum where they kept their victims captive, was sparely furnished and dimly lit. Nicolai Stolov was lounging on the couch, dressed to kill, in his customary black shirt and slacks feeling smug that, inexplicably, he had concocted the correct antidote that saved Fedor's life. With his arms and feet bound, Fedor reminded Nikki of a religious leader he could not recall. He was humming "Sympathy for the Devil," recalling that when he was five, he used to chop the heads off roaches and watch them scurry about. At twelve, he used to rip the heads off rabbits and see how far he could throw them. His record was 69 meters. Great childhood memories. Those were the days.

He heard Alejandra's heels click into the room. She was appalled at Fedor's condition - stripped down to his boxers, strapped to an anchored bar chair, flanked by a chrome-plated stand holding the saline solution in an IV bag. It was a pitiful sight of torment. There was rheum accumulating in his eyes, around which were dark sooty circles that looked like the result of a twelve-round beating from a heavyweight boxer. He was perspiring profusely, and the room reeked of sweat. Despair hung about him like a shroud. He was feverish and kept pining for his wife. He had never endured such pain. "I can't move my legs," he bleated.

Alejandra was guilt-ridden, and so repulsed by Nikki that she almost gagged in disgust. None of this used to bother her; but for some reason, this did. Fedor was unique. He did not have sex with her, and he truly wanted to help her. She did not think he deserved to die. "Is all this really necessary?"

Nikki glared at her. No response. She was not expecting one. Normally she would be attracted to men like Nikki, with his tall frame, broad shoulders, and classic European looks. But he thought he was a genius and could do no wrong.

"I swear to God, your heart must have been installed by a machine," she exclaimed. Iouri swaggered in, carrying a racing helmet.

"You two behaving yourselves?" he asked, aware of their growing animosity, then turned his attention to his prisoner.

"Fedor, I have a reward for you for giving us valuable information The truth serum worked perfectly. I just wish I could have seen the look on your partner's face when I told him about his Zurich account and girlfriend. I am going to put this helmet on, and we will pipe in some classical music to make your stay more comfortable," he said, then slid the helmet on. He could have given a rat's ass how Fedor felt; he just did not want him listening to any of their conversations.

Iouri was a cocksure individual with the arrogance and obstinate confidence of an aristocrat. His peacock strut made every room his spotlight; the world became his stage and his alone. A handsome, athletic Russian, he was chiseled from head to toe. His body was his temple, He worshipped money. He revered money. He would do anything for money. Anything.

Unlike Nikki, Iouri did not enjoy the savagery. It was merely a perfunctory necessity, a means to an end. He believed mankind was headed toward changes of apocalyptic proportions, with secret societies such as the Illuminati and Skull and Bones becoming more prevalent. The New World Order was evolving into a plausible reality. The U.S. government and its imperialist ways was a growing tumor, engulfing everything in its path. Iouri was out to get his, and the rest of the world could go to Hell, wherever that was—he was an atheist. He loved money, and held the United States in the highest contempt. They murdered his father.

Ivanovich Malakov was a Special Agent of the KGB Executive Committee, also known as Department V, in charge of political murders, sabotage, and kidnapping. He had become a top-ranking agent rising up the rungs of the KGB by inventing Maskirovka. In order to fool electronic surveillance, they built phony airfields, hangars, and bridges, entire tank divisions out of tinplate and plywood. Because of his father's status they became members of Vlast, the privileged ones. With a small taste of the good life, Iouri had his nose pressed against the shop window of high society and wanted in at all costs.

Ivanovich had brought Iouri to visit the cloak and dagger Promised Land, the world of shadows and suspicions at Number 2 Dzerzhinsky—KGB Headquarters. They were chauffeured in a black, armor-plated ZIL limousine with green-tinted, bullet proof windows. Iouri toured the notorious Lubyanka prison, where he heard the bloodcurdling screams of tortured prisoners.

"Iouri," his father said, "Do you know why they refer to my business as wet work? Because there is so much blood involved." This made an indelible mark on the young Iouri, who began to think of murder as a regular part of business and life, almost as mundane and inconsequential as taking out the garbage. He did not go out of his way to murder just anyone; he did not get his kicks out of it, like Nikki; but if it had to be done to achieve a goal, so be it. Morality was a quaint concept. Something to be debated in a Liberal Arts class. There were two sides to his personality: one displayed his charm, the other, his fangs.

Acting on an erroneous tip, the CIA had eliminated his father for reasons Iouri said, "I will take to my grave. No one would believe me, anyways." He was jailed at the age of twenty-one as a political prisoner, a convenient charge Russia levied against its own when it could not conjure up a legitimate reason, and unceremoniously released when the Berlin Wall fell in 1989. He promptly fled for the U.S. to seek his fortune and exact revenge, taking with him only his childhood friend, Petrov Kuvayev.

The classical music in Fedor's helmet was soporific, giving him solace for the first time in several hours

"Listen, Mr. Pharmaceutical," Iouri said, pointing at Nikki, "No more games with your drugs; he is not your lab rat. We need him alive until I receive the money. I will be in Command Central if anyone needs me."

As Iouri left the room, Nikki stared at the slumped helmet. Evil thoughts slid into his mind, like dark, oily serpents. Normally, he had visions of blood that blossomed into reality; but this time, he had different ideas. He would be the spider, Fedor, the fly. He wanted to watch him twist and turn. He wanted to drink his panic in long slow gulps. I could attach a virtual reality game to that helmet and drive him insane. Or maybe trigger a heart attack. Or better, I could make him so crazy, he would beg to kill himself. Now wouldn't that be the perfect crime? He beamed his Cheshire-cat smile.

"Whatever you're thinking can't be right, or normal, Alejandra said. But whatever it is, cut it out! You heard Iouri. Fedor's not your guinea pig!" She was determined to ensure that Fedor stayed alive.

Entering Command Central, Iouri said to Petrov, "You were right. He does get carried away. I have to watch him or he will create a one-man Holocaust in there. Anything?" Iouri inquired, seeing Petrov fixated on his computer screen.

"Not yet." Petrov was the opposite of Iouri; it was an oddity that they were such good friends. They were like chalk and cheese. But they did possess something significant in common: loyalty. Iouri demanded unwavering loyalty and Petrov reciprocated willingly. Petrov was slender, with little muscle definition, but surprisingly fit for not exercising. He had engaging, emerald eyes, long, straight hair worn in a pony tail, a Belgrade beard and chevron mustache and a pleasant, almost shy, demeanor. For him, his body was simply a shell, a carrier for the brain. The cerebellum was where it's at. Knowledge was the ultimate power.

Petrov truly believed this. Proud of his brain power, he was the master of the technical quirks of any computer. With his long, slender fingers he would slide along the keyboard with the skill and speed of a concert pianist. Unlike Iouri, he did not crave the limelight; he hovered below the radar. Well respected in the hacker underground, he was integral to Iouri's extortion plans. Iouri often raved, "If it was ever entered into a computer anywhere in the world, Petrov will find it!"

Intellect was critical to Iouri, but he was also the epitome of Russian chutzpah: brains, brawn, self-confidence and charm. Iouri used his Svengali-like charisma, laser-tuned mind, superior negotiating skills and sophisticated criminal instincts to advance his cause at every turn. He could finesse anyone because people were drawn to his Pied-Piper charm.

Iouri and Petrov landed in New York City in late 1989. They settled in Brighton Beach, formerly a stronghold of Italian families. It was transmuting into the East Coast Russian Mafia— Red Mafiya—headquarters, where the Russians came not to live the American Dream, but to steal it.

The Italians with their Omerta culture—silence or death— had never seen anything like the Russians. John Gotti claimed, "We'll kill you, but the Russians are crazy. They'll kill your whole family." Startled New York cops claimed, "They'll shoot you just to see if their gun works, then use your balls as cocktail olives."

Iouri was reunited with another crony, Nicolai Stolov. The two shared similar experiences. Both attended Russian Military School, achieved high marks, and became crack marksmen. It was in New York that Iouri rose to the top of the Russian Mob, which was metaphorically called the "warm spot", after Evsei Argon, Brighton Beach's first don. In time, the Russians and Italians learned they had more in common than heavy chains and open collars. They pooled their resources and fought the Feds.

Because of Operation Daisy—the name of the Fed pursuit against the Red Mafiya, Iouri formulated his strategy for wealth and revenge; but he would implement it on the West Coast. He wanted to get out before their faces ended up on Red Notices - wanted posters distributed by Interpol.

When the three migrated West, Iouri discovered that many Russian-Jewish socialites were defectors. As a front, he established two businesses: an international rebar firm and a commercial fish tank installation company. Iouri used his architectural education and concrete construction experience to advance Rebar International, seeking out his father's contacts; it actually earned a handsome profit.

Exotic Tropic World, in which he partnered with Nikki Stolov, was not financially lucrative, but served two purposes: It opened the doors of many fine restaurants; Iouri loved fine wine. Also numerous Exotic Tropic World's clients were the traitors Iouri was pursuing, defecting Russians who abandoned their families for capitalism in the Evil United States. While Petrov manipulated the computer to scout the financial assets of their targets, Iouri would survey them personally.

His plans were emerging nicely, but he needed someone else, someone to complete the team. She sidled in one day while he was entertaining clients at Morton's in Beverly Hills. Actually he had seen her before, but, that day, she raised a blip on his sinister radar. An minor actress in Russia, she aspired to the Big Time in Hollywood.

Iouri was unconcerned with her ambitions. His only focus was that she was gorgeous, more specifically, other men would find her alluring. Iouri fancied more petite women, but he knew men would succumb to her voluptuous figure and natural sensuality.

They dated for awhile. She fell in love with Iouri's style and cosmopolitan ways, and he loved the sex. It took some time before Iouri could trust her, but when he divulged his agenda; he was surprised at her immediate acceptance.

"I think I'll like this cloak and dagger stuff; besides the modeling and acting is going slow and I need the money. Everyone's telling me that, at twenty-eight, I've waited too long to get started. No one cares that I had any success back home," were her only comments.

Little did she know she had signed a contract with the Devil. So, with the inclusion of the seductress, the cadre was complete. Alejandra became the fourth member of Iouri's Fifth Column.

Since Iouri's lucky number was five, the number of years he spent at Kronstadt prison, he decided he would extort his victims in series of fives, taking a short hiatus between groups. Iouri had one final Herculean ambition, much grander than their current exploits, with which he was becoming bored; but he was not ready to disclose the details yet. He merely entitled it, The Big Score.

CHAPTER 3

Petrov had married a curvaceous blonde with classic beauty, named Anna, a veritable Marilyn Monroe, and they had a daughter named Katerina. Iouri never understood what she saw in Petrov. He just knew they were passionate for each other. Iouri never understood it, assumed it must be love, whatever that was. He never loved anyone or anything but money, until recently.

Halfway through a fashion show he attended, reluctantly, for an important client, after several glasses of Chateau Margaux, boredom had set in and Iouri became enamored of one of the models. One particular model. Who is that? I have to meet her. He almost jumped up on the runway; but Iouri never lost control. His temper flared from time to time, but he never relinquished total control. The only criticism he had ever received from women was that he was as spontaneous as a rock.

Her name was Marina Minsky, a petite waif with strawberry-blonde hair. Confident, ladylike and sensuous, she aroused feelings he had never had for any woman. Gazing at her lithe figure, he admired her delicate shoulders, slender neck, compelling blue eyes and rosebud lips. He had to have her. He would not be denied.

Amazed at his sudden, inexplicable obsession, he finessed his way backstage with a verbal onslaught of requests for a date. Marina realized that he would not take no for an answer, admired his persistence; so she relented. Later, they were married.

Soon, she was expecting, living in their London townhome. Marina was not fond of America, and preferred to be closer to her mother in Moscow. Since Iouri shuttled frequently to Europe; the arrangement sufficed for them.

Iouri's sudden nuptials hurt Alejandra, but she was the ultimate professional and knew her place. She also knew that the only probable release from this cabal was death.

Nikki had no permanent love interest nor would he ever have one. He was addicted to sex, and his favorite woman was always the next one. He suffered from anaclisis, a neurotic attachment to women who were reminiscent of his mother, who died when he was five. Alejandra despised Nikki because he was a bona fide psychotic. His favorite sport was a blood sport: Murder. He loved to kill. Anything. Anyone.

The three men thrived on the adrenaline rushes during a job, but not Alejandra; she needed her sleep. She dawdled into the sanctum, yawning, wiping her eyes after a brief nap; gasping when saw the black helmet bobbing and wobbling violently. Fedor had ripped his right arm free, and the intravenous line was whipping around like a clothesline in a tornado. He looked like he would be swallowed up in a maelstrom if he were torn loose from the chair. Nikki was gone.

"Nikki...NIKKI!" she screeched, then heard him sprint up the marble staircase. "Look!" was all she could say in horror. Nikki grabbed Fedor's head and yanked the helmet off, ignoring the frantic, muffled groaning from inside. How the hell did he rip off those nylon straps? Nikki wondered.

Fedor's face was pale purple as he gasped for oxygen. The helmet had sealed itself around his neck, jaw, and chin, the moisture from his perspiration creating a vacuum. After breathing for a few minutes, his color lightened to a prison pallid. Any evidence that he used to sport a tan had vanished. His white whiskers and silver hair gave the image of a senile porcupine. Muttering indecipherable words that sounded like sandpaper on concrete, he motioned Alejandra over.

"Pl--please. Help." She put her ear close to his face. "Please, may I use the bathroom. And have something to eat?" His pitiful request touched something deep inside Alejandra. She spun around and glared at Nikki.

"Unstrap him and take him to the bathroom. Find him another pair of shorts; and I will get him something to eat, Besides, you heartless animal, this room smells like a fucking latrine."

Nikki was crazy, but not stupid. This was one skirmish he was going to lose, so he kept his mouth shut. He snipped the ties from Fedor's left arm and unwound the rope from around his abdomen. When he removed the intravenous line, Alejandra hissed, "Be careful when you reinsert that, I don't want him to get phlebitis."

"Why do you care so much about this guy?"

"None of your damn business!" Nikki had never seen her so animated.

They talk about me like I'm not even here, Fedor thought. Almost as if I'm dead. It was his first coherent thought since Alejandra sedated him. When he opened his mouth, he could smell his own fetid breath. Still, without total feeling in his legs, Nikki had to haul him, dragging him down the hallway.

Iouri was in Command Central, attending to regular business, growing impatient." Seventeen hours. Where is the money?"

"Nothing yet," Petrov responded.

Petrov held Iouri in high esteem, even tried to emulate him, but he was very unpleasant to be around when he was agitated.

Iouri grabbed the cell phone and voice scrambler.

"Where is the money!?" he growled.

"The money was wired four hours ago. Honest."

"If I do not see the money in one hour, you will have one pissed-off wife on your hands and you will never see Fedor again."

Intense silence filled the room. Petrov made no comment. He never missed a good chance to shut up.

Iouri wanted the money, but he was wary of being traced and tracked down, so he maintained a 48-hour window. If the ransom was not received in that time frame; the mission was canceled and they regrouped for their next prey. Iouri decided to call London to diffuse his anger.

"Hi honey…ah, I miss you too," he said in obligatory fashion.

Passing Command Central with Fedor's food, Alejandra cringed. Her heart pinged with jealousy. She thought Iouri's greeting was sincere. Clenching her fists and punching a throw pillow in the sanctum, she had tried to alleviate her frustration. But it was no good. Her silent tirade ended with a tear rolling down her cheek. I've got to get out. But how? she wondered. I don't know, but I just have to.

With the sixteen hour time difference, it was morning in London. Marina was due next month; it would be her second, but Iouri's first. Her son, Stephan, was eleven years old, the consequence of a one night stand that she refused to abort, although Iouri wished she had. Iouri tolerated him out of respect, because she truly loved her son and was a good mother. She had fallen prey to the notorious casting couch of a fashion show producer, who promised her success. He had had his fun and moved on. It shattered her naïveté; a bleak and brazen initiation into the modeling world.

"It'll be alright," Marina said weakly, "I'm at the end of my last trimester and everything aches. Walking is difficult. I'm just ready to get it over with."

"You do whatever the doctors say, and try to stay off your feet. Ah, your mother is there to help, no?"

"Yes."

"I will be there as soon as I finish some business. I will call you before I leave. Goodbye." Though Iouri rarely said I love you, his infatuation with Marina long passed, and typically emotionally unyielding; he was genuinely concerned about her health. She found that endearing, but he was primarily concerned that she was carrying his first child.

As Fedor was re-strapped to the bar stool, he was awash with emotions. He was exhausted and unkempt. The shorts Nikki had given him were little solace after festering in his own feces and urine for eighteen hours. His raw skin was biting with eczema and roseola. The air was caustic.

He thought his mind was playing tricks on him. What are those? Are they rats? His face was contorted with fear, and his eyelids fluttered when he strained, unsuccessfully, to raise his legs. Distressed beyond belief, he thought his dementia was recurring. Or was it permanent? Did Nikki's concoction of drugs make him deranged? After awhile, he realized his phobia was images cast on the walls by shadows from Nikki's loafers as he traipsed about the room.

Monumental terror swept over him. He prayed for this nightmare to end. Although never a religious man, he began praying: "Yahweh, please help me. I don't want to die."

Fedor knew he was grasping at straws; but he was desperate and willing to try anything. Ironically, he could hear his father say, "Fedor, some only find The Way when they're in trouble, when they're dying, or when they're in prison. And it's usually too late. Don't be one of those men."

Outside, people were living another day - working, eating, flirting, vacationing. Life continued, in spite of what was happening to him. It seemed, somehow, it should have come to a halt. The clocks should have been stopped, the mirrors covered, the doorbells silenced and the voices reduced to a respectful hushed volume. But life was not that way. He felt he had been born a loser and had gone down from there.

He was perspiring profusely, the sweat stinging his eyes. Alejandra wiped his face with a cool, damp kitchen cloth. She noticed his nose was bleeding and an annoying fly was circling his head like a buzzard.

"Here, I hope this makes you feel better," she whispered, avoiding eye contact, fighting the guilt within her. She was trying not to get too emotionally involved, but it was probably too late for that. With armor that protected her from guilt, she had made herself internally cold for too long. But her new, emerging conscience was melting the ice in her blood, and deep down in her bone marrow.

When Fedor felt the wet rag, and smelled her perfume, they were like hammers breaking the chains of his anxiety.

Ooh, that feels good, he thought, as he strained to smile. He had heard Iouri's diatribe on the phone with his partner and suspected that the funds were imminent. Alejandra's unexpected act of kindness gave him hope that maybe they would let him live. Maybe.

CHAPTER 4

Fountain Valley is a serene, old-money city nestled among the palms between Newport Beach and Huntington Beach in the heart of Orange County, tempered by the Pacific Ocean breeze. Newcomers to the area, the Taylors were entertaining guests at an estate Tom Taylor had purchased there three years ago. It was his pride and joy.

"Come on in, man," Tom said warmly, waving him inside.

"My God, Tom. Couldn't you get anything bigger?

"Cost me my last nickel and then some. But it was so worth it. Listen, I've been giving tours as people arrive. Want me to show you around?"

"Sure, why not. It should only take us a month." Tom laughed. Pat hummed along with the trio performing in the sunken reception area, admired the pearl-white piano Tom had purchased in honor of John Lennon. It was reminiscent of the one included as a poster in the *Imagine* album cover.

Tom Taylor was a classic rock aficionado and trivia fanatic. Also an accomplished guitarist. He had not performed professionally in ten years. Disillusioned with the music business in general, he had grown especially tired of the drug scene and become obsessed solely with making money. He would not be happy unless he died a gazillionaire.

Pat was a tall, lanky man with wavy salt-and-pepper hair, a matching mustache under a pronounced nose. He had quiet gray eyes, a sincere smile and small lines on his face that added character. Ten years Tom's senior, Pat McGinnis was a twenty-five year veteran of the Southern California car business. He marveled at Tom's rapid rise in the finance sector of the business. Tom was the Finance Director, his expertise—Special Finance; Pat was the

Sales Manager or "Desk Man". They worked at West End Chrysler/ Plymouth/Dodge, referred to as a six-pack because it contained all Chrysler's franchises. Passing the laundry room, they stopped at Tom's den, which resembled a prestigious law office and was filled with Tom's diplomas and certifications of achievements in the car business. Notable were his Masters' Degrees in Accounting and Finance and a Top-Ten sales award. In his best year, Tom had sold three times the national average in California, a monumental achievement, since California was the largest auto market in the U.S. All the usual clichés pertained to Tom: He could sell ice to an Eskimo, fur coats to Hawaiians, and reading lamps to the blind. He was a tough act to follow and this catapulted him into the finance division where he had achieved unparalleled success.

Tom loved to show off, a trait bordering on pretention, sometimes downright arrogance. Although garrulous and friendly, he was maniacally ambitious and focused. He could be manipulative, even a little Machiavellian. Shrewd and clever, his imperious body language overtook a room when he entered. He was one of those people who seemed bigger by the sheer force of his personality.

Tall, blond, with unmistakably determined blue eyes, he was a little overweight, but the weight was distributed proportionately throughout his body. He was in better shape than he thought, but not as good as he should have been. With the sun glaring in his face; he could just make out the silhouette of his lovely wife gliding toward him.

"Hi, Pat, thank you for coming. You look very GQ tonight," she said with her radiant smile, Cupid's bow lips and white Chiclets teeth. Tom is mesmerized by her. Pat grinned broadly in appreciation. For all his shortcomings, Tom was passionately committed to Sabrina. The love he had for her was deep and flowed like a great river. She truly was the woman he had been looking for all his life.

Sabrina was a welcome relief to Tom's second bachelorhood. She was trying to break him of his Puritan, workaholic ways, coaxing him to relax and enjoy life, something he had never been able to do. They were married in mid-April in a quaint ceremony on the Eastern edge of Maui, an area unmolested by civilization. Flown to their destination by helicopter, the small entourage included the pilot, a female minister, and a musician. It was a very touching event captured on videotape for their future children.

Tom loved to recount how they had met. He was the Finance Director at Inland Chrysler, and she was a new saleswoman. One day he was in the conference room making entries in the Finance Log. Sabrina came bouncing in and stood directly across the table from him, frustrated by his inattentiveness. When he looked up he was exactly eye level with her bosom, and she was showcasing a low-cut sundress. "You new?" he managed to get out. "Name's Sabrina," she replied, sweetly. "Well, welcome to the Garden of Eden." Not the best of lines, dork.

She smiled. "Does that make you Adam or the snake?"

Quit wit. I like that, he said to himself. "Can I ask you something?"

"Ask away."

"Are those, uh, real?"

"All factory equipment. No aftermarket parts here."

They both laughed. She scampered away with pinkish cheeks. Later that day, Tom asked her out

Rob and Joy Cafferty arrived.

"Well, here comes my favorite person," Tom muttered under his breath. "I wonder if he'll have that surgically removed?"

"What's that, dear?" Sabrina asked.

"The ring through his nose that she attaches his leash to."

"Now, be nice," she said, preparing to greet her guests.

Joy Cafferty sauntered in like she was walking on a yacht, backlit by the sun's rays.

"Hi Joy," Sabrina said as they embraced.

Joy looked like an exquisite bird about to take flight in her impeccable, snug white jumpsuit, revealing a significant amount of cleavage. Her avaricious eyes were like those of a tigress on the prowl. But Tom was not fooled by her beauty.

"Hi Tom," she said with a flirty, cannabis grin. Tom nodded and greeted her husband, Rob, who was one deferential step behind his mistress.

Joy was Sabrina's best friend. They had worked as saleswomen in San Diego, and moved to Orange County a few years before Tom met Sabrina. They shared an apartment until Joy moved in with Rob, leaving Sabrina with a lease she could not afford. Why Sabrina continually tolerated Joy's disloyalty irritated Tom. Rob, a tall handsome Texan, recently left the car business and joined a commercial leasing firm in order to spend more time with their three-year-old son, Austin. Affable, attentive, and a good father, Rob kept his testicles in Joy's purse. She was his trophy wife, and ordered him around mercilessly.

Tom's face was deadpan as Sabrina escorted them to the bartender in the back yard. He glanced at Rob and felt sorry for him. He took a long look at Sabrina. They shared something most people did not - they understood each other very well; and they shared an awareness that happiness is fragile and good fortune a gift. Life was good.

CHAPTER 5

"Hey Iouri," Petrov said casually. "It's a hit. Look. Two million dollars." Petrov pointed at the computer screen. Iouri moved closer to see for himself. He reveled with exhilaration the moment the money arrived. He never tired of that feeling. His steel-blue eyes shone with sheer delight.

"I will take that high-five now," he said, excitedly. Petrov obliged him. Quickly and with surgical precision, Iouri went to work transferring the funds. Every movement was controlled, his mind ahead of every move. I will leave fifty-thousand at Kasikorn Bank in Thailand, a hundred-and-fifty-thousand in the Bank of Cyprus, three-hundred-thousand in the Bank of Zurich. Gotta love those Swiss; they know how to keep a secret. He continued dispersing the two million to locations that made tracing them impossible. Besides actually receiving the money, this was the part he loved the most.

"All the money is transferred," he announced, still savoring the euphoria. This was more intoxicating than fine wine. "I would give the two-millions dollars to anyone that could unravel what I just did." Petrov nodded. Iouri was a master at diverting assets.

Nikki looked at his watch. The money must be here by now; maybe they're ready for me. He gazed longingly at Fedor's sagging head. He had asked to keep the helmet off to avoid possible asphyxiation like the last time. Nikki had sedated him and he was still sleeping.

Alejandra disdained the gleeful glare in his eyes. It sickened her. How can anyone so handsome be so repulsive? Every time she looked at him, she saw an eyeless skull and the rotting corpse he would eventually become. She suspected it was time. Time to save

Fedor. Time to save her soul. She knew she was just postponing the inevitable.

I really have to get out. I like the money, but there's been too much death - at least twenty bodies that I can remember. She was disgusted with herself for being part of Iouri's Death Odyssey for so long. She had to save Fedor's life. She knew it was the right thing to do. But how? There's got to be a way. Think. Then, like a flash, she had an idea. She knew it was a long shot, but one she had to try.. "Hang in there, Fedor," she mumbled, looking at his slumped, tortured body. She walked out and saw Petrov in the hallway. Good timing.

"Petrov?" she whispered, "Come with me. I need to talk to you." He followed her downstairs to the spot near the fireplace where Fedor had fallen.

"Listen, I need your help. I know you're the most sensible and humane of the three and Iouri listens to you."

"Sometimes." He was very composed, wondering where this was going.

"Fedor is a gentle old man who didn't hurt anyone; he surely doesn't deserve to die. Yes, he walked out on his wife and two kids back home; but that was a whole lifetime ago. He's made good and done well. I mean, he's a self-made man who's created a lot of jobs for people. And, my God, he has a wife and two children here. There's been too many killings. We've got our money. Please help. Please. Talk to Iouri, Okay? Please?" Her eyes were a beseeching blue, a pleading blue, a fierce and almost painful blue. Petrov nodded while she spoke, but his face displayed indifference. "I'll do what I can." He truly was ambivalent about the situation.

"Thank you," she said softly, looking for signs of hope

"I'll go talk to him now."

Petrov shuffled into Command Central and swung his chair towards Iouri. "Iouri," he began, "Alejandra pulled me aside to ask me to ask you to spare that guy's life. For some reason, she's really begging for mercy for this, um...Fedor." Iouri listened impassively. Although amoral, he did not enjoy the killings. Purely on Nikki's insistence, he agreed that the murders minimized their exposure.

Even though he realized Nikki had his own demented agenda, the eliminations still served their purpose. After a brief discussion, Iouri made his decision.

Fedor was groggy, his mind cloudy and his mouth was so dry he felt like he was eating dust. He could tell by Alejandra's face that there was tension among the others. Impending doom seemed to coagulate in the air. Alejandra's mood was gloomy and forbidding. She keeps staring at me. His sad eyes were no longer hazel; they looked ash-gray and begged to know: Did they get the money? As if reading his mind, Alejandra said soberly, "They got the money."

A colossal calm came over him, as if he saw land after being lost as sea. They've got their money and now I can go home. He reflected on his life and had a renewed fervor to improve himself. He would spend more time with his wife and children. He truly loved his wife. Reminiscing about their honeymoon on Paradise Island, Fedor relaxed for the first time in almost two days. He was genuinely happy for the first time in many years.

Iouri strolled in without looking at Fedor and whispered something in Nikki's ear. He left as quickly as he entered, smiling at Alejandra on the way out. Afterward, Nikki's face was downcast.

She still looks okay, actually happier than before, Fedor thought, sensing the worst was over. He felt someone approach from behind. Good, they'll cut me loose and I'll get the hell out of here.

"Ready to go, old man?" Nikki asked. Alejandra's eyes widened. Nikki bumped the chair from behind. She turned away. Everything went black.

Why did they put the helmet on me? Maybe they don't want me to see the house when they take me out. Wait a minute. I've seen the house! Momentary confusion shifted to frightful clarity, as he felt the rope tighten around his throat. Fear washed through him. Gasping for air, he thrashed about ferociously. His involuntary attempt to release himself only exacerbated his oxygen shortage. Feeling his lungs inflamed with pain, and his heart palpitating erratically, his oxygen-deprived brain clung to the last strands of consciousness. He kept mewling: "I don't want to die, I don't..."

There was no white light. Only sparks of pain in his eyes. Then darkness. Pure and true. Final.

Nikki stood smiling over him with vicious delight. This was almost as enjoyable as sex. Almost. No, actually, it was more enjoyable than sex. Nikki let go of the rope and used his hands around Fedor's neck as a final measure. He had an orgasmic reaction when he thought he felt Fedor's flesh splitting under his knuckles.

"Why didn't you just drug him? Alejandra cried out, sobbing. "Or use that strychnine stuff you used on the others?" She was horror-stricken, pressed against the wall, as if an invisible force held her there.

"What fun would that be?" Nikki shot at her. Fedor stopped convulsing. Nikki grabbed his wrist. Amazingly, there was still a faint pulse. "This guy's like a cockroach after a nuclear war. He just won't die." Picking up a medieval-looking device that resembled a pair of hedge clippers with curved blades, he said, "I always come prepared for times like these." His maniacal laughter reverberated in Alejandra's mind.

Nikki actually asked Iouri for a guillotine after reading in, "Soldier of Fortune", an article which stated that when the spinal cord was severed, there were still electrical pulses in the brain. Nikki wanted to order a victim to keep blinking as he released the blade to see if the eyes would keep moving once the head hit the floor. Iouri told him he was crazy but relayed an equally sick story he learned from his father. The KGB used to poison their targets with thallium that had been subjected to intense atomic radiation that caused the metal to disintegrate into little particles. The radioactive particles, when ingested in food, or drink would permeate the system with deadly radiation and the subject would melt from the inside out in the most gruesome death imaginable. Nikki thought it would be fun to watch.

Placing the invention around Fedor's neck, he pulled the rip cord on the handle, which collapsed the blades with a loud, crisp, satisfying snap, slicing through Fedor's neck—muscle, bone, and cartilage—like a tomato. With one tug of his right hand, Nikki had transformed the sanctum into an abattoir, a place of butchery.

A single jet of blood spouted from Fedor's mouth, spraying the inside of his helmet. The carotid artery spurted blood, splattering his chest, back and arms, dripping eerily off his elbows onto the tarp Nikki had put there. Fedor's head hung on his chest by only a few spinal cord strands.

"Who are you, Hannibal Lecter!?" Alejandra bellowed, a screech so guttural she startled herself. Somehow, she found the strength to break her paralysis and to move her legs. Everything was so surreal, she felt like she was moving in slow motion. Disgusted and nauseated, a lightning bolt of unrelenting hatred and rage exploded in a blood-freezing scream. "You sick bastard!"

She ran past Iouri and Petrov, down the marble staircase, slamming the huge front door as she left. The house shook as if it had been struck by a wrecking ball. She felt like she had just crossed through the doorway from Hell.

"I can't believe I tolerated this for so long. I'm such a fool," she sobbed as stumbled down the driveway to her car a block away. "I tried, Fedor. I really did."

"Where does she think she going?" Nikki snapped. We need to cut her loose or one of these days she'll turn us in."

Iouri said. "She will be back to pick up her money. We have more important things to be concerned about now," he said, pointing at Fedor's dead body. "What did I tell you about using that thing indoors?" he yelled.

"I used a tarp," Nikki said innocently.

"It does not matter. I told you about the Luminal the Feds have."

"What's that?" Petrov asked.

"It is a chemical solution that can detect blood up to twenty-years-old on any surface. All they have to do is pass an ultraviolet light over it and the blood stains show up."

"Really?" Petrov said his eyes riveted to the blood-soaked tarp.

"But I also know if the surface is scrubbed clean with another compound such as alcohol, they cannot lift an adequate DNA sample, so be careful moving him and scrub this room when you get back. Petrov, go get the surfboard."

Petrov left and returned with the surfboard. They wrapped their victim's lifeless body in a plastic liner and secured him to the surfboard with long nylon cords. Iouri returned with two little pills "Remember to take these."

Petrov took his and handed the second one to Nikki. They carried the surfboard with their mummified victim out to the garage, unaffected by its jerking from posthumous spasms, loaded it into the back of Petrov's black Nissan pickup. It was equipped with a camper shell, a baroque canoe strapped to the roof, and camping supplies. They appeared to be three men out for a weekend of carousing and male bonding.

Petrov and Nikki drove the Nissan pickup, Iouri following in his Cadillac. Storm clouds crept in, befitting the mood, as they exited from Interstate 5 to Highway 99. The journey usually spanned six to seven hours. Halfway up Highway 99, a California Highway Patrolman moved in between Petrov and Iouri, unsettling everyone. Iouri called and instructed them to remain calm. The officer hit his red lights. His siren wailed. The headlights seemed like two huge suns in the darkness.

Petrov pulled over. Iouri continued on, pulling over on the shoulder when he was out of sight. I hope Alejandra did not do anything, he thought, recalling her thunderous exit from the house. She would not be that stupid; she likes the money too much. He could not fathom anyone thinking anything was more important than money.

"License and registration please." Officer Cannon, a fifteen-year veteran, took the documents Petrov handed him. "I'll be right back."

Petrov and Nikki glanced at each other. Nikki gripped his tubular steel weapon, watching as Officer Cannon meandered back towards his patrol car, stopping to look at the full moon. Iouri was listening intently on his cell phone. The trio had rehearsed a plan for this possibility. Petrov had his cell phone set on hands-free. His left foot was prepared to strike the button on the floor if necessary.

A few years ago, Chino, a Mexican gangbanger known for mayhem in Los Angeles, came into Petrov's shop. Petrov was a computer programmer by day and installed stereos part-time.

"Hey dog, check dis," Chino boasted, plopping down in the driver's seat. "Now stand back, my man, I don' wanna break no legs. Tis is the latest shit from South Africa."

Petrov heard a click, and a five-foot steel rod rocketed out from the undercarriage near the door frame with enough force to maim or kill anyone nearby.

"Primo, huh? Let any fool try n' jack tis mathafucka."

Petrov reported back to Iouri. They immediately installed it on all three of their vehicles.

Petrov had his window open. Iouri listened for the sounds of another vehicle. Maybe Officer Cannon had called for backup. Silence. Apprehension.

Then Iouri heard the officer's door slam and his footsteps as he approached the pickup. If Bob Cannon said, "Please step out of the truck," or "May I have a look in the back," he would be instantly incapacitated. If necessary Nikki would jump out and deploy his weapon, which contained a glass ampoule filled with prussic acid.

The officer returned to the car. "Where you guys headed?"

"Yosemite. Camping," Petrov said flatly.

"Kinda late, no?"

"We got a late start. Is there a problem, officer?"

With his flashlight, the officer made a cursory inspection of the camper shell, crouched down to take a look at Petrov's passenger. "Can I...?" the officer started to say. Petrov began to depress his left foot when the officer interrupted himself, remembering he was supposed to meet a colleague.

"Nah, that's okay."

Petrov stopped himself just in time and glared at the officer. You don't know how close you came to never walking again. Or death. Nodding to the officer, Petrov pulled away, flashing his headlights to alert Iouri.

Exiting Highway 99 to the 41, they entered Yosemite National Park, following the serpentine roads. Iouri liked to think he had a reason for everything he did, and usually that was true. He had chosen Lake Eleanor because he was an avid Beatles fan and Eleanor Rigby was one of his favorite songs

Petrov parked the pickup close to the lake, removed the canoe and set it in the water. The lake was a huge sheet of dark glass. Nikki removed the surfboard with its mummified surfer, attached fifty-pound weights to Fedor's abdomen and feet, wading in knee-high cold water. Fedor's head was barely attached. Nikki wrapped duct tape around the neck and from shoulder to shoulder over the head.

Petrov threw Nikki a rope, which he tied to the surfboard. Petrov paddled out to the middle of the lake as Nikki guided the surfboard

Iouri stood sentry on the shore, surveying the perimeter through a night vision device. He also had a battery-powered, directional rifle microphone that could detect voices up to a quarter-mile away. And he used a heat analyzer, a sleek-looking, futuristic ray gun with a two-inch diameter lens instead of a gun barrel. Moving the viewfinder across the landscape, the device would show heat from living sources larger than fifty pounds.

Petrov quit rowing and they floated to a stop. Nikki flipped the board over, brandished his prized switchblade and sliced the cords, remembering the glee he felt when his Medieval contraption had produced so much bloodletting.

"Merry Christmas, Fedor," he gurgled, doing his Boris Karloff Impression, as their two-million dollar deposit sank into the black water.

CHAPTER 6

"What do mean you can't fund the loan?" Tom growled into the phone, whipping through a file on his desk.

"They have a job gap," the voice said. "You know I need five years of continuous employment for a Level 1 loan."

"How long was the job gap?"

"Four months."

"Big deal. At least she had a job for four years; that's more than most of our customers."

"But it's a Level 1 approval."

Tom grew impatient when lenders chose their guidelines over common sense. "So, what are you going to do?"

"I'll have to send it back."

"Why!?" Tom shouted. "Your damn rep is in here every other day begging for more business, and this is the third one this month you want to kick! Look, just charge me an extra boarding fee and fund the goddamn thing. She needs this vehicle to get to her job."

"Okay, I'll see if my supervisor will sign off on it."

"Make it happen, or that's the last loan from West End Chrysler you'll see as long as I'm Finance Director."

"Yes sir," she said.

"Tom, lines one and two," Jan announced in her sing-song voice. Jan was a cute, genial Latina, working her way through college. Recently, she had read a Wall Street Journal article that listed the ten most stressful jobs, and finance director in a major metropolitan auto dealership was number eight. She constantly cautioned Tom to take it easy. "I don't know how," was his standard response.

"Do you know who's on what line?"

"Glenn's on line one, and I don't know who's on two."

"Put two on hold. I'll take Glenn. Hey Glenn, what's up?"

"That paystub should be on the fax any minute."

Glenn was the best clandestine proof of income guy in town, but prone to mistakes. They still joked about the paystub he once designed that displayed a pay period ending February 30th; and the bank still funded the loan.

"Great, then I can fund that loan."

"Can you drop me some money today?"

"Sure, I'll send Bonnie to the bank after lunch."

"Do you need a deposit slip?"

"No, I have plenty. Listen, gotta go."

"Later, dude." And Glenn was gone.

"Lakeisha Johnson, line two," Jan said.

"Where the hell's Sabrina. I need her to take these stupid calls. It's Monday and I gotta be on the phone talking to the banks."

"She's on her way."

"Hi, Lakeisha," Tom said into the phone, drumming his fingers on his desk. "What's doing?"

"Tom," she whined, "the bank called and left a message. Do you know what they want?"

"Let me look." Tom grimaced, feeling a pain in his abdomen, as he reached behind for her file. "Have you done your customer interview?"

"What's that?"

"After the bank has verified your job and residence, they do a brief Interview, and then you get a statement or payment booklet in the mail."

"They's not gonna' take my car, is they?"

"They will if you don't call them."

"Shouldn't they do all that before you gives me the car?"

"No, that's not the way it's done." Tom knew any further explanation was useless. "Please, after you talk to them, call Sabrina and let her know you've done your interview."

"Okay." Lakeisha seemed satisfied.

"You okay?" Jan asked, peeking in. Tom nodded. "Always."

"Here's this morning's messages; and Jack wants to see you asap," she added, handing him a stack of memos. Tom pulled the fax from the machine, inspected it for accuracy. It was a Glenn creation. Another paystub.

The 1990's ushered in a new division in the car business called, appropriately, Special Finance. It quickly became Tom's area of expertise. It was the fastest growing, most lucrative segment of the auto industry, brought on by record bankruptcies, extreme personal credit balances defaulting and an escalating divorce rate, all of which created a rapidly growing population of credit bandits, who still needed to purchase vehicles. Consequently, a raft of high interest lenders sprang up, along with geysers of easy cash from the investment pools throughout the country. They supported their loans by selling them to the various markets on Wall Street.

Good credit was considered to be a FICO score of 700 or higher. In some liberal financial circles, a score of 650 was still considered good credit, but a FICO score of 700 was the universally accepted benchmark.

Special Finance dealt primarily with FICO scores between 450 and 550, considered the dregs of the credit world. The lower the score the tougher it was to find a lender and the greater the funding difficulty; but Tom enjoyed the challenge and was one of the best.

Within this new market, there was a subculture outside the Special Finance Lender's guidelines that, with a little ingenuity, could be made to fit in the box. A lot of people, many of them minorities, had irregular incomes or unreported cash; and some had illegal incomes. Many also had a Mafia Don's regard for the Tax Code. Paradoxically, very often, their incomes were far more substantial than that of the normal customers.

Tom was brilliant, and also streetwise. He invented a clandestine circle of thirteen employers that confirmed customers' employment, for a fee, of course; and from the unlikely referral of a bank representative, Tom met Glenn, a master of fraud and forgery, who was available 24/7. Very often, bad-credit clientele who generally were irresponsible, had lost their drivers' licenses along the way, an essential stipulation in funding an auto loan. Tom was not judgmental of his customers' plights; he considered himself an apologist for deviation. He understood that shit happens.

Tom's crew would cut and paste licenses from other, valid driver's licenses, expired driver's licenses and identification cards. As a last resort, he had an inside woman at the DMV, whom he used sparingly, due to the high cost and extreme risk involved.

The money charged to customers was called "program money"; it was cash only, and, after expenses, Tom would pocket the excess. The system was very lucrative for him, his team and his owner, Jack Steinwell.

"Yeah, Jack?" Tom said, hustling into his owner's stark, utilitarian office. Jack was a distinguished-looking, Jewish man in his early seventies, shrewd and confident. His long, white hair, mustache and beard made him resemble a caricature of a Quaker.

"I've got flooring this week," Jack groaned.

"How short are we?"

"$400,000.00."

"Not too bad."

"You've got two days," Jack said sternly.

"But I usually have a week."

"What can I do? Chrysler just called and said they would be here in two days, and I can't float them any checks."

Jack was known to be miserly, but he was generous with Tom because Tom was the best Finance Director he had known in his fifty years in the business. Savvy with numbers and a tough negotiator, Tom always rose to the challenge. Also, his system enhanced Jack's income statements by several million in the past three years. Tom was grateful for the remarkable income, but wished Jack would upgrade the facilities.

Back in his office, Tom figured that, at $20,000 per average loan, he had forty-eight hours to fund twenty loans. His record was sixty fundings in a week. These hurdles used to be challenging; now they were just hassles. Twelve years working up to one-hundred hours a week were beginning to take its toll. The once illustrious car business was fading fast.

Grabbing at his stack of messages and separating out the urgent ones; he picked up the phone. "Honkas!" Sabrina cooed, with a smile, poised in his doorway. Tom's tension dissipated immediately, as relief had arrived in the form of his gorgeous wife. She was like a fragrant candle illuminating the darkest night. Tom laughed and set down the phone.

"Honkas! "she said again, this time laughing. Every couple had its own private word or saying, and 'Honkas' was theirs. One time while Sabrina was getting dressed; Tom squeezed one of her luscious breasts; instinctively, she yelped: "Honkas, honkas," mimicking a circus clown's horn. Since then, "Honkas" had evolved to mean anything sexual, and the comical way she said it made them both laugh. Sabrina used it to lighten him up when life became too serious. "How're you doin' honey?"

"It's Monday." Tom groaned. "Please call Lakeisha Johnson and prep her for her customer interview." He handed Sabrina the file. "I have to stay on the phone; Jack needs $400,000 in the next two days."

"Yikes, well, you know I'm here to help. Tom truly loved his wife and did not know what he would do without her.

After what felt like a thousand phone calls, Sabrina shuffled into his office. The pep in her step was gone. "Can we go now?" she asked. A nine-hour day was more than enough for her.

"Yeah, let's get out of here. See you at home."

"Beat you there."

Tom cruised up his driveway, pressed the garage door opener. "That's odd," he remarked. Sabrina's car was missing. Maybe the cops finally got her. He checked his cell phone. No messages. He went inside, then heard the garage door open, drawing him back.

"How'd I beat you home, Mrs. Andretti?"

"I stopped at the drugstore."

"I thought you got your drugs from Joy."

"Funny," she said with a sly grin. Tom kissed her, followed her back inside. He loved to watch her hips sway in that fascinating way of hers; she was not only sexy, but very ladylike.

Sitting on the side of their bed after his workout, Tom was gathering the energy to take a shower. Sabrina scooted into the room, a glow on her face, holding something in her hand.

"Honey, remember how we said we wanted to have a child someday?"

"Yeah?" Tom said, suspiciously.

"What if that day was today. Look! It's pink!" she said, holding up a pregnancy test.

"So that's why you went to the store."

"Is that all you have to say?"

"Well, I'm kinda in shock, but I guess it's okay as long as it's a boy."

"That's up to you. You placed the order."

They sat silently, letting the news settle on them.

"Didn't you use...?"

"Honka-stuff? Of course. That's all you have to say? I thought you'd be more excited.

"I am. I am!"

"You always said you wanted a family. Have you changed your mind?"

"No, of course not."

Because her womanizing father divorced her mother after twenty-two years of marital discord, Sabrina was still disgusted with her father's behavior. Tom knew people got restless, strayed and broke each other's hearts, but thought that, in a perfect world, they should be like penguins and mate for life. Sabrina's overwhelming fear was infidelity and being replaced. For Tom, this was absurd; she was flat-out gorgeous, loving and loyal, and the perfect partner for him.

They kissed and stared deeply into each other's eyes, a look that meant everything to them. It was their special moment; they were going to have a baby. Then, he hugged her so close that, after a while, he could no longer feel the tender beating of her heart, because it had become one with his.

CHAPTER 7

"You son-of-a-bitch," screamed a livid Alejandra.

"Do not talk to me that way." Iouri snapped.

"You said five-percent, that's one hundred thousand dollars."

"Calm down," Iouri said. She was so furious she looked like she would pounce on him. "I said I would think about it, but it is still three-percent - sixty-thousand dollars. Don't tell me you cannot live on that."

"That's not the point. You promised!"

"I never promised," he said, with a pompous smirk.

Iouri did not part easily with money, no matter how much he had. She thought about slugging him with all her might, but that would be like walking into a bar full of Marines and spitting on the American flag. What she really wanted was him. And to do something else for a living. Was it love? Obsession? She did not know anymore. But her attraction to him was too dangerous for her in so many ways now. She was growing a conscience. She felt some of her had died along with Fedor. The notion that she could have done more to save him still plagued her.

"So did you have fun in London?"

"It is always nice to see Marina, and the baby is fine; thanks for asking."

"How is the whore?"

He grabbed her arm and held it behind her back, twisting her like a top. "Now, you've gone too far." he hissed, then released her. She turned around, looking at him with sad, contrite eyes.

"Alright, alright. I'm sorry. I shouldn't have said that."

She was staring at her white Nikes, feeling her eyes well. She was possessed by a strange mixture of energies: desire, fear, and disgust in equal measures. She saw something in him that was never there before. Or perhaps she had never noticed it - a bottomless pit of pure hatred ingrained in every atom of his being.

"That is right. Now take your fucking money and get out!" Iouri whispered, through his teeth, spots of saliva on his lips.

Sensing it was foolish to stay any longer—it was definitely over now—Alejandra fumbled for her prized designer purse. They exchanged stubborn parting looks like jilted lovers. Clutching the tightly packed one-hundred dollar filled package, she slammed the massive front door, creating a thunderclap echo throughout the house.

Alejandra's angry and animated exit caught Rafi Hassan's attention, as he struggled to carry out a garbage can not much shorter than he. Rafi had been suspicious of Iouri and his neighbor for four years. Iouri never spoke to him, and people came and went at odd hours. A brown-skinned Middle Eastern man with a cherubic face, Rafi talked to everyone and everyone liked talking to Rafi, so he was baffled when he tried to strike up a conversation with Iouri that he was so unreceptive. Rafi took his silence as rudeness. Rafi also noticed Iouri's consistent absence for weeks at a time. No wife. No kids. Only Russians. Strange.

CHAPTER 8

On Saturday, Sabrina went to her doctor's appointment. The home test results were confirmed: she was with child.

Although she enjoyed working with Tom, she hated working Saturdays, but knew her presence made his day more bearable. It took her a year to coax him into taking Sundays off. The lunatic slaved seven days a week most of his life.

"It's official," she announced, as she dashed into his office, a huge smile on her face. "I'm going to get fat."

"That's great, but did you have to say it like that?"

"C 'mere you big dummy and give me a kiss!"

His initial apprehension now was replaced by anticipation.

"How many have we sold today?" Sabrina asked.

"Two so far," Tom replied.

The clicking roll of the printer shattered the moment, dampening her euphoria. At work, Tom was all business. This made him great; but it could also make him unbearable. She respected this Tom, but she adored the Tom away from the office.

"Um, can we talk? I don't see anyone waiting to see you."

"Sure. What's up?" he asked, noticing the tentative expression in her eyes.

"Did you ever think of leaving?".

"Leaving what?" For a moment, Tom thought she meant her.

"The car business."

"Actually, I've been thinking about it a lot lately."

"Really?!"

She was genuinely surprised. Although they discussed most matters openly, this question had entered unchartered waters.

"I mean you're forty and you've never taken weekends off."

"I know, believe me, I know," he said wearily. "I'm forty on the outside, but my insides must be a hundred and forty. Besides, I've always said this is not the best business to raise a family around."

"I know you've said that before, but I thought you were just trying to appease me."

"No, I was serious."

Sabrina was relieved. This was going much better than anticipated. She was going to be a mother, and she might actually get Tom away from his insane hours.

"So when and what will you do?"

"I don't know but we'll definitely discuss and plan it soon."

"Okay. Let's try and get out of here early and celebrate."

"Done."

CHAPTER 9

It was close to Valentine's Day, and Iouri had just returned from a month in London, where, for the first time, he witnessed the miracle of birth. Marina and he named her Natalya. A profound and unforgettable experience. He was greeted by a disconcerted Alejandra. Like a dormant volcano, the pressure had been building for some time, and now burst into an exchange of insults and name-calling. Iouri had married Marina on a whim, which infuriated Alejandra; but he did not care. It was his world and they were lucky to be a part of it.

Following his interlude with Alejandra, he picked up his gold, French phone; he had been trying to reach Marina since before Alejandra arrived.

"Hello," Iouri said.

"Did you have to leave so soon after the baby was born?" Elena whined.

She was his mother-in-law and not fond of him, for no particular reason; he just did not warm up to her like a son-in-law should. But he fathered her a granddaughter, and her daughter seemed happy.

He was aware of this, but, being Iouri, could care less.. The only thing he loved as much as money now was his daughter.

"Let me speak to my wife," Iouri said, curtly, smiling when he heard Natalya in the background making baby sounds.

"Sure, I'll get her." She was not about to argue with him. Her respect for him bordered on fear, sprinkled with some distaste.

"Hi, Iouri."

"How is the baby?"

"She's doing fine. My mother's been a big help," Marina said. loud enough to make sure Elena heard her.

"How are you feeling?"

"Fine, just tired. Natalya won't be sleeping through the night for awhile.

When will you return to see her?"

"Probably in two or three months."

"That long? Iouri, she'll grow up without you."

"I told you, in a few years, I will not be working, and I will spend all my time with Natalya and you. And the next time I come back, we will go to Moscow and buy that apartment for your mother." That should shut her up for awhile.

"Thank you Iouri; that will make her very happy."

He hung up and browsed around his palatial Encino mansion. It screamed, "Look at me, I am Iouri and I am King." He was proud of procuring the property from a Saudi businessman who, inexplicably, fled the country and let the house slide into foreclosure. It was a scaled-down Taj Mahal, a place big enough to house the U.S. Congress. Architectural Digest recently had called to ask if Iouri would allow some photographs for an upcoming issue featuring LA area homes. His estate cast an impression of majesty. It exuded money, and money made the man.

Rafi Hassan was walking to the curb to place some outgoing letters in his mailbox, when he saw a familiar black Nissan pickup arrive. The driver had brown hair, a medium frame, and casual clothes. He had seen this man before.

Iouri's neighbor was involved in many civic organizations and its members disliked Iouri's continual shunning of their invitations to get involved. One of Rafi's cronies commented that Iouri "looks Russian Mafia to me." The whole neighborhood was worried about this mystery man. Knowledge spreads. Evil knowledge spreads faster.

CHAPTER 10

"Another Monday," Tom moaned, sipping his tea. It was 7:30 a.m.

In thirty minutes, the phones, people, and fax machine would create a cacophony lasting until late evening.

"Morning, Tom," Jan said, flashing her infectious smile. "Before you get started, Jack wants to see you."

"Jack's here before me? On a Monday?" This can't be good, he thought, as he headed to Jack's office.

"You wanted to see me?"

"Have a seat." Jack's face was as expressionless as a hard-boiled egg. "I'll get to the point. I'm selling," he said, flatly. Tom thought he was being fired, although the result might be the same.

"I don't know if the new owner will retain you, but I don't know why not. You have a great reputation."

"How long before the changeover?" Tom asked, his mind racing with the news. His face showed no emotion. He did not know how he felt.

"Thirty to sixty days; so clean everything up. Don't deliver anything you can't fund in ten days."

"That's my usual benchmark," Tom said defensively. He was not enjoying this conversation; Jack's voice had a threatening, ominous tone.

"Well, you get a little crazy out there sometimes. Just keep it conservative."

"Will do," Tom said, then returned to his office. Sabrina wanted me to get out of the business, maybe this is a sign. Like John Lennon said, "Life is what happens to you while you're busy making other plans."

46

Tom's thoughts were interrupted by a sudden apprehension: I hope some of the shit we've been doing in the past few years doesn't unravel after he sells. If it does, I'll probably be out of the business. He tried to transition back to things he could control. But the tracks in his mind still ran in an indecipherable tangle. He had to know what he was going to do next. He was always in control. Besides, Sabrina was pregnant. He thought a while longer. Then it came to him. I think I'll take Bob up on his offer. "Jan please hold calls for the next fifteen minutes."

He dialed the phone. "Bob? Tom Taylor. Still looking for a partner? My owner just informed me he's selling, and Sabrina wants me to get out of the business. And, well, in fact, you're the first to know, she's pregnant. Also, I'm tired of working 24/7 and want to be home on weekends. What do you think?"

"Congratulations, my man. I thought you'd forgotten about me. Actually your timing is spot on. I just came from the doctor's. My back's acting up again and my arthritis is getting worse. I've only got seven or eight years before I'm essentially crippled."

"Geez, I'm sorry to hear that."

"Thanks. Such is life."

Tom admired Bob's fortitude, given his medical situation; it was impossible to tell from his attitude that he was going to be incapacitated soon.

Bob Beem, an MIT graduate, computer genius, and Teutonic master salesman, was president of SJCC. Starting his firm sixteen years ago, they serviced three different markets: security and safety products to dealerships, security computer installations to medium-sized companies and Search-Tec, which was his bread and butter. Search-Tec was the premier aftermarket for GPS in Southern California, and Bob's franchise, Search-Tec's oldest, covered the whole southwestern United States. Three years ago, Bob's health worsened, he had lost control of his small sales force and was no longer able to pound the pavement like he used to.

Compounding the situation, his two sons, Jake and Jason, although competent computer technicians, were not picking up the sales slack as they had promised. But they were still drawing excessive salaries. Bob had too much pride to make any changes. Love can be a family entrepreneur's nemesis.

Bob was uncharacteristically crestfallen one day when he came to see Tom.

"What gives?"

"What do you mean?" Bob asked, self-consciously.

"You seem out of sorts. I can usually count on you for a healthy dose of optimism, a joke, or at least a smile."

"That obvious, huh?"

"A little."

"My rheumatoid arthritis is getting worse, sales are slipping, and my kids are getting rich. They're going to break me. I've worked too hard for too long not to be able to retire comfortably. What I really need is a partner, someone with your sales ability and drive. Would you be interested?"

Tom was caught off guard. "I've never thought about doing anything else, but I'll keep it in mind. You never know, I might make a change one day."

So that day had come. They decided to meet later that week to discuss the details. Reflecting about a new chapter in his life. Tom heard a commotion. "You are?" Jan chirped loudly as a office women clustered around the receptionist's desk.

"Well, congratulations," the business manager said.

"Tom, how come you didn't tell me Sabrina was pregnant?" Jan yelled.

He approached the gaggle of women, greeted Sabrina with a kiss.

"You'll be a good dad," the accounts payable clerk said.

"He already is," Sabrina announced.

"Thanks Sab. Come on in, I need to talk to you."

"Yes, your Lordship. Right away," she said and marched like a toy soldier toward his office, accompanied by laughter from the gallery.

"Jack's selling. He told me first thing this morning."

"Wo! When?"

"Thirty to sixty days; but he must have been planning this for awhile. Dealerships take six months to a year to change hands."

"So, what are you going to do?"

"Remember I told you about Bob Beem and SJCC? I just talked to him and he still needs a partner. I'll make a lot less money, but I'll be home on weekends and you can stay home with the baby."

"So you're really going to leave the business?"

"Yep, it's time to go; but we have to be careful the next few months."

At a breakfast meeting with Bob Beem, the new partners agreed on Tom's capital investment and ownership percentage. Bob was pleased with Tom's enthusiasm, but concerned with one of Tom's directives.

"You know your sons are taking advantage of you."

Bob said nothing. The personal implications hurt more than the financial drain.

"They're going to have to work for a lower salary plus commission and/or we'll find other computer techs."

"I know, I know, but please break it to them gently."

Tom thought it was interesting how Bob assumed that Tom would be the one to tell them, but gladly obliged.

"I will," Tom assured him.

He drove home, thinking of the most pleasant way to awaken Sabrina - the familiar silken rhythms of lovemaking at which they were so sensuously adept.

"I'm going to get me some," he could already hear her say.

"Honkas," he said to himself, as he opened the door. She was not in the bed.

It's still early, where could she be?

"Honey is that you?" Her voice was filled with horror.

Tom followed her voice around the fireplace. He was halted by a heartbreaking wall of dread and witnessed the saddest sight he had seen since they lowered his mother's casket into the ground. It burned across Tom's mind. Sabrina was crouched in pain on the commode.

"I think I'm miscarrying. I think I've lost the baby!" she cried out. Each word felt like a dagger in Tom's heart. He did not know what to say when he knelt in front of her. He reached for a damp wash cloth to soothe her blanched face. "I'm calling 911."

"No, I think I can get up," she whispered in anguish, "I think I can walk."

Shimmery lenses of tears had formed in her eyes and her voice quavered.

Fortunately the hospital was only two miles away.

"Your progesterone level is below 1000, I think you did miscarry, but we're not a hundred percent certain." The nurse was solemn and professional but comforting. "Stay off your feet for a few days, and you should be alright; but if there's any bleeding, come right back."

My body will heal soon, but my heart will take much longer, Sabrina thought when she looked at Tom. Grief was a vise that was squeezing her heart.

"Let's go," she said, with watery eyes.

The day, which felt as long as a bad week was spent in quiet solitude. No phone calls. No visitors. Tom did his best to console her. Their usually lively home was silent.

During the next couple of weeks, he went to work as usual while Sabrina convalesced at home. The challenge was gone. Replaced by drudgery compounded by Jack's growing stolidness. Tom was concerned that the idyllic lifestyle he had worked so hard to build was beginning to show cracks, or worse, disappearing.

Tom went home one day and Sabrina was smiling. Almost giddy. He had not seen her smile in three weeks.

"I went to the doctor because, well, I know this sounds weird, but I felt I was still pregnant. He told me my progesterone level had shot up over 1000. I'm still pregnant.

"Amazing. C 'mere, little mommy," Tom said, then they hugged and exchanged a warm, tender, lingering kiss.

"This is gonna be one tough kid. He refuses to give up."

"Or she."

Three weeks later, the sale went through. Twelve intense, extremely profitable years were gone. No fanfare. Nothing. A mere obligatory "Good luck," from Jack Steinwell, a man for whom Tom singlehandedly made millions a year for years. Tom felt his send-off was unacceptable. But one door was closing and another was opening. Nonetheless, he walked away at the pinnacle of his success. And income.

He wasted no time adjusting to his new partnership and making his presence known. SJCC was managed out of two locations: a small warehouse off Avenida Pico, and the rear of Bob's stately home in San Clemente, which he had converted into a sizable office. The house was perched on a hill overlooking the ocean. Tom broke the news to Bob's sons. They took it rather well, confirming Tom's suspicions that they knew they had been taking advantage of their father.

Wow, what a view, Tom thought, gazing out at the Pacific Ocean. Cris, the office manager, was Bob's wife in name only - a curiosity they had adjusted to, and something Tom grew to respect. Bob went through a womanizing phase and they separated, but Cris, a native Ukrainian, feared deportation if they divorced. So they stayed married and remained friends through the years.

Tom's salary was fifty-percent of what he was used to, but he knew he would improve sales, so that would change. SJCC had tremendous untapped potential. Also, he had ample savings, and he thoroughly enjoyed the weekends he now could spend with Sabrina.

"Bob, I'm going to Capistrano Ford, I have some friends there and I think they'll sign up for Search-Tec."

"Good move," Bob said.

"Then I'm going to the doctor's with Sabrina at 3:00. Call if you need me."

Tom grabbed a few Search-Tec brochures and hustled out the door, where he was confronted by two LA Sheriff's Deputies.

"You Thomas Taylor?" one of them asked.

"Yes," Tom said. "What's up?"

"We have a warrant for your arrest."

"For what?!"

CHAPTER 11

"Hey," Petrov greeted Iouri in his mild-mannered way.

"How are you?" Iouri said, opening the door, a package under his arm glad to see his childhood friend. Lifting the package to his nose, Iouri thought, I never tire of that smell. His eyes filled with delight as he handed the package to Petrov. He loved everything about money. Even trivial items. He actually knew it would take exactly 517,578 one-hundred dollar bills to cover an American football field.

"Here's your money."

"Is it all there?" Petrov.

"All two hundred thousand. Why, have you been talking to Alejandra?"

"No, why?"

"Not important."

Iouri doled out ten-percent each to Nikki and Petrov, covered all expenses of their projects, including vehicles and kept the rest. They knew their positions in the terror trio. Iouri was the dictator and they were his vassals. They were surprisingly reticent to question Iouri's hegemony and glad for what they received. All three were millionaires, Iouri a multi-millionaire. Nikki Stolov made a fortune for murdering, and Petrov was able to keep his gorgeous wife satisfied so she would not leave. For all his sophistication, Petrov was insecure about his marriage. He knew he was wealthy, but he was self-conscious about his pauper-like appearance, which plagued him with self-doubt. He felt he had won the Ultimate Wife lottery and did not want to lose his prize.

Nikki and Petrov also accepted that the only way out was either death or prison - not a major concern, because their loyalty to each other was formidable. Betrayal was unthinkable.

"Let's celebrate the baby," Petrov suggested. Iouri handed him a snifter of vodka and poured himself a flute of Dominus '87 he had brought back from Europe. Petrov started rambling about some of the particulars of the upcoming Big Score. "What are you going to do with your palace?"

"I will sell it."

"After all this work?"

"I will make money. Besides, I will be able to live anywhere. With money, you can do anything." Iouri was a capitalist first and a human being second. Or last.

"I once told you I didn't have your reverence for money," Petrov said. "But you were right; it is an acquired taste." Iouri's grin said, I told you so.

"Listen, I've seen some new Dell hardware and ultra-hi-tech software that will help me hack into the title company's system."

Iouri respected Petrov's computer skills, but when the conversation turned to gigabytes, firewalls, and random-access memory, Iouri tuned out. His thoughts strayed to Alejandra. She was more upset than when she left the Woodland Hills home. Not only upset, but seemingly hurt, worse than he had ever seen her. Almost possessed. He was curious if he would ever see her again, she had left in such a furious rage. Worse yet, she appeared unstable enough to turn on him. Shakespeare said, "Hell hath no fury like a woman scorned," he thought. No, no woman is crazy enough to betray me.

While Petrov called his wife; Iouri stretched out on the sofa, admiring his small palace with pride. Then, he noticed his neighbor.

Rafi Hassan was staring in, standing like a sentinel at the end of Iouri's driveway. "What the hell does he want? He is so goddamn nosy and he always tries to talk to me. Maybe I should put him on my endangered species list.

He stomped off to his bedroom and grabbed the head of his pet greyhound. Setting it on his desk, it yipped twice as he twisted its head and yanked it off. It came off with a weird popping sound. Then he removed his favorite toy. The dog was a gold-plated statue that doubled as the mansion's safe-deposit box. It was the closest thing to a pesky animal Iouri would ever allow in his castle.

He returned to the living room with his Remington 9mm with a pipe-type silencer, a five-inch, gleaming, black cylinder. He stood in front of his window like he was at the firing range and Rafi's forehead was the bullseye. The warm steel felt good in his hand. His blue eyes were hard and cold as icebergs. Unwavering. Soulless.

Petrov hung up. "Iouri, you're not serious."

The only sound was the ominous, metallic click of Iouri's hand releasing the safety. "You know I can open the window and hit him right between the eyes." Iouri could shoot the balls off a mouse at two-hundred yards. He glanced at the horrified Petrov.

"Do not worry. He cannot see me. The windows are tinted."

"I'm not worried about him seeing you; I'm worried about you shooting him."

"Nobody would hear anything."

"You know better than that. Ballistics would prove where the shot came from. Iouri, please. You'll ruin everything"

Iouri lowered the pistol. His face was hard. "I know, you are right," he conceded. "Even I, Iouri Malakov, am allowed a brief moment of irrationality," he said in his aristocratic tone. He paced around, still looking out of the window, his eyes now black as the plague. There is something about him I detest, he thought, the 9mm still dangling at his side. The feeling was mutual.

CHAPTER 12

"Fraud and Embezzlement," one of the deputies announced. The reflected glint of his silver badge hit Tom's eyes like a laser, momentarily blinding him.

"This is nuts," he answered; but he knew they did not think it was crazy. They were just doing their jobs and had heard it all before. It felt surreal, like a nightmare.

"Can I tell my partner what's going on?"

"Well, alright," the same officer said, "but hurry up."

Tom rushed inside. "Bob, would you call Capistrano Ford to reschedule, and call Sabrina and tell her I'm being arrested."

'You're kidding." Tom shook his head.

"Of course," Bob said, in shock. "Whatever you need."

They Mirandized and handcuffed Tom, his heart hammering so hard he thought it would shatter his ribs. His mind sprinted in circles in a whirlwind of emotions. Transported to the Whittier Police Station, it was there that his suspicions were solidified. Why would Jack do this? He tried to figure out as the phone rang on his one legally-allowed call. The police station smelled of loser sweat and Pine-Sol.

"Sabrina?"

"Honey, you alright?" She could hear in the background the chaotic chatter of the police station.

"Never better. Listen, bail is twenty-thousand, so I need two-thousand. Please call Rich; he'll know a bail bondsman." Rich Randall was the best repo man in the business. He and his colleagues ran in shady circles, so they knew all about jails and bail bondsmen.

Sabrina and Rich quickly bailed Tom out; frantically, he searched for an attorney. His first call was to Louis Gutierrez, an old roommate, and a top-notch finance manager.

"Lou, it's Tom, I need the number of that lawyer, the one who helped you get your sales license back."

"Hold on a sec; alright, here we go. John Hunt, 714-555-1000."

"Thanks a heap, man."

"What's going on?"

"I'll let you know as soon as I know."

Tom called Mr. Hunt's office and they set an appointment for 8:30 the next morning. Mr. Hunt said he would make a few calls to obtain some background information on the charges.

Hunt's office was in a large Victorian mansion, dignified in spite of its aging façade. As Tom crossed the threshold, a melodic chime rang out. The receptionist emerged from her office and shook his hand.

"Welcome, Mr. Taylor. Mr. Hunt will see you now." She led him into the anterior office, excused herself and closed the door.

"Tom, Randy Hunt."

"Pleased to meet you," Tom said, admiring the gold stitched "RJH" monogram on his shirt cuffs.

"I know a lot about you already. I was legal counsel for Long Beach Nissan when you were the Special Finance Manager there. I know you have a great reputation, but you are, let's say, ambitious and aggressive. I know you can be creative, and I suspect your creativity is what has gotten you in trouble."

"But Jack knew what I was doing; that's part of the reason he hired me," Tom replied defensively.

"And you trusted a car dealer to stand by you if he had problems? That was your first mistake." Tom sat there, silent, absorbing his statement. Randy Hunt had an aura of strength, calmness, and competency that was reassuring. Tom was enthralled by his stentorian voice; he felt like he was listening to a James Earl Jones impersonator.

"Hey, Darth Vader, forgot your mask?" Tom said a little surprised at his own impromptu outburst. Startled at first, Randy smiled when he realized it was a compliment. "I bet that voice is an asset in the courtroom."

"Doesn't hurt," Randy said, modestly. Unfortunately, Mr. Hunt's copper nose and pockmarked complexion marred an otherwise commanding presence.

Tom gave him a synopsis of his system - how he provided employment documents, driver's licenses and proof of income for countless customers.

"Actually, it's a brilliant system, albeit slightly illegal," Randy remarked. "The interesting thing is that it's a victimless crime, with the possible exception of the banks." He scanned a legal document.

"The charges are Fraud and Embezzlement. I can understand the fraud aspect, but how do they get the embezzlement charge?" Tom wanted to know. "Apparently, some of the customers found out that the dealership was sold, and in their infinite wisdom or stupidity, take your pick, decided to stop making payments. There's been a rash of repos. The first thing a bank looks for after a repo is fraud. Evidently they discovered some of the jobs and pay stubs were bogus because, get this, the customers confirmed." Tom's eyes rolled back. Fear swept through his brain, which felt like Jell-O. He was nauseous. He didn't know whether to scream or throw up or cry. What idiots, he thought.

Struggling to maintain his composure, he asked, "But why a criminal matter, and not civil, and where does the other charge come from?"

"Good questions. The money called "program" money is the essential problem. Any money that comes into the dealership must go through the dealer's coffers first. Any sidestepping, even if the dealer is complicit, is technically embezzlement. It's a criminal matter, because it's easier for Jack Steinwell to recoup the money he had to recourse to the banks."

"What do you mean?"

"If he can obtain a criminal conviction on you, he can go to the insurance company and they have to pay him; and they pay

relatively quickly. No fuss. No muss. If he were to sue you civilly;
it would be expensive, take years, and he probably wouldn't win."

"But he knew what we were doing; I made him an extra million
a year for three years." Tom said, explosively. There was fury in his
face as he jumped up, clenched his fists and paced in front of the
lawyer's desk.

"Listen, have a seat," Randy said, calmly, waiting for Tom to
settle down. "I've been handling buy-sell agreements, and a myriad
of other legal issues for auto dealers for twenty years, and dealers
only care about two things: themselves and money—nothing else."
He stopped to let this sink in. "And Jack Steinwell is one of the
worst; you had to know that - you've been in this business awhile. If
you didn't, I'm sorry, but there's nothing I can do about that now.
My job is to keep you out of jail."

The word, *jail*, resounded in Tom's head and pulverized his
mind, causing his heart to hammer so hard, so loud, he thought
he would lose consciousness.

CHAPTER 13

The Pomona Superior Courthouse was an august, fifteen-story, rectangular, stone structure that towered over the other downtown municipal buildings like the Washington Monument. Tom's chill worsened when he walked up the concrete steps and witnessed the reddish-brown bloodstains of the C.H.P. officer recently shot by a gangbanger while exiting the courthouse. Tom had heard about it on the drive over. The gravity of Tom's situation hung heavily, pressing down on him with a seemingly infinite weight.

Defendants and their families scurried about like frightened ants on a molested anthill. The tension and uncertainty were palpable. Terrified, Tom suspected that some of the horde waiting to go through the metal detector would not go home that day. Please don't let me be one of them, he prayed silently.

They rode the elevator up, spotted Tom's attorney on a payphone near the courtroom door. "How're you doing?" Randy said, shaking Tom's hand.

"Nervous. Randy, this is my wife Sabrina."

"Pleased to meet you," Sabrina said in a subdued voice.

"We should go in; they'll be calling us any moment," Randy said. They shuffled past the deputy standing in the small vestibule and took their seats. There was a row of benches on both sides of the cramped aisle. A platoon of attorneys, the Assistant District Attorneys, were preparing to do battle. Tom felt his throat constrict when he glimpsed somber, roguish-looking defendants behind a decrepit Plexiglas cubicle. They were attired in various colors of jail uniforms. Red was for murder. The hairs on Tom's neck stood up as he imagined himself in jail clothes. He was increasingly overcome with helplessness. The courtroom had the dead, parched smell of dust in an ancient tomb.

"Listen, I know one of the D.A.s," Randy whispered, a little raspy from cigarettes. "I'm going to ask him to see if he can grab your file when it comes up in rotation. He's been here awhile and he's a pretty fair guy."

Randy strutted through the small wooden gate in the center of the courtroom, greeted a rotund, middle-aged man with a face like pudding. The D.A. seemed genuinely glad to see Randy. They spoke for a few minutes, laughed heartily about something, then Randy sauntered back. "Alright, he's going to grab it," Randy said. "Now, when they call us, you stand by me, enter your "not guilty" plea and then we'll go out in the hallway."

"Okay," Tom said quietly. "This seems like a car deal," Tom whispered to Sabrina's. "Doesn't anyone go to trial? This seems to be going too fast." He was interrupted when the bailiff snapped to attention and announced, "The court is now in session, the Honorable Judge Forkin presiding. All please be seated and remain silent."

The bespectacled Judge Forkin had straight, thinning gray hair that looked like steel wire. The clerk called the first cases - the in-custody cases. When the jailed defendants were finished, they were ushered through a side door, shuffling away as if they just had their last meal. Tom wondered where it led.

"State of California vs. Thomas Taylor...Case Number CA02020202." Tom's heart began pounding like a pneumatic hammer as he followed Mr. Hunt up to the defendant's table. "How do you plead?" The judge asked perfunctorily. Tom glanced at his attorney. Randy pointed to a microphone.

"Not guilty," Tom said, in the most sincere sounding voice he could muster.

"Your Honor, I request a short recess. I would like some time to discuss a possible resolution to this case with the District Attorney. Mr. Taylor is a professional, a homeowner, and this is his first offense.

"Alright, the court is in recess for thirty minutes," the judge proclaimed with a swing of his gavel, then stood up to leave.

Tom and Sabrina followed Randy out into the hallway and sat at a long, bench. Tom eyed his attorney and John Zubek, the D.A., as they conversed down the hallway. Proficient in evaluating body language from many years of studying couples debating a vehicle purchase, Tom thought their meeting looked positive. The D.A. was smiling and nodding. The conversation had the casualness of two guys shooting the breeze. But still, Tom felt a wave of fear hurtling toward him with the speed and power of a freight train.

"Okay, I'll talk to him." Tom heard Randy's words echo as the two men separated. Randy knelt down by Tom, clutching a file and talking with the urgency of basketball coach during a time-out.

"This is where we're at. Tom, you're a first-time offender; that's good. But you're obviously guilty." 'Guilty' echoed in Tom's mind. His stomach felt like it was filled with sour milk. "Three years probation, 300 hours of community service and a $15,000 fine; you've got the money, right?"

"Yeah, but hold on," Tom said, a flutter of fear in his voice. He couldn't help but feel he was being hustled. "Jack knew what we were doing."

"Doesn't matter."

"What if we fight this, and like, um, go to trial?"

"We could, but you'll pay me twice as much, and if we lose, you'll do one to three years in county jail. You don't want to go to the Los Angeles County Jail, it's a filthy, nasty, human dog pound," Randy explained. "It really is Abbadon. Do you know what *that* is?"

"No."

"It's the lowest level of Hell. A level of Hell even Dante didn't know about. Besides, Sabrina's pregnant."

Tom was already looking at her little bulge when he heard Randy's words. "Give us a minute, please." He and Sabrina stared out the enormous courthouse window. "It doesn't seem fair," he murmured.

Sabrina gazed up at him, tears in her eyes. "I can't have you gone. I know you don't think it's fair, but can I make a suggestion?"

"Since when could I stop you?"

She managed a smile. "You've always told me that a wise man picks the battles he knows he can win. Honey, I don't think you can win this. You should take the deal."

Tom knew she was right, but he was not ready to concede defeat yet. He excused himself and went into the men's room. Washing his hands, he looked into the mirror. It as it appeared to transform, turning black like the tinted windows of a police car. Gazing into the darkness, he saw himself as a creature driven by greed and vanity. His blue eyes burned red with anguish and anger.

In tough times, Tom always reflected on his mother's short life. You grow up fast when you are measuring your allotted time on earth in minutes, not years or months. His mother's untimely death when Tom was eighteen launched him on a fanatical mission to grab all the gusto life had to offer. At all costs. Grief changes a person like a volcanic eruption changes a landscape.

Success is a concept that is often misunderstood. Sometimes a man is trying to solve the wrong puzzle. And as he climbs the ladder of success, he often finds his ladder is leaning against the wrong building. Bending all the rules, ignoring all the rules, even breaking all the rules, hustling at the speed of light, all in the name of getting ahead, now culminates in a criminal conviction. He closed his eyes and had a silent talk with his mother, something he had done many times in the past twenty-three years. Time to make a change.

He headed back to Randy and Sabrina In a voice thin with misery, he said, "Let's get this over with."

Entering the courtroom, he had an unsettling and surreal feeling, like he was walking into a cemetery toward a grave marker with his name on it. The court was called to order and Tom entered his "nolo contendere" plea - no contest. Judge Forkin enumerated the conditions of his probation. The entire proceeding took ten minutes. In that ten minutes, a part of Tom died.

CHAPTER 14

An FBI Special Agent since he returned in 1992, Lt. Carl Farland had been a Sergeant in Desert Storm, discharged with enough medals and ribbons to make a quilt. A bulging, barrel of a man, his chiseled chest and enormous biceps stretched the limits of his Kevlar vest. He looked like he was hewn from a massive slab of oak. Even the skin on his neck had muscles.

Today, he assembled the largest group of special agents and sharpshooters he had ever seen since joining the force, so large, it dwarfed the size of the squadron he commanded near Baghdad.

Date: February 19th. Time: 0515 hours. Location: 17060 Oakview Drive. Encino, California. Personal residence. Suspect(s): Iouri Malakov, Petrov Kuvayev.

Another cadre of agents was dispatched to a Woodland Hills residence to arrest another accomplice, Nicolai Stolov. The three original targets shrank to two when Lt. Farland's source received word that Kuayev was at the Encino residence. The attacks were to be coordinated so the perpetrators could not tip each other off.

Lt. Farland surveyed the silent sea of black helmets stationed behind bulletproof shields, a battalion of zealots in a trance before a Crusade. Mission: To seize the suspects without disrupting the wealthy neighborhood, which soon would be preparing for the workday.

At 0615 hours, Lt. Farland squeezed the button on his radio: "Go! Go! Go!"

The front line, armed with a battering ram, made easy work of Iouri's palatial front door; after they smashed their way in, it looked like Swiss cheese blasted by shrapnel.

On the sofa, sleeping off the effects of last night's Stoli, Petrov was jolted awake as if his blanket was on fire. He did not believe it was real until he was handcuffed and shackled, lying face down on the oriental rug.

The mists of sleep rapidly vanished. His green eyes bulged. In shock, he was deluged with chaotic thoughts: What would he tell his wife? When would he *see* his wife? When will his see his Katerina? How did these guys know he was there? And worst of all, what do these guys know?

A second phalanx of agents found Iouri in his Versailles-like master bedroom. Adrenaline-stoked, his first inclination was to grab his nine-millimeter. But when he looked out the window and saw a virtual army, he knew it was futile. Surprisingly, they allowed him to dress. Iouri perceived their sense of decency as weakness: "soft Americans." He was silent as they escorted him out in handcuffs. He was more concerned about the FBI ransacking his mansion.

Approaching the white van, he could see Petrov was slack-faced, like a dead man walking. But Iouri's look told him to keep silent and be strong. Dumb Americans! You do not know what you are doing or who you are dealing with, he thought.

Iouri and Petrov were fastened to chains to the floor of the van. Iouri scowled at the two agents who loaded them and kept giving Petrov reassuring glances that everything was under control because Iouri Malakov was in charge. His ego was bolstered by the army of agents they used to capture him. He wanted to know why they had not used more. He was not afraid. The hunter never feared the rabbit. And nothing could be as harrowing as the prison in Kronstadt.

As the van sped down Oakview Drive, a gratified Rafi Hassan paused by his car, attaché in hand, and watched the cavalcade of FBI vehicles ramble away, a sly smirk on his face.

Lt. Farland heard on the radio that Nicolai Stolov had resisted violently, like an enraged Rottweiler. He was eventually subdued, but not before three agents were seriously injured, one critically. Iouri and Petrov smiled and gave each other a look: "That's our Nikki."

For Lt. Farland, Mission Accomplished. Reading the field report and arrest warrants, he said to himself, man, these guys are no joke - definitely to be taken seriously. He turned around to observe the two suspects. One was quiet, almost timid. The other had an insolent look, very haughty. The second one kept his head high, appearing to ignore his arrest, as if he was not cuffed and tethered to the floor.

His eyes attracted the most attention. He looked like a vanquished lion who gave the impression that he would and could leave of his own accord when he wanted to. As if the steel chains were imaginary.

Unaware and unconcerned that Lt. Farland was watching him, questions pulsed like a strobe light through Iouri's brain: Who ratted us out? Alejandra? Rafi Hassan? That asshole! But what did he know? I wonder if that CHP officer was suspicious and put a tail on Petrov's pickup? I do not know, but he did not sound that smart or that ambitious. Iouri's mind kept racing through a labyrinth of possible enemies and rats. He even considered his mother-in-law, whom he considered inconsequential. I know she does not like me, but what the hell could she know? The big question was, what do they know and how much do they know? His thoughts were interrupted when he sensed Lt. Farland's eyes.

"What are you looking at?" Iouri barked at him. Startled, Lt. Farland quickly turned away, embarrassed, mumbled something that sounded like, "asshole."

The van arrived at the Los Angeles Metropolitan Detention Center. MDC was a ten-story hi-rise in the heart of downtown LA, adjacent to Dodger Stadium. A maximum-security, Federal Pre-Trial Facility, it was an impregnable fortress, whose architecture could best be described as modern Southwestern mortar-proof. The B.O.P. boasted: 'It would be easier for an inmate to get into heaven then escape from the M.D.C.'

The van pulled up to the security gate, and a guard used a long, aluminum pole affixed with a mirror to inspect the undercarriage. This 9-11 really has these stupid Americans spooked, Iouri said to himself. What a charade. Don't these federal employees know their own government attacked those buildings?

Lt. Farland looked in his rear view mirror and saw a familiar van pull in behind him. "Look, boys, the third member of your party has just arrived," he announced, trying to bait Iouri. In part, as payback for his outburst. Iouri was silent.

"All clear," the guard declared. A pair of Dutch steel door with serrated edges opened, one submerging into the ground, and the other rising up, giving the illusion of a dragon's mouth. The vans roared down a steep concrete ramp into the bowels of MDC. They stopped in front of a behemoth, three-inch thick, steel overhead door that looked capable of withstanding a bazooka barrage.

Before they descended, Iouri, who was eidetic, already was casing the building, cataloguing everything he saw, every detail of the scene soaked into his memory like indelible ink. He wondered if they would grant him bail. Probably not. He had the resources, but the judge would most likely deem him a flight risk. Innocent until proven guilty. What a farce. If they do not let me leave, I will take matters into my own hands, he decided, constantly surveying what his limited movements permitted him to see.

The overhead door rose with a metallic grind and the vans advanced into the receiving area. To the left was a gray cinder-block wall, with chain-link fencing bolted to the top, rising all the way to the corroded steel beams supporting the ceiling. To the right, he saw an inmate entrance. Like a digital recorder, he embedded everything he saw of importance in his memory. When he blinked, it was like a camera clicking.

"What we got?" inquired C.O. Fields.

"Three new guests," Lt. Farland replied.

Correctional Officer Fields was a burly black man with a pot gut. His white B.O.P. uniform was stained was souvenirs of that morning's breakfast. It was simply another monotonous day at a mindless job. He felt he was doing time along with the prisoners.

Lt. Farland, his driver, and the Special Agents from the second van stowed their weapons in the security firearm boxes and escorted the Russians inside, sequestering them in a black, steel cage. The three Russians did not speak as they were issued white jumpsuits and plastic sandals called jellies.

I guess I will not be wearing any designer clothing for awhile, Iouri thought. Petrov was silent, and Nikki disgusted, his eyes as angry as those of a captured dog. Behind a locked door was a crush of inmates - stragglers with strange, faraway stares.

"Now what?" Petrov asked dejectedly. His spirit seemed atrophied. Assuming the air of a confident, soft-spoken attorney, Iouri said, "They will probably put us in isolation. That will make communication difficult; everyone will have to be patient. I will call Victor Goldman, and you both will have to call your attorneys." Petrov had a knot in his stomach the size of the Kremlin.

"When we go to court, we will not get bail, because we will be deemed flight risks. Like I told you, though, these people are idiots. You know what we will do." They both smiled at Iouri as the implication was obvious. Always thinking ahead, Iouri had a contingency plan for this. He had done his research and learned that Victor Goldman was the premier California attorney for high-profile and/or murder cases.

The three were marshaled to the dilapidated freight elevator that lifted them to the fourth floor: R&D, Receiving and Departure. There, they were placed in separate holding cells.

Petrov's heart was pounding hard and his throat had clutched up. He was in despair. After a few hours, which felt like eternity plus a few minutes, all three were fingerprinted and photographed. Then, they were ushered through two security doors, down a dark hallway that smelled of disinfectant and despair.

Iouri monitored the number and location of security cameras as they entered the decrepit freight elevator. On the way up, all three faced the rear as ordered. They remained silent. The only sound was Petrov's anxious breathing and his thumping heart. The elevator stopped.

"Malakov, this is your floor," said the accompanying C.O. All three moved to leave. "No, no. You two stay. Malakov only."

CHAPTER 15

Still smarting from his conviction a week ago, Tom's mood elevated when he saw the other two loves of his life, Samantha and Tommy, who had arrived from Chicago for a visit. Tommy, at twelve, looked just like his father, slimmer and unblemished. Videogames were his passion. Samantha would be seventeen next month. She had bloomed into a stunning young woman. 5'8", slender and athletic, with radiant eyes the color of blue glass. She looked like she was peeled off the cover of a young woman's magazine.

On the second night of their visit, Samantha went to gossip with Sabrina, whom she considered a big sister. The two Toms sat dangling their legs in the pool. "Mom says you were arrested. What happened?" Tommy asked. Tom looked a little deflated as he contemplated his answer.

"Well, we did some things at the last dealership I worked at; the owner knew about them, but after he sold the dealership and the problems were discovered, he pointed the finger at me."

"That doesn't seem right."

"No, it's not; but I shouldn't have been doing what we were doing."

"Are you going to jail?" Words a father never wants to hear from his son.

"No. I could have; but I took what is called a plea bargain. And now I'm on probation, which basically means I already have one foot in jail, so I have to be real careful."

"Well, I'm glad you're okay," Tommy said thumping his father's arm.

The visit was fun for them all and went by quickly, highlighted by Samantha's driving Sabrina's Mercedes down the Pacific Coast

Highway. It was a picturesque California postcard day. Their stay culminated in a two-day trip to Disney's California Adventure. The next day, Tom drove them to LAX. They said their goodbyes and he experienced his customary moment of melancholy as he watched the plane take off.

On their way home, Tom suggested to Sabrina that they take a stroll along the Huntington Beach Pier. They stood at the end of the Pier. Seagulls wheeled about them in a raucous cloud, filling the air with their wing beats. They tossed bread crusts, like two children on a picnic. As they embraced, in her excited state, Sabrina's nipples had hardened and darkened pushing through her cotton shirt. Tom ran his hand down her back. Her body was as smooth as a rose petal. He was learning to relax and realize that sunsets were more than just wavelengths and frequencies. He could sense the immense timelessness of life; calm and balanced, everything in equilibrium. They exchanged a kiss against the breathtaking backdrop. They were in love. Life was good.

The next morning, the doorbell rang. Tom went to the front door, where he was greeted by a thirtyish, black female and a middle-aged Caucasian male, probably early fifties, both in casual business attire.

"Mister Taylor?" the woman asked

"Yes," Tom stuttered, with a sinking feeling. He knew that tone. He had heard it recently. Too recently.

"My name is Inspector Harley, and this is my partner, Inspector Glenn.

Can we have a word with you?" she asked as she held up their U.S. Postal Inspectors' badges. It did not sound like a question.

"Am I under arrest?" Tom said, instinctively, disgusted this could be happening again.

"No," she said, "Can we come in?" This time she was very forceful and put on a starched smile.

Tom was relieved, but suspicious. His legs were rubbery.

"Do you know a Tony Jones?" Inspector Harley asked, holding up a picture. Not a mug shot. Inspector Glenn stood silently, observing.

"Yes, I do," Tom replied, cautiously.

"Tell me about your relationship."

"I sold Tony Jones a mini-van when I worked at Inland Chrysler. He asked me if I would pay him if he brought us customers. We talked briefly and I told him, 'okay, but let's see how it goes'. He evolved into what the car business calls a 'bird dog'."

"Uh-huh," Inspector Harley said. Her voice was so low it sounded like a grunt. Her brown eyes glared at Tom with the intensity of a laser. She was reaching for signs of dishonesty.

"Did you ever accept any social security checks?"

"From him?"

"Him or other customers."

"I don't recall taking any directly from him, but from customers occasionally, sure, why?"

The two inspectors looked at each other. Tom suddenly felt like he was playing a chess game in the dark. "Do you mind if I call my attorney?" he said, realizing that this could lead to his wearing silver bracelets again.

"If you don't cooperate, we can tell your probation officer. We know you're on probation, and he can have you thrown in jail immediately."

That was a lie. Whatever they were insinuating that Tom was involved in probably occurred before his probation began, so he could not have violated his probation. He was falling victim to one of law enforcement's primary investigative tactics: Deception.

Filled with trepidation, but standing his ground, Tom called Randy and explained what was happening. Cupping the receiver Tom asked, "Am I a target of this investigation?" Apparently that was a question they had to answer honestly. They hesitated, then replied in unison, "No." Tom relayed their response.

"As long as they cut to the chase, tell them you'll continue talking,"

Randy advised him. "Tom, is there anything I should know?"

"Nothing I'm aware of."

"You sure?"

"Positive."

"Alright. Be careful, and call me when they leave."

They knew they had to come clean. Harley decided to turn up some of their cards. She removed an encyclopedic volume from her brown leather bag, the book of Federal Statutes. Thumbing through, she plopped it on the table, turned it around and slid it to Tom.

"According to 18 USC 3583 (B) (2) you could be guilty of receiving stolen property," she announced, conveniently omitting discussing the paragraph concerning intent. Smoke and mirrors. Tom glimpsed the words in the massive Federal Code Book. It was having the desired effect on him: Fear.

"So what you're saying is that Tony Jones was dealing with or handling stolen social security checks?"

"Yes," they replied.

"And because I may have handled them, I'm guilty of a crime?"

"Yes."

"Even if I didn't know they were stolen?" Tom asked. Blank faces.

"How much are we talking about?" Tom's voice went up a notch in volume.

"Approximately $7500 at your dealership," Inspector Harley said.

"Well, I made a lot more than that in a month. Why would I steal any social security checks? I didn't need the money; I made more than enough on my own."

"So you know nothing about any social security checks?"

"Absolutely not!?"

Silence. Every second seemed to linger.

"But you do acknowledge handling them."

"Maybe two or three a month; but I'm not certain they came from Tony."

They explained that Tony Jones allegedly had a ring of women at several L.A. post offices stealing social security checks. Meeting over. They handed him their cards.

"We'll be in touch if we have any more questions."

"You know where to find me."

Tom was understandably shaken when he told Sabrina what had happened. "Sounds like Tony's in deep trouble."

"Looks that way."

One month later, Tom arrived home from work to find a phone message from Inspector Glenn. Standing with the cordless receiver to his ear, he closed his eyes and all the blood drained from his face. He turned dead white.

"Honey, what did he say?"

"He said, I've been indicted."

CHAPTER 16

Iouri was brought to Five South. The unit was triangular shaped, with two levels of cells on two of its sides. In the center, on the main floor, were cafeteria-style tables anchored into the concrete floor; the place was occupied by inmates playing board and card games, bordering a small recreational area. The voices formed an indecipherable babble of male posturing, an atmosphere resembling a gathering of Vegas crime families. Definitely not the Country Club, Iouri thought.

The rec deck contained a ramshackle weight system and half a basketball court. A basketball bounced angrily, resembling the thumping of a sledgehammer. The inmates were glued to the perimeter. They looked like they would skin snakes with their teeth for their cigarettes. Nice place.

"Name?" the C.O. grunted.

"Iouri Malakov."

"There's no cells open right now," the C.O. said, and pointed to a filthy, scratched-glass room overhead. Iouri strode up the stairs, entered the TV room, his bivouac. Inmates lay around gawking at a Lakers' game and arguing. A bunch of high paid monkeys throwing a ball around, he said to himself. He did not care for sports, television and most people.

He set up his cot and ventured out to see if there was intelligent life among these aliens. His hopes were not high. Busy businessman had no time for TV. Iouri was a voracious reader. Although the Kronstadt prison was a living Hell, a sympathetic guard, who had met Iouri's father at a Moscow assembly, supplied him with a steady stream of books, most about the Evil Empire - the U.S.

Glancing around his new quarters, he saw inmates playing billiards and horsing around, as if they enjoyed it here. But many

were young, early twenties and thirties, angry, cynical, lost in space
and time. What he really saw was a teeming mass of impoverished
humanity, pawns in the U.S. government's chess game of corrupt
justice. This is only temporary, he reassured himself. Whatever it
takes. But how did they know? It plagued him. He would find out.
Somehow.

He told himself not to worry, and since it was getting late,
he would try and get some sleep. Settling down on his cot, his
mind wandered to his days in Kronstadt. Rolling onto his side, he
spotted something peculiar behind the T.V. room door. A hole at
the height of the door handle. He jumped up and sauntered over,
put his hand in the hole.

This is unbelievable. His face looked like he had just made The
Big Score. The damn place is built with drywall! It was never built
to be a prison. He laid back down on his cot, with a childish grin
of delight. This will be like cutting paper with a chainsaw. Then
he went to sleep.

The next morning, he rose and did a quick one-hundred push-
ups, just like at Kronstadt, where he would complete as many as
one-thousand in a given day.

He hustled down to the guard's desk "I would like to make a
call," he said.

"Do you have a PAC number?" the C.O. asked, setting down
his novel.

"What is that?"

"It's your Personal Access Code number, like a bank PIN
number."

"I just got here last night."

"Oh, well, you'll have to wait for your PAC number."

"How long does that take?"

"About a week to ten days. And then you'll have to fill out one
of these," the C.O. said, holding up a blue form.

"But I need to call my attorney," Iouri insisted.

The C.O. glared at him - Another inmate who thinks he's the
fucking President. "Alright. Go up to the door before the T.V.

room where you slept and see the Counselor. Tell him I said you need to make a legal call."

Iouri jogged up the steps and stood outside the door. A plump man with a face as shiny as an eight ball was blabbing on the phone. Iouri stood in the doorway and waited.

"We might buy the house in Englewood..."

Another federal employee stealing our tax dollars, Iouri thought.

Noting Iouri's arrogant attitude, Counselor Brugnone interrupted his rambling and snarled, "What do you want!?"

"I need to make a legal call," Iouri said, calmly.

"Come back in a hour."

"One more thing..."

"I told you in a hour!" Brugnone snapped.

"But...?"

"One hour!"

And like a wave from the ocean depths, Iouri screamed with all the Russian fury he could muster, "CHERNOZHOPY!" (black ass). His voice rang out like a cannon. He stomped away, and down to the rec deck to work off some steam.

The receiver slid away from Brugnone's hand. His mouth hung open like the back of a garbage truck. He was dumbfounded by Iouri's contemptuous tone.

He did not know what he had said but he was certain it was not "Happy Birthday."

"Victor? Iouri Malakov."

"Are you alright?" Victor asked sincerely. "Where do they have you?"

"LA Metropolitan Detention Center How did you know?" Iouri asked, perplexed and impressed. His question boosted Victor's ego another notch.

"I make it my business to know. No, actually, the LA Times. I have it right here. You're on the front page, and it's a three page article. They have a picture of you as they're hauling you out of your house. Nice house."

"When can you come see me?"

"Tomorrow. 10:00 a.m. I will take immediate steps to protect your house before the Feds get their corrupt, grubby little paws on it. Since you do have substantial legitimate income, it will be difficult for them to prove the house was purchased with illegal funds."

"Thank you, and very good. One more thing. Would you please call my wife in London and let her know that I am fine, and that it will be two weeks before they process the paperwork so I can call her." Iouri gave him the phone number.

"Will do. See you tomorrow. Now I don't have to remind you not to say anything about your case. With your picture on the front page, you'll be a celebrity in there, and probably asked a lot of questions."

"No, no, of course not."

Iouri had an LA Times subscription in London so he could read it when he was visiting Marina. She did not read it often but on the obscure chance that she saw that day's front page, he did not want her to worry. He wanted a chance to downplay any sensationalism that was printed. But his primary concern was that she would reveal the skeletons in his closet before he had a chance to muzzle her.

CHAPTER 17

"This is fucked," Tom yelled, his face still ghostly white. Sabrina was speechless. The next morning, Tom called his attorney. "Randy, I got a call from one of those postal inspectors, Inspector Glenn; he said I've been indicted. What the hell does that mean and what the hell is going on? How the hell can they do this?"

"Apparently, the grand jury felt they had enough evidence to prove a crime had been committed, and the AUSA felt he had enough evidence to get a conviction."

"English, Randy. Speak English!"

"They think you're guilty."

"Of what?"

"I don't know, but I'm sure it has something to do with those social security checks. Let me call them and find out what's going on. Stay there and I'll call you right back."

Tom called his partner. "Hey, Bobby, it's me. It seems I've got myself some more trouble, something to do with those postal inspectors who came to see me last month. My attorney is trying to sort it out. I'll keep you posted. I'm really sorry about all this."

"Don't worry, pal, just take care of it. Sales are up thirty-percent since you came on board, so I'm not worried. Just let me know."

"I will." Amazing guy. I hope he doesn't think I'm a jerk like his sons, Tom thought. He hung up. And froze. Sabrina was weeping. This was all so unfair to her. Especially being pregnant.

"Honey, c'mere." Tom held his wife, stroking her hair, trying to comfort her. He felt horrible. This was all his fault. He promised himself he would play it straight. He was playing it straight; but his world continued to crumble. The damage had been done. Fear throbbed through her.

"Honey, what's going to happen?"

"I don't know," he said with visible discomfort, wishing he had a better answer. His mind tumbled chaotically from one possibility to another. Fear etched his face, and his soul. The phone rang. Tom answered.

"Here's what's going on, Randy informed him. "You've been indicted on receiving stolen property in the amount of $1875.00 of stolen Social Security checks. It's rather petty…"

"But I didn't know they were stolen!" Tom blurted out.

"Apparently they think you did. Like I was saying, it's a petty indictment for a Federal crime. I find it hard to believe they're even prosecuting you. Now I haven't handled many Federal cases, but this should be easy. You'll probably get probation, just like with your other case. I've arranged for you to self-surrender at 9:00 a.m. on Friday at the Federal Courthouse in downtown Santa Ana. It's right near my office, so be here at 8:30 and I'll drive you over. They should grant you bail, but you should know, the Fed system is different; it's not the simple matter of a bail bondsman. You usually have to pledge some real estate, like your house. I'll have more details by Friday."

Friday, Tom woke up early from a restless night's sleep, went downstairs and made up a cup of tea. It was still dark. His mind was spinning. All he could do was pray and hope that everything would work out that day, and he would come home again.

The Ronald Reagan Courthouse was a one-hundred million dollar behemoth in downtown Santa-Ana, California, an earth-toned, marbled edifice. Walking up to the courthouse in step with his attorney, Tom saw the silhouette of Inspector Glenn. He really did have an unfriendly face, pinched and perpetually frowning.

Tom was photographed and fingerprinted, and had a brief interview with a young lady, whose title was, Pre-Trial Officer. She asked some biographical and financial questions, and then he saw his attorney.

"I just spoke to the AUSA. He's offering probation and bail if you plead guilty."

"But I didn't know they were stolen."

"Doesn't matter."

Tom had heard these words before. This did not feel right.

"It's this or a year in jail."

"Do I enter my plea today?"

"No, in two weeks."

"So, I'm not going home today?"

"No."

The word "no" gripped his throat like a chokehold. Tears of despair pooled in his eyes, and the hammering in his chest forced him to gasp for air as he tried to speak. "Please break the news to Sabrina gently," he said, in a voice pinched with pain and disappointment. She was supposed to be here by now."

"Of course I will."

They spoke for a few more minutes, but gone was his attorney's customary confidence and assuredness. When he spoke, his words sounded prepared, and his eyes wandered to the same vague spot in the air beside Tom. In a recent conversation, Gene, his older, wiser brother warned him about attorneys. "Attorneys can be like carrion. They sense people's despair, vulnerability, and cash, so always be careful." Tom prayed that this was not happening to him. But something did not feel right. Not right at all.

He was brought before the Federal Magistrate and stood there, scared stiff. The place had the hushed feeling of unfettered power. With great reluctance, he pled, "Guilty," and another court date was set for formal sentencing and bail. He was still in his suit, shackled and handcuffed, as he was ushered out of the courtroom. He spotted Sabrina on the way. The anguish in her eyes was painful to see. A tear tracked down her cheek. Gut-wrenching. He mouthed, "I love you."

He was brought to the Santa Ana Jail, a local facility leased by the Federal government. The units, called Modules, looked like dorm rooms. He was no legal expert, but common sense suggested that a person should not be in custody if he had accepted a plea bargain for probation. Something is wrong, Tom decided.

Sabrina visited regularly, tried to keep her chin up. But the visits were strained. Their conversations were limited to light banter, each trying to keep it afloat for the sake of the other, talking via telephones through a reinforced plate glass window.

On one visit, Sabrina arrived, glowing, with a photo - a copy of her ultrasound. It was a boy. They bantered about names, decided on Tyler. Tyler was on his way. Two weeks later, no bail and no Randy Hunt. A phone call revealed that he had accepted a huge retainer from the owner of an Indy Cart Racing Team, was out of town and would be traveling for at least the next two months.

CHAPTER 18

"Flight 929 to New York, with continuing service to Moscow will be boarding in forty-five minutes," the voice announced. Alejandra had arrived at LAX three hours early for her flight. She waited with the seething mass of humanity crowding the International Terminal, constantly on the alert and trying to remain calm. Her eyes wandered briefly to the empty seat next to her. The name Malakov on the front page of the newspaper seized her attention. Her heart raced. She grabbed the paper. Her eyes darted around nervously as if she might be under surveillance.

Reading an exaggerated account of Iouri and her former cronies, of Russian extortionists and murderers, she became jumpy as a cat. She scoured the article for her name. Nothing. Thank God! She let out a sigh of relief, and felt a sudden calm. She continued reading. No bodies. She knew she was leaving just in time.

She had conflicted feelings about leaving her friends; but she had tired of Iouri's hegemony and Nikki's maniacal love of death. The sad truth was that she still loved Iouri. The LA Times stated that, "The FBI had received an anonymous tip from a reliable source." Her only hope now was that someday she could beg forgiveness, and that Iouri would excuse her for what she had done.

CHAPTER 19

The next morning, Tom stared at a phone book, the traditional Yellow Pages. Can't hurt at this point, he thought. He opened it to: Attorneys - Federal, ran his finger down the page and stopped on a large advertisement: Steve Reid, Federal Attorney, twenty years experience. His office is right across the street. He called Sabrina and she connected Tom to Mr. Reid's office via three-way. Luckily he was in. Tom presented the synopsized version of his plight.

"A lot of attorneys take on federal cases that don't have a clue how the system works. State and Federal laws are like apples and oranges," Mr. Reid stated with authority. Now, someone tells me, Tom thought.

Steve Reid's voice was a lot more stellar than his appearance. Middle-aged with a boyish face made him easy to talk to, but his dark, brown eyes were a contradiction. Regardless, he seemed to know what he was talking about. "I'll pull your file at the court building. Also I know John Hogan, in charge of the AUSA's office. I'll go over right now and talk to him after I've reviewed your file." His voice was encouraging, and there was something avuncular about him.

"Don't go anywhere, I'll be right back." Tom had the most befuddled, upset look Steve had ever seen on a client.

"I was just kidding. Relax. I'm going to get you out of here."

After researching Tom's case, and a brief conversation with the AUSA, Steve returned a few hours later.

"Listen, the good news I that I can get you out of here; but the bad news is that Mr. Hunt should not have had you plead guilty. That was unnecessary.

If you truly didn't know the checks were stolen, I could have gotten you acquitted. It really is a chickenshit indictment. But just because you're indicted, doesn't mean you're guilty. The government can indict a ham sandwich if it wants to."

"That's what I thought," Tom said, relieved, but realizing that he'd been scammed. Mr. Hunt had been paid in full.

"Here's the tough part. I have to get a substitution of counsel signed by Mr. Hunt, and if he's on the road with that racing team, who the hell knows how long that could take. Judge Sunland, that's who's been assigned to your case is a stickler on counselor's substitutions. I absolutely need his signature."

After two months, with Steve Reid staking out, even camping out, at Mr. Hunt's office, an embarrassed John H. Hunt signed the substitution of counsel, and Steve expedited its processing. On December 17th, at 6:30P.M., after 121 nerve-racking days in custody, Judge Sunland granted Tom bail. He was released the next day.

CHAPTER 20

Although Tom had not been gone that long, he felt like an astronaut who had landed on an alien planet. It took a few days to adjust to normal life. He and Sabrina enjoyed a quiet Christmas, the house, wrapped in lights and adorned with figurines, looked like a wedding cake. Anticipation was high as they prepared the nursery for the baby's arrival.

In mid-January Sabrina's mother arrived from Columbus, Ohio to help out and witness the birth of her first grandchild. Renee Cardell, although plump and matronly, at sixty-three still refused to lose her beauty. She was a brassy blonde with striking green and yellow eyes, almost feline. She was born in Paris and still retained her accent. Tom found it endearing, Sabrina found it annoying. "Thirty-five years in this country, and she still sounds like she's at some Paris café."

Renee was an ardent Catholic, and believed that Hell's fire awaited all sinners. But Tom knew her heart was in the right place. For him, she was as idealized and genuine as any grandmother in a Disney film. But according to his wife, Renee goes around driving people crazy.

Tom returned to work. His partner, Bob, who was steadfast and loyal to a fault, was glad to see him. He was a man with infinite understanding and Tom was grateful for that. All he said was, "Now quit hanging around with that rough crowd and get back to work."

Tom worked hard to make up for lost time while Sabrina and her mother shopped for a crib and some last minute items. On February 1st, Tom was having lunch with a client when his phone rang.

"Honey, my water just broke," Sabrina said calmly. "Mom and I will meet you at the hospital."

"On my way," Tom said.

The baby was being stubborn; he was not coming out on his own. "We're considering inducing labor, but I'm concerned about something," the doctor explained, eyes fixed on the fetal heart monitor. "His heartbeat is irregular. It even stopped once. If it stops again, we'll have to do a C-section. If it does happen again, we'll only have seventeen minutes to save the baby."

A hush gripped the room. Then, the fetal heart monitor screamed.

"Let's go, stat!" the doctor ordered. Medical staff rushed in and whisked Sabrina away. Tom paced the room, back and forth, back and forth. He and Renee stared at one another. Not a word.

Forty-five minutes later, the doctor appeared in the doorway. "Dad, would you like to see your son?"

"They're alright?" The relief was indescribable.

"It was close, but he's fine."

"And Sabrina?"

"She's fine, too; but she'll be sore for awhile."

They were escorted to a post-op nursery, where Tyler was swathed in a blue and white blanket in a small crib-like plastic container under a lamp. Tom's heart fluttered when he saw his son for the first time. He reached in and put Tyler's little hand around his pinky finger

"Hey, Tyler, it's your Dad," he whispered.

Tyler squeezed Tom's finger ever so slightly. A tear rolled down Tom's face

"It's...I mean, he's a miracle."

"There's my two guys," Sabrina called from the doorway.

"You cooked a good one," Tom said.

She shuffled over, kissed him, and they stood admiring their new baby boy.

"He's so beautiful," she whispered.

"So are you," Tom replied. Tyler was still holding onto his finger. All memories of legal problems had vanished. The world could have stopped and they would not have known.

On March 17, Tom was sentenced to three years Federal probation. On the way out of the courtroom, Steve Reid showed them into a conference room reserved for defense attorneys and their clients. Tyler was with them, sleeping in a portable carriage.

"What's wrong?" Tom wanted to know.

"Nothing. I just wanted to give you some advice. I'm a legal counselor; it's what I do. Now that you're on State and Federal probation at the same time, you have to be extremely careful. If someone doesn't like the color of your tie, you could find yourself in prison or jail."

Sabrina and Tom both nodded.

"I will send a letter to your state probation officer and ask him terminate you early. There's no practical reason for you to be under two umbrellas. The State usually defers to the Feds anyways."

"Much appreciated," Tom said. Steve glanced at Tyler."

"Beautiful boy."

"Thank you, counselor," Sabrina said, proudly.

"Now, you two get out of here; and I don't want to hear from you, Tom, unless it's to send me new clients."

"Thanks for everything, Steve," Tom said. "I mean it".

"Glad to have been able to help. Stay out of trouble."

CHAPTER 21

"Hey, dog, you Iouri, man?" sputtered the large Mexican with spittle at the corners of his mouth.

"I am not your dog."

Iouri despised the arcane prison language. It was too crude for him. His face was a mask of stone.

"Man, are you Iouri or not?"

"I am. What do you care?"

"You gotta a phone call in my house."

Iouri sensed whispers as he followed the inmate to his room. It had to be Nikki or Petrov. Iouri hopped up on the chrome piping fastened to the wall that snaked up from the commode, disgusted by the stench in the cell. Balancing himself, he was face-to-face with a one-foot square vent. He spoke in Russian.

"Hello?" Iouri pointed to the door, dismissing the Mexican.

"Iouri?" Nikki said excitedly, "You alright?"

"I've been better; but we will be just fine," Iouri said evenly. "You are on Nine South, No?"

"How did you know?"

"I make it my business to know everything. Do you think I am wasting time?"

"No." Nikki smiled a toothy grin.

"And Petrov is on Six South."

"Yes, I just talked to him."

"Which is good; at least we are all on the same side of the building."

"Did you hear?" Nikki asked.

"The death penalty?"

"I heard. This government is seeking the death penalty, but they do not have the bodies; they also do not have any real evidence. Supposedly someone tipped them off."

"How do you know they don't have any bodies?"

"Victor told me. And this death penalty business, it will not matter."

"Do you have any ideas?"

"This is me, Iouri. I already have a plan."

Iouri laid out a brief summary of his plan. To Nikki it was a simple solution to a mind-bending problem, something that seemed impossible at first, but blatantly obvious once revealed. Only World War III would stop Iouri from carrying out his scheme.

""Sounds very good," Nikki said, impressed at Iouri's ingenuity.

"So the first thing I am going to do is get a copy of the blueprints. Then I will need the number and placement of all security cameras, inside and out, and then the work schedule of all the C.O.s. Speaking of that, I have seen a few Russian and Armenian C.O.s around, I think for the right donation they will play for us."

"If they are true countrymen, they will," Nikki said. "Time frame?

"As soon as possible, but it will take some time."

"Where in Russia are we going hide out?" Nikki inquired.

"I am not giving up on the Big Score," Iouri replied, emphatically.

Nikki was dumbstruck. "How the hell, are we going to pull that off?"

"Think about it." Iouri always felt he did his best when the cards were stacked against him. "Everyone will think we fled to Russia; no one would think we'd be crazy enough to stay in the country, especially only fifty miles away. It's actually brilliant, if you think about it."

"Yes, I think it is brilliant," Nikki admitted."

"So, there are two things you and Petrov can help with."

"What things?"

"First, you need to get into cell 913, and Petrov needs to get into cell 619 and I need to get into cell 518. If you do not understand, go look; the reason will be self-evident. If not, I will explain at a later time. The second thing we need is a person."

"Huh?"

"There is bound to be someone here that has never done any serious time, and is not a real criminal. Maybe a white collar guy. They are usually greedy, but not too smart; that is how they get here. Someone I could pay off, who blends well in the area, someone we could use and get rid of, depending on how it goes."

Nikki's scalp tingled, and his heart began beating fast at Iouri's words 'Get rid of'.

"So you want me and Petrov to look around for this guy."

"Yes. Do not ask too many questions. Just listen. You are a military man. You know how to do it.

"Should be an American, a white guy would be best."

"Correct," Iouri replied. "We cannot use any of our Russian associates, because they certainly will be contacted once these idiots know we are gone."

"Then who?" Nikki asked.

"Don't know. Perhaps, whoever we are looking for is not even here yet."

CHAPTER 22

A few days later, Tom was preparing to go to work. He hurried downstairs and saw Sabrina feeding the baby, and a woman in professional attire he had never met before.

"Tom, this is Vickie Stanford," Sabrina said pointedly.

Tom recognized the name; it was his Federal Probation Officer, there for an unscheduled visit. Overweight and frumpy, she had frizzy straw-blonde hair tied in a pony tail that hung halfway down her back.

"Pleased to meet you," Tom said coolly, and reached to shake her hand.

"Mr. Taylor, you have a beautiful home, a beautiful wife and a darling little boy. You are a very lucky man." She said, with a smile as phony as a three-dollar bill.

"I sure am," Tom said, concerned at her comment. He did not like her tone. She seemed angry, bitter and vaguely accusatory. Still raw from his previous brush with the law, Tom's imagination went into overdrive:

"So, who do you think you are, Mister Taylor, standing there in your tailor-made suit, your Versace tie, and with your million-dollar home?"

"What are you insinuating? You're looking at me like I'm Al Capone or John Gotti."

"How, do I know you're not really a gangster or a drug dealer?"

"I don't drink, I don't smoke, and I've never taken any illegal drugs."

"I'm supposed to believe that from someone who used to play in a rock band?

"I'll give you this house if you can find anyone who says they have ever seen

or known me to do drugs."

"Of course, I won't find any; they're all dead from overdosing."

"What's your point?"

"And your wife here, your beautiful young wife. I know you've been married before. Did you run out on her for Sabrina?"

"Tom. Tom," Sabrina blurted out.

"Sorry. I was distracted."

"Vickie was reminding you to make sure you had your monthly probation reports filed on time and in her office by the fifth of each month," Sabrina said embarrassed.

"Yes, you wouldn't want to give me any reasons to violate you, now, would you?" Vickie said with a smirk. The syrup was thick.

"Of course not," Tom said, plainly, putting on the best smile he could come up with under the circumstances.

A week after the visit, Vickie Stanford insisted that Tom go in for a drug test. When he arrived at the Ronald Reagan Building, he waited in the probation office on the fourth floor. She came out and asked him to follow her.

"You know I don't drink, smoke, and I've never taken any drugs; it even said so in my Presentencing Report."

"I know, but I'm allowed to test any probationer up to three times." It was the best she could come up with. Tom stood there, dumbfounded. On the way home, he had the clear sense he had ended up on her radar.

After 9-11, a barrage of businesses in the emerging field of biometrics sprang up all over the country. The nation had become hyper-paranoid and security trumped everything. One of these firms was Tele-Voice, which held patents on voice verification. Doors could be opened with a person's voice and only that person's voice. The technology was so advanced that even a digital recorder could not fool the system. It was state-of-the-art, and Tele-Voice was one of Tom's accounting clients. He had been running ads for his CPA, payroll and other small business services, to try and make up for the income he'd lost. Late one Thursday evening, after having been at their office, he received a disturbing phone call when he arrived home.

"Mr. Taylor?"

"Who's calling?"

"This is Peter Nesbitt of the Secret Service."

First, the LA Sheriffs, then the U.S. Postal Inspectors, now the Secret Service; who's next - the CIA? He had visions of a SWAT team squatting around the exterior and sprawled on the roof, ready to infiltrate his home at any second.

"This is a joke, right?"

"No joke, Mr. Taylor. Are you familiar with Tele-Voice in Dana Point?"

"Yes. Why?"

"What is your relationship with them?"

"I prepare their payroll and monthly statements. Can I ask why you want to know?"

"We found your name at the office, and, this evening, one of our agents saw you leave the premises. We also know you're on federal probation," he said, his tone dripping with menace.

"Am I a target of your investigation or whatever is going on?"

Silence. Tom had used the magic words.

"Do you know anything about any counterfeiting?"

The question shook Tom up. "What do you mean?"

"We raided Tele-Voice and confiscated their computers."

"Scratch them off my client list."

"They had been printing one-hundred dollar bills. So you're saying you knew nothing about it?"

"Absolutely not!" Tom said, forcefully, almost rudely. "I show up two Thursdays a month for payroll, and once a month I prepare their income statement for their venture capitalist." Apparently their venture capitalist wasn't providing enough resources.

"You're not having any financial difficulties?"

"No, why?"

"You're working two jobs," he said plainly, obviously trying to bait Tom.

"Well, as you probably know, I was gone for four months after being indicted for receiving stolen property that I didn't know was stolen; and the amount was only $1875.00. I'm not making the same as in the car business, but I still have considerable wealth.

Also, I want to be home on weekends with our new baby." Tom felt violated, having to explain his life choices to a federal agent.

More silence. "Alright," Nesbitt said, "we'll be in touch if we need you."

The next day, following a long and detailed discussion, Sabrina and Tom decided to take the equity in their house and invest in an apartment building. They loved their home, but it had served its purpose. It was time to be more practical.

That evening, Tom came home from work with severe, abdominal cramps. Sabrina made him soak in the bathtub, and called Tom's sister, who was a nurse. After hearing Tom's symptoms, she advised him to go to the hospital first thing in the morning if his condition persisted.

The next morning, he felt worse, and they went straight to the hospital.

"You have two, very large kidney stones and an Elyes," the internist said, holding up an X-ray and pointing at the stones.

"What's an Elyes?" Tom asked.

"Basically, your system has shut down, because the stones are so large."

"So now what?"

"First, we have to insert a stent, to prevent the stones from dropping and blocking your kidneys."

"Geez! Then what?"

"Then we'll perform a lithotripsy."

"A what?"

"Lithotripsy. Don't worry, it's not as painful as it sounds." We sink you in a tub of water and blast the stones with a laser beam, so they'll break up into small pieces, and then you'll be able to pass them."

"Where does the stent go?"

"In your...um...groin," the doctor explained.

"Yikes!"

The stent was inserted and Tom was released. The lithotripsy was scheduled for the following week. Tom was given a prescription for Vicodin.

He remembered that, when Vickie Stanford drug tested him, she told him to inform her of any prescription medications. The next few days he played phone tag with her, so Sabrina faxed a copy of the prescription to her office with an explanation of his medical condition.

The next day, sitting in his office, he dialed Vicki's office again. Voicemail.

"Vickie, this is Tom Taylor. I'm still trying to return your call. I sent a fax regarding my prescription. I hope you received it; I'm at the office and I'll be leaving for a doctor's appointment." While he was talking, a message popped up on his cell phone. It was Vickie Stanford. "Mr. Taylor. I need you to call me immediately."

Tom decided to call her after his doctor's appointment. He strolled out the door and was greeted by three U.S. Marshals.

"Tom Taylor?" His face was instantly gray. This can't be happening. He was speechless and rigid.

"We have a warrant for your arrest." The words hit Tom like a sledgehammer. He spun around and rushed back into the office, taking off his watch, wedding ring, and removing his wallet and placing them on his desk.

"Cris, please call Sabrina; tell her I've been picked up. Again."

Cris was in disbelief, as Tom went back outside and they handcuffed him. Two marshals loaded him in the van. The other marshal drove away in a sedan.

"So what am I being arrested for?" he asked, blinking like a deer in the headlights.

"Dunno," replied the first marshal.

"Probation violation," mumbled the second.

"Probation violation for what?" Tom asked, incredulously, his head spinning.

"We don't know. You'll have to ask your probation officer."

The van made its way to the Santa Ana Jail, behind the Ronald Reagan Courthouse, the place he had left almost seven months ago. He felt like he was in the middle of nowhere on the way to the end of nowhere. Tears filled his eyes, but he did not blink. He remembered the last time he was there; he'd had a cracked tooth extracted and discovered that there were no medical facilities other than for medications and crude dentistry.

"Listen, I just had a surgery a few days ago, and I had a kidney stent inserted," Tom explained. Both marshals nodded. Tom was escorted through the security entrance, and waited in the small reception area for new inmates, fighting the constant need to urinate, while the marshals conversed with staff members.

"Well, you can't stay here," announced the first marshal.

"Where to now?"

"MDC LA."

"What's the MDC stand for?"

"Metropolitan Detention Center."

"Where is that?"

"Los Angeles."

Handcuffed and crouched in the back of the mini-van, Tom glimpsed the freeway signs, After exiting on Los Angeles Street, the van pulled up to a towering, gray, concrete structure that looked to be ten or fifteen stories. They drove underground, and Tom was stowed away in a screened-in cage off in the corner. He felt like an animal at the zoo.

A rotund black man waddled over; Tom could smell him as he approached. He wore the uniform of the B.O.P. - white shirt and black trousers. "We're waitin' fa count," he explained.

"What's that?"

"Evryday between tree-tirty and four o' clock, evrytin' stops and we havta count you guys to make sure no one's missin'."

Can I use the bathroom?"

"Right ova' der," he said, pointing to a filthy, one-piece, aluminum toilet.

The stent produced the constant urge to urinate, but sometimes, it caused blood to mix with his urine.

"Count's clear," the C.O. grunted. "Put 'tis on."

Tom took off his shirt and tie. The C.O. handed him an oversized, white jumpsuit. It smelled like it had been washed in Drano. His shock crumbled to despair as he entered a freight elevator that took him to the fourth floor. There, he was thrown into a smaller holding cell flooded with the caustic smell of urine.

Processed and photographed, he then was allowed to use the phone. No answer. He tried another number.

"Mike, it's me." he said to his brother, "Would you call Sabrina and let her know I'm at MDC LA."

"For what?"

"Probation violation."

"How long are you lookin' at?"

"I don't even know what the violation is."

"Sure, of course I'll call."

"Thanks."

Stepping on the elevator, facing the back, as ordered, he went up one floor.

"There's no room; he'll have to sleep in the T.V. room," the C.O. said.

The reality crushed Tom. His mind spun, when he saw the dirty, glass room, smoke billowing, inmates strewn about like refugees. He felt like a ship torn from its moorings, thrown adrift in a raging sea.

Chapter 23

"Chow time!" a voice yelled, startling him awake. Breakfast was cold cereal and crumb cakes scraped off industrial-sized metal sheets. The chow line was a hundred-plus tired, lost-looking men shuffling along, resembling the charity lines of the Great Depression. Tom wolfed down his food without tasting it.

"You Taylor?" asked a pleasant, bespectacled, Hispanic inmate. Tom nodded.

"You'll have a cell after breakfast. My name is Miguel Ochoa; just call me Ochoa. I'm an orderly," he said. "Orderlies are inmates that help run the floors and keep the place clean; we get a little extra food and privileges. C'mon, you're in 518," he said, "I'll introduce you to your cellie. His name is José Garcia. You don't speak Spanish, do you?"

"Pocito," Tom answered.

"That'll help." They walked up the small flight of stairs to the back of A Range. "518 is back in the corner; it's quiet and next to the stairway, so don't get any ideas."

"What do you mean?"

"Escaping. You know. By the staircase to the outside."

"I shouldn't be here long." Famous last words.

"What are you here for?"

"Probation violation. At least that's what they tell me."

"Here we are," Ochoa said, as they stood in the doorway of Tom's cell.

"José, este es Tomas. Es un buen tipo, y habla pocito," Ochoa said, introducing Tom and telling José that Tom speaks a little Spanish.

"I'm going to try and get you some clothes and get you out of that jumpsuit," Ochoa said as he walked away.

"Hola José," Tom said, shaking his hand, "Que haces?" His soft brown eyes were timid, and his whole demeanor was that of a man, lost and forgotten, in a strange country. Jose told him he made picture frames out of the foil from potato chip bags, and sold them to other inmates, so they could display photos of their families and loved ones. Tom admired his ingenuity and hustle.

"Gotta present for you," Ochoa said, reappearing in the doorway, holding a bag stuffed with clothes. "Throw me that jumpsuit once you've taken it off," he said, before leaving. Tom quickly changed into his inmate clothing, noticing the white tag on his shirt announcing his eight-digit registration number. Guess I'm a real federal prisoner now.

He meandered out of his room to survey his new surroundings. The raucous din of prison lingo spewing from cartoon-tattooed inhabitants depressed him.

"Oh, yeah, he my dog."

"Killer's my homeboy. He on Six South."

"Yo, Frenchie, wanna get high? Oh yeah, I forgot. You always high."

"I hear Joker's back; he got a dirty after a fourteen-year bit."

Tom felt like he was walking through the Valley of Death. He limped out to the rec deck, grunted as he picked up a basketball. He tried numbing himself by shooting hoops. No good. The kidney stent hampered his mobility. He leaned against a wall, staring with empty eyes. Days like these remind me I am going to die, he thought.

"A&O. A&O!" a voice bellowed. All new inmates to the dining area."

"That's you," said an inmate, pointing at the cafeteria tables.

"I don't know what the 'A' stands for, but the 'O' is for orientation."

Tom stood up and gasped. The stent caused discomfort after any abrupt movement. He hobbled to the dining area, where about twenty inmates milled around. At a table, a muscular man stood ramrod straight. His voice boomed.

"I am Lieutenant Danko. I am in charge of operations. I'm here to go over some rules and regulations."

With speech that was measured and precise, he articulated procedures regarding social and legal visits, the chapel schedule, use of the law library, and the strict no drug and alcohol policy; the last was received with snickers.

"Two final comments," he said, pacing stiffly raising his hand displaying two fingers in vintage Nixon fashion.

"First. Keep your rooms, the floor, and your person presentable at all times. Second, and most importantly, respect my staff at all times, and we will treat you with respect. Remember we are not the reason you are here, we are merely your keepers. If you're upset you're here, look in the mirror.

CHAPTER 24

"Taylor," the C.O. hollered.

"Yes sir?" Tom asked as he hurried to the officer's desk.

"You have a legal visit. Don't forget to put your green shirt on."

Patted down, he was escorted to the first floor registration table.

"Name?"

"Taylor."

"Legal visit, Room 11. Right here," the C.O. said, tonelessly, pointing to a glass-encased office.

"Hey Steve," Tom muttered, grimacing as he sat down gingerly across from his attorney.

"Morning, Tom. Uh, you alright?" Steve asked.

"It's the stent."

"Sabrina told me about it."

"You talked to her? How's she doing?"

"She's alright. She's worried about you, and afraid, being alone with the baby and all. That's why we have to get you out of here. Soon. Also, you need proper medical care, and you'll *never* get that here. Listen I received a copy of your retainer from Vickie Stanford. I think she's being real petty, and she appears to be attacking you personally. I don't know what you did, but she doesn't like you. But don't feel bad. She doesn't like me either. I brought her up on sanctions twice in front of Judge Sunland, and won, which should work in our favor. I tried talking to her already, but she wouldn't give me the time of day." He stopped to make sure Tom was following. "Uh, there are four items on the detainer," Steve said, handing Tom a copy. "First, police contact. You're supposed to report any police contact within 72 hours, so the conversation you had with the Secret Service, technically puts you in violation."

"I didn't know," Tom said in disbelief.

"Nobody does. That's one I've never understood myself. Here's the real irritating thing about that, Tom. There are three classes of violations: A, B, and C. But C violations do not necessitate custodial time. In other words she didn't have to arrest you. Second item, Appearance of New Criminal Activity. That's not a violation. New criminal activity is "the appearance of new criminal activity;" that's just B.S. Now, it's possible the Secret Service will still charge you; but they have no evidence. You say you didn't do anything, and you only look suspicious because you were on federal probation. Third item, she claims your probation reports were late. Now, they have to be in by what date?"

"The fifth of the month."

"Are you sure they were timely?"

"I fill them out and mail them on the first."

"I thought so." Lowering his voice and leaning closer to Tom, he said, "I have a friend in her office; I might be able to get copies. I'd love to catch her in a lie; but I don't know if I'll have it in a couple of days. Now, the fourth item, I have some questions…"

"Resisting arrest!?" Tom shouted, reading from his copy.

"She claims you hid behind the bushes at the office when the marshals came to pick you up."

"That's a total lie. It's impossible!" Tom snapped.

"Why's that?"

"Behind the bushes at the office is a two-hundred foot drop, I'd have two broken legs or worse."

"What a bitch!" Steve said he would see Tom in a few days.

Tom filled out the paperwork for the Inmate Telephone Service. Counselor Brugnone, dialed the number, handed Tom the phone and said, "You have exactly fifteen minutes," then left his office.

"Sabrina?"

"Honey is that you?" Her voice was filled with relief and fear. "Are you alright?" she said, her voice breaking a little.

"All things considered, I guess I'm okay."

"I got through to medical. They're supposed to give you pain meds."

"You're amazing," Tom said, forever grateful for his wife. "I saw Steve this morning. He's going to try for bail in a few days."

"I know. He told me Vickie doesn't like you and for some reason you've become a pet project of hers."

"What do we do if I get stuck here?"

"In the short run, I'll use the P.O.A. you filled out in case of emergency; and

I'll handle the closing myself. I'll tell the family you're traveling on business. They're used to you not being home much anyway. Did Steve say what we're looking at?"

"Probably four to eight months; fourteen months, tops, if the judge finds me in violation." Tom was not going to approach the possibility that the Secret Service might charge him, which would mean two to three years. He did not feel he was lying since Steve reassured him that the probability was as likely as finding a vegetarian tiger. No point in upsetting her unnecessarily.

"How's Tyler?" Tom asked.

"He's great and he loves his daddy. Listen, you stay strong for me in there, I'll handle things out here. Tyler needs his father sane when he gets out.

After 3:30 p.m. count, Tom was called to the Pill line.

"Mr. Taylor," said the P.A., "I have some Tylenol with codeine and some Bisacodyl."

"Bisaca-what?" Tom said to the petite Filipina.

"Bi-sac-o-dyl," she reiterated, enunciating slowly. "Those are the tiny brown pills. They're very strong laxatives. If the stent hasn't already caused you problems, the codeine will constipate you." Great, Tom thought. Problems at both outlets.

Having a little time before Count, he went to see what was on TV. Sitting along the same wall, Tom felt the eyes of a bulky Mexican riveted on him. It was obvious and uncomfortable. The Mexican shot up, barged over and planted himself next to Tom.

"Dino," he said, jutting his hand at Tom. He shook Dino's hand Tentatively, wondering what this was all about. "I saw ya' go to pill line today, whad're dey giving' ya'

"Pain medication for my kidney stones, and a laxative," Tom replied.

Dino was an immense man with hands as big as shovel blades, arms the color and size of whole hams. His head was shaved and the hair had fallen to his chin in the form of a goatee.

"What kin' pain medicashun?"

"Tylenol with codeine." High-octane Tylenol.

"How many?" His eyes and voice softened.

"Six tablets two, three times a day."

"Ya' need all doze?"

"No, not really," Tom said hesitantly. "Why?"

"Uh, maybe we cummake a deal."

"Like what?" Tom asked, not wanting to get involved, but sensing he had no choice.

"What do you need?"

"Nothing yet, I'm hoping to leave."

"Uh-uh, everybody says dat. What ya' like to eat?"

"Um, tuna fish, I guess?"

"Ahright, evra' two tablets for a tuna pouch, okay?"

"Okay, I think."

"You deliver the tablets to my house, and store is on Mondays. He patted Tom on the shoulder, then hustled off to his cell. Tom was acutely conscious of the primal threat emanating from him.

Later that evening, shuffling through the ranges, Tom heard guitar playing from a cell near his. Leaning on the doorway, he listened to a bearded inmate strum a passable rendition of Garth Brooks', "The Dance."

"Mind if I sit in?" Tom asked.

"You play?" the inmate responded.

"A little," Tom said, glad for a chance to show off. Maybe it would band-aid his ego for awhile. He played Joe Cocker's "Feelin Alright", and Johnny Winter's version of "Johnny B. Goode," to resounding applause from the circle of hooch-swigging inmates. He left the room, thinking he needed to start playing again.

"Taylor...court," the C.O. said, tersely, after opening the cell door. The kidney stent pinched Tom's groin, cramping his abdomen as he rose to get dressed. Pray for bail, he said to himself.

At 5:00 a.m., they were marshaled to the fourth floor, strip-searched, and their 'greens' were exchanged for courtroom 'blues'. After a series of eternal delays in a myriad of holding cells, Tom was shackled and loaded into a white van, bound for the Ronald Reagan Courthouse.

At the courthouse, he endured a five-hour wait before they were ready. Let's get this over with," Tom said, bracing himself as he entered the courtroom. He smiled at Sabrina in the gallery. She smiled back. He took a seat next to his attorney.

"How are you doing?" Steve asked, sincerely.

"Been up since four," Tom answered, yawning. He saw his probation officer, the pre-trial officer, and the AUSA huddled. The court clerk strolled in. "This court is now in session, the Honorable Judge Sunland presiding. Case No. 001322789, USA vs. Thomas Taylor."

Judge Sunland entered, adorned in her black robe.

Steve expounded to the court that, although Mr. Taylor was guilty of police contact, a very minor infraction that did not require incarceration, he had a new child at home, and a wife, motioning briefly to the gallery.

Moreover, he was not a flight risk, nor a danger to the community. Also he was in dire need of proper medical care.

Vickie Stanford, dressed for battle in her gun-metal business suit, countered ferociously, with a vendetta-like tone that startled both Tom and

Steve. She enumerated the issues on her detainer, three of which were false, and closed with a ridiculous letter from the Medical Director at MDC stating that Mr. Taylor was receiving the "utmost in proper medical care."

"Then why do I still have the stent in? It was scheduled to be removed a month ago," Tom muttered to himself.

Being a conservative jurist, Judge Sunland erred on the side of caution and denied bail. As the gavel hit the bench, two marshals lifted Tom from his chair

and ushered him out of the courtroom. The last thing he saw was Sabrina weeping quietly.

"Now what?" Tom asked Steve through a mesh screen. He was handcuffed, fettered to the floor, perched on a stool in an enclosed cubicle.

"Here's what we're going to do. We need pictures of that drop behind the bushes in the back of your office. I'll have Sabrina get those. I'll need to get a letter from your personal physician and a copy of your medical records at MDC. Once we have all that, I'll set a date. And I'll try to get a copy of your probation reports from the inside. If I catch her in some lies and/or get her to lose her temper like I've done before, Judge Sunland will have to let you go. In the meantime, keep your chin up and try to stay healthy.

The marshals shepherded Tom back to MDC LA. Processed through R&D at 9:00 p.m. Tom dragged himself to Five South. He entered his cell and bumped into a barricade of thirteen banker's boxes. Like spires on the Kremlin, there was a stack of Architectural Digest and Conde Nast Travel magazines atop the monument of boxes.

Thirteen boxes of discovery; must be a serious case, Tom thought. Tom's discovery was about two-inches thick, if that. An inmate making up the bottom bunk heard Tom shuffle in. The athletic figure stood up with poise, and turned around as if someone had just illuminated the spotlight for the debut of his Broadway show. His eyes had a steely look, as fierce as eagle eyes. His aristocratic nose and robust jawline produced such a forceful presence, he looked like he could levitate and rearrange the thirteen boxes if he simply willed it to happen. He had a polished air of resilient nobility. "Hello, my name is Iouri," he said, extending his hand. His grip was cold and felt like a vise.

Chapter 25

"Hi, Iouri, I'm Tom."

"Ah, yes I know."

Tom did not know exactly what he meant, but let it slide.

"I hope you do not mind that I moved in. Garcia shipped out, and your cell is away in the corner and quiet. I did not want to wait until you came back, as someone else would have taken the spot." Iouri spoke as if the topic was not open for discussion.

And if I mind, then what? Tom thought. What's the difference; one cellie's as good as the next.

"Sure, no problem," he said.

"A Range!" a sonorous voice boomed.

"Hey, they're serving lunch. I'll let you get situated. You gonna eat?"

"No, I would never eat that crap."

Well, la-de-da. What do you eat? Tom wondered as he left the cell.

After lunch, Tom informed Iouri of his kidney stent and general medical condition; he explained that his constant use of laxatives made for frequent and inopportune need for the toilet and asked for his cooperation and understanding. Iouri acted like it would not be too much of a problem.

"I'm going to work out," Iouri announced, "I usually work out from ten to three o' clock." His days were planned like a military maneuver.

"I ride the bike as much as I can," Tom said, not to be completely outdone.

"That is good. And I'm going to teach you how to eat right."

Yes sir, Tom said to himself.

Iouri's diet consisted of vegetables, massive amounts of tuna fish and protein products, as much as he could get hold of. And, as a general rule, no sugar. He was a voracious reader, listened to classic rock and the BBC News Station. He did not watch television. He felt Americans were uncultured, lazy Neanderthals who had been nurtured at the nipple of the Boob Tube.

Tom suffered through dinner chow with two inmates he had met recently, Brian Siefert and Dr. Shah. Brian was from Madison, Wisconsin and finishing a five-year sentence for money laundering. Dr. Shah was a chiropractor with a business partner who allegedly had forged Dr. Shah's signature on some fraudulent bank loan documents and fled the country with the money.

"Ever notice how much he works out?" Brian commented.

"Wants to look good when they strap him down," Dr. Shah replied.

"Seems kinda arrogant, though."

"You know he was my cellie."

"Oh yeah, that's right. Lucky you."

"Who are you talking about?" Tom asked.

"That Russian guy they've got here for five murders. He was on the front page of the L.A. Times when they arrested him.

"I think you're talking about my new cellie," Tom informed them.

Brian and Dr. Shah's eyes locked.

"Be careful," they warned Tom in unison.

"Why?"

"He's extremely wealthy, and wealthy inmates are very dangerous. They prey on guys like you; besides; he's apparently a killer."

Tom tried to process what he'd just heard, then turned in his tray. At 9:00 p.m., he called Sabrina, which was fast becoming a nightly routine. A far cry from his former routine of Jacuzzi and Honkas.

Shortly after lockdown, Iouri switched off the light. Tom wished he could have switched off his mind, which was caught in pre-trial purgatory. He watched as Iouri darted back and forth in the cell with unwavering assuredness. He wears his MDC uniform and struts around like a ship's captain; he's either nuts or knows something no-one else does.

A couple of days went by without a word from Iouri. Tom found him as elusive as smoke. He was as disciplined and unemotional as a robot. After his workout and shower, he styled his hair, put on his lotion and posed in front of the mirror, as if fashioning himself for a Mr. Olympia tournament. His body looked rock-hard, void of any hint of fat. When he moved his head, muscles and tendons rippled like snakes.

Iouri suddenly stopped pacing and faced Tom. "My attorney says your attorney is a jerk. He says you are only fighting a violation and should be out."

"My P.O. is lying; I'm trying to get out with my probation terminated, "Tom replied. "I hear you're on a big case, that the government is trying to give you the death penalty."

"Ah, yes, your government is stupid. It is really a matter between Russians.

Your government should not be involved."

"It's not my government."

"You are an American, right?"

"Yeah? So?"

"Then it is your government."

"So did you do what they claim?"

"What do they say?"

"That you were on the front pages of the LA Times, and you killed five
people."

"That is preposterous. We are just computer hackers settling scores from the old country. Your government does not have any evidence; nor do they have any bodies." Iouri sounded totally credible. "Let me tell you about your country. You may be very smart and college educated, but you have been brainwashed by their system."

Tom was intrigued as to where this was going, and wondered how Iouri knew he was college educated, as he had never told him.

"Your country is called the United States of America. It should be called the United States of Hypocrisy. You are aware that your country was founded by a bunch of slave owners proForkining they wanted to be free."

Tom had never looked at it that way.

"I just read in, the San Francisco Chronicle, an article about a senior intelligence officer, who was accused of devil-worshipping; and he admitted it!

You have devil-worshippers in high places, helping make policy decisions that run the country. Too bad they are not as good at raising the IQ in Washington as they are at raising money."

Tom seemed unfazed by that one.

"And your famous War on Drugs, that is one of the biggest jokes. Do you Know that twelve hundred metric tons of refined heroin, worth ten percent of America's GNP, are shipped from Thailand on U.S. Air Force Cargo planes every year? Some War on Drugs. Your DEA agents are just criminals with guns and badges." Iouri was animated and on a roll. "Now this is one of my favorites, and I have many. Who shot John Kennedy?"

"Lee Harvey Oswald."

"Wrong."

"Who, then?"

"A man named William Greer."

"Who's that?"

"He was a secret service agent two cars behind Kennedy?"

"You're kidding."

"No, I am not; I have seen the original film. All the films you and the American people see have been doctored. There is no way from where Lee

Harvey Oswald was with the kind of rifle he had, that he could have killed Kennedy."

"Wow." Tom said. That's pretty amazing if it's true; or maybe the guy's just whacked.

"I will tell you that Lee Harvey Oswald was in Russia two days before he

allegedly shot Kennedy."

"How do you know all this?"

"I read a lot. And my father was a KGB agent."

"Where is he now?"

"Your CIA killed him."

Silence. Iouri's speech became cold and functional. "There are many things you do not know, Tom, obviously."

"You seem okay with being here," Tom said, vaguely rattled by Iouri's conspiracy theories. Recalling Inspector Harley, he had learned the U.S. Government did what the hell it wanted and found ways to justify it later.

"What do you mean?" Iouri inquired.

"Being in jail and facing the death penalty."

"This is not jail. This is Disneyland."

I've been to Disneyland. Many times. And this ain't no friggin' Disneyland.

"I did five years hard time, pacing back and forth, using a bucket for a

Toilet; if I screwed up or mouthed off, I would be counting trees." Iouri's tone was spirited almost incensed.

"Counting trees. What the hell does that mean?"

"Counting trees means they would have thrown me on the ground in

Siberia face up so I could count trees as I froze to death. The last thing that happens before you freeze to death, is you stop blinking, which enables you to count even more trees."

A voice beckoned him from the wall. Actually, it echoed from the vent. Iouri leaped up on the plumbing, cupped his hand around his mouth and started speaking Russian into the vent. Tom sat on his bunk, observing

his enigmatic roommate. We supply our own drugs? That doesn't surprise me; but the Secret Service shooting JFK? Why would they? There's always been a controversy about his death, but that's a stretch. Or is it?

Tom had heard that other inmates communicated through the vents, but had never seen it done before. Who was he talking to? Probably some- one on his case. When Iouri was finished he jumped down and said, "Tom," which sounded like, 'Tum'." "It is late, I have court in the morning." He turned off the light.

Tom pondered his new cellie. He was respectful of Tom's medical condition, his constant urination. Iouri was confident, stoic and arrogant. Or was he delusional? Or a good actor? Tom tossed and turned, trying to get to sleep, wondering if the man sleeping in the bunk below him was a mass murderer.

CHAPTER 26

When Tom awoke, Iouri was already sitting up on his bunk, waiting for the C.O. to open the door. It was 4:00 a.m. Tom shuffled out of the cell, still half asleep, agony in his groin. He saw someone running the length of B Range, which connected to A Range, like the base of an isosceles triangle. His arms were flailing like an escaped mental patient and he was blubbering incoherently.

He crossed into A Range and mumbled something unintelligible, which sounded like, "My life…above here."

Then Tom deciphered that he has said, "Tell my wife I love her."

His hands and neck were bloody, his sparse hair standing up in comical wisps. He kept loping toward Tom, who was frozen in place. He squatted on top of the white, tubular railing, looking eighteen feet down onto C Range.

"Don't do it!" the C.O. roared.

Inmates were dumbstruck. Some taunted him, chanting: "Do it!" There was a frenzied commotion as C.O.s and medical staff flooded the floor. Tom wanted to do something, but his body would not respond. What should he do? What could he do?

Preparing to jump, the man appeared to have second thoughts. He angled himself toward the adjacent set of railings and lunged, trying to grip the bars. His bloody hands slipped. Tom could hear the thud of his body, and the smack of his head, bouncing like a bowling ball off the tiled floor. The sound was apocalyptic. The impact carried with it everything ugly the prison system had to offer: despair, hate, oppression and death. Immediately, an army of C.O.s removed the inmates from the floor, ushered them into their cells and locked the doors. The last words Tom heard were: "I can't breathe," a strained gurgle, the sound of a man drowning in his own blood.

The medical staff snapped open a gurney. Tom sat on his bunk, contemplating what he just witnessed, raw evidence of what the system can do to people.

There was a conspiratorial air of camaraderie as Iouri, Petrov, and Nikki greeted each other like they were at a reunion of the Boy's Club. They were down in the basement of MDC in a holding cell, waiting to be escorted through a tunnel to the Roybal Court Building. The lighting was grim and harsh, and the aroma had the stench of a portable toilet, but the three acted like they were at a Malibu beach party. They spoke in Russian: "Can you believe these idiots, putting us in the same holding cell?" Iouri said. "In Russia they would not have let us be in the same building." The other two acknowledged with smirks and nods.

"Tell me about your new cellie, Nikki said. Will he work?"

"I think so." Iouri murmured.

"What's his name?"

"Tom. Actually, he's perfect. I haven't had much time to work on him yet; but I have started. He lives in Orange County, and he's only fighting a probation violation. Victor told me he has a court date on December 16th, and he should be released then. We are getting close to Thanksgiving, so I will move fast. I will try to have him locked in the next two weeks. I'm planning a New Year's Eve departure."

"When we're finished with him, we will eliminate him?" Nikki asked in anticipation.

Petrov shook his head. Some things never change.

"That may not be a necessary, or even a good idea," Iouri responded.

"Why not?"

"We will be escaped fugitives forever, and will need someone who can move about freely and legally. If this Tom proves trustworthy, he will be worth more to us alive than dead."

Petrov nodded. Iouri was probably right, once again.

"Is Anna hanging tough?"

"Tough enough, I guess." Petrov's doubts about his marriage were flaring up.

"Tell her not to give up; it will not be too long."

"What about Marina?"

"She says she is being patient, but I sense she thinks she will never see me again," Iouri said plainly, "I think she's planning to move on. And if she does, so be it. I will deal with her when I see her."

The inmates on Five South were locked down until 2:00 p.m. The buzz around the unit was that it was Irv Rubenstein who attempted suicide. It inundated the local news. Carey Tobin, another inmate, explained to Tom that Irv had a co-defendant, Earl Steelburg, whom Irv had believed the Feds had pressured into being a turncoat, and promised leniency if he would testify against Irv. For Irv, it was the last straw. As a result he was looking at a life sentence.

Tom returned to his cell, and was making a tuna fish sandwich when Iouri arrived. "How was court?" Tom asked him.

"Usual shit; just filing motions." Tom was still on a need to know basis.

"You know what happened this morning?"

"Some Jew tried to kill himself."

"What do you think?"

"What do you mean?"

"Is he a coward or an idiot?"

"He is neither. It is your life; if you want to end it, it is your choice," Iouri said, icily. Tom was taken aback at his coldness. It was clear that he was a man who faced the world on his own terms. He did not look for or care about the approval of others. He knew it had a short half-life. Those who did not believe in an afterlife tended to lean very hard on this one. A complex, mysterious and dangerous man.

CHAPTER 27

The next evening, tired of watching T.V., and too early to call Sabrina, Tom sauntered back to his cell, and was stopped cold. Again. Two C.O.s and an Asian inmate Tom did not recognize, were huddled with Iouri, smoking cigarettes, looking at pictures and some paperwork. Everyone except Iouri, whose face remained impassive, glanced at Tom with an unsettled look, as if he had caught them all having group sex. "Excuse me. Be right back," he mumbled, doing an about face and leaving.

Back in the cell, the meeting was disbanding. "Thanks for the Allen-wrench," Iouri said quietly. The Asian inmate stood sentry in the doorway while the two C.O.s shook Iouri's hand and whispered, "Thanks for the loot. It'll be a good Christmas for our wives."

"Maybe for your wife; mine will never know," said one C.O.

"This meeting never happened," Iouri snapped. His gaze was serious, remote and impersonal.

"What meeting?" The three left, not speaking to each other.

After calling Sabrina, Tom returned to his cell to find Iouri engrossed in a novel. He ignored Tom, who climbed up on his bunk and started reading the newspaper. Then, suddenly, Iouri stood up suddenly and tossed down his book. "You know what is going on, do you not?"

"Are you referring to your little powwow earlier tonight?"

"Right."

"No, I have no idea."

"I am trying to get out of here."

"We're all trying to get out of here."

This is not going to be as easy as I thought. Iouri was annoyed by Tom's flippant comment. He decided to use the direct approach.

"I have an escape plan."

"You're kidding."

"No I am not, and I need your help."

"Thanks for considering me, but not interested."

"Ah, what would it take?" Iouri asked, matter-of-factly. He believed that every man has his price.

"What do you mean?"

"How much money?"

Tom tried to think of the best way out of this, and flipped back, glibly, "Oh, a million bucks."

"A millions would be fine," Iouri replied, unruffled.

When Iouri's words sank in, Tom's mind froze. "Come on, you don't have that kind of money. Besides, how're you going to pull this off?" Suddenly, he had a lot of other questions, and wondered if he had lost his mind by even thinking about it. This is nuts!

"I am not telling you any more at this point; but I thought you knew or had figured it out."

"How would I know?"

"Do you think three Russians would sit around and let your country kill us?"

"Hadn't given it much thought."

"A millions dollars would be no problem, and my plan is perfect. Getting out of here should be easy as long as everyone follows my directions; but I will not tell you any more until you tell me we have a deal. One more thing: I do not have to tell you to keep your mouth silent, correct?"

"Of course not," Tom reassured him; but it was clear that Iouri's question was a not-so-veiled threat.

CHAPTER 28

"Pill line," an Asian voice announced. Tom shuffled down to the medical station, tried to exchange pleasantries with the affable P.A., Mercedes, but she appeared to be in a mood.

"Hey, dog," Dino growled, as Tom shuffled back onto his floor. "What da' Hell ya' tryin' ta pull?"

"What do you mean?" Tom asked as he passed Dino his tablets. He was baffled when Dino took a belligerent stance, blocking his movement.

"Ya ben sellin' dees to Bandit, ain't cha'."

"No."

"I seen 'im wit some."

"I'm not the only one that gets them, you know."

"Ya' shure ya' ain't ben givin' 'em to him?"

"Yes, I'm positive."

"Oh, okay. Jus' checkin'." Dino said, then plodded away.

Tom hustled toward his cell.

"Hey Taylor," the C.O. said. "Social visit."

Even in casual attire, Sabrina looked well-dressed and beautiful. She kissed him. "Honey, if you shaved, you missed your face," she announced with that dreamy smile. Tom sat down, tousled Tyler's hair. Tyler smiled and giggled. "How're doing?"

"Fine. Freaked-out, insecure, neurotic, angry and/or emotional - take your pick," she said, then laughed.

"You forgot, 'gorgeous'. Did I tell you about my new cellie?"

"I didn't know much about the last one."

As Tom told his Iouri story, her warm smile disappeared. "... so then he asked me to help him escape," he finished, lowering his voice.

Her face went from upset to total disgust. "Are you NUTS!?" she yelled, then spat out a verbal onslaught, leaped up, clutching Tyler and stormed to the exit.

Tom sat there, defeated. "I never said it was a good idea," he muttered as he struggled to get up. Truth be told, the more he thought about it, the more enticing the money became. I'm sure she didn't hear the million dollar amount.

He returned to his cell, distracted by Iouri speaking Russian into the vent. Tom was beginning to recognize a few words. "Da" meant "yes" and "nyet" was "no". Occasionally he heard, "kto," which meant "who."

Iouri jumped down and paced a few times back and forth like a pitcher winding up. Tom knew what was coming.

"How did your visit go? Do we have a deal?"

Tom wanted to say yes, but prudence dictated that he should stall. Wisdom insisted he say no. Greed was dueling with common sense. Iouri waited. Tom felt a choking sensation in his throat; Iouri did not look the type to take no for an answer.

"Sabrina wants to think it over. And I want her approval before I say yes." The green goblin of greed was luring Tom. The million dollars was emblazoned in his mind, calling to him. Iouri was still, his eyes boring into Tom.

"How do I know that, if we help you, we won't be hurt?" Tom asked him.

Iouri's face grew harder. The question irritated him, but he knew Tom was coming around and did not want to scare him away. "Listen, ah, the things we did were to settle scores with people who were traitors from Russia; we did not kill anyone. Part of what I was doing was in memory of and out of loyalty to my father.

"Why did the CIA kill your father?"

"I cannot tell you."

Silence. Tom felt like he might have poked a stick into a hornet's nest.

"If you are as smart, resourceful and ambitious as you appear, I have a large job set up, and your cut would make the millions dollars seem like, how you say, pocket change."

CHAPTER 29

Thanksgiving in prison. Yuck, Tom thought, when he opened his eyes in the morning. He opened some cards from his older children and his partner Bob Beem. Cris, the office manager, had the pictures developed showing the precipitous drop behind the office. She was fired up to testify, if necessary.

Tom was apprehensive as he approached the bank of phones. He had not spoken to Sabrina since her agitated exit from the visiting room. As the phone rang he was expecting a cold reception.

"Hi, honey." She did not seem upset. "How are you holding up?"

"Never better."

"Keep your chin up, I know it's no picnic in there, but, according to Steve, you should be home by Christmas. Hang in there; I'll see you Tuesday or Wednesday. I love you."

"I love you too," Tom echoed, smiling when he heard Tyler cooing in the background.

Tom decided he wanted more information from Iouri. "Do you really think an escape is possible?"

"You were a contractor; what do you think?" Iouri said, guardedly.

How did he know that? I never told him I was a contractor. He was beginning to believe Iouri had a complete dossier on him.

"In case you have not noticed, this place is built with drywall."

"I can see that."

Iouri looked disgusted. He did not want to divulge any more information without Tom having agreed to a deal.

"Maybe you don't realize that this is crazy, but I do. I just want to know it's possible."

In a professional tone, Iouri enlightened Tom on the history of MDC.

"In the early 80's, your government built this place to be the West Coast headquarters of the bankruptcy division of the IRS. For reasons I cannot uncover, but are not essential, the building sat dormant for a few years, and in 1984 they revamped it into a prison, or federal holding facility as they call it. Prisons are built from concrete slabs and cinder block, Tom. This place was built to be an office building, not a prison, so yes, it is very possible."

Although he did not know the specifics, Tom was beginning to believe him.

"Do you have the money?"

"Do we have a deal?"

"I'm putting my freedom on the line, so I need to know you really have the money. And if you do, how you're going to get it to me." He did not realize that, under the new conspiracy laws, he might be putting Sabrina's freedom at risk, and endangering the well-being of anyone close to him.

Iouri removed the lid from one of his banker's boxes and pulled out a stack of papers. Tom could see they were account statements and general bank records. He noticed an expression of almost religious ecstasy on Iouri's face as he flipped through the papers. "Ah, look at this," Iouri said, gruffly, showing Tom a sheet of paper. "The Feds took $969, 323.00 from the Bank of America where I had three domestic accounts for my one company, called Rebar International. It's a legitimate business and they had no right to steal that money."

"What are those other accounts?"

"Those are from my global accounts - from the Bank of Zurich, Kasikorn in Thailand, Credit Suisse in Geneva, and a bunch of others."

There must be thirty to thirty-five million dollars in them.

"They didn't levy those accounts?"

"They cannot, and they are very upset, and I am glad they are very upset."

Well, looks like he has the money.

"You understand, your government is evil, one of the most evil and corrupt in the world. So if you have any, how you say, compunctions, about doing anything against your government, do not give it a second thought. As you probably noticed, I love to read. Knowledge is one of the ultimate powers. There is a truism from an author I like, W.H. Auden, who said, "'Those to whom evil is done, do evil in return'."

"Eye for an eye, tooth for a tooth."

"Something like that. Something else I want you to think about: In this country, justice is for a select few. You and I are not part of that group. We are not Kennedys or Bushes or Clintons, so there is no real justice for us. The fact that you are separated from your wife and newborn child is absurd. For a probation violation? That is not justice.

"Who do you talk to in the vents?"

"Do we have a deal?"

"I will talk to Sabrina this week and close her on the deal."

"I know you can, and I know you will," Iouri insisted.

Tom was uncertain whether that was motivational or threatening.

"I have two co-defendants, Nikki and Petrov. Nikki has a little girl that he is legal guardian for, his niece, and he has to be able to get her before the end of January or the Feds will put her up for adoption. Petrov has a gorgeous wife and a pretty little girl. Nikki is on Nine South lined, up directly above us, and Petrov is on Six South. He is trying to get into the cell right above us. This is imperative for the plan to work."

This confirmed a hunch Tom had that Iouri had been scheming to move into Tom's cell all along because it was pivotal to his plans.

"What if Petrov can't get in line?"

"Then he will not go."

"He has a wife and kid; I mean, if I'm helping I want him to come with."

"It may not be up to you."

Tom nodded. He now believed that Iouri had the money and that an escape was possible. But there still was one more obstacle - Sabrina.

CHAPTER 30

The next morning, Tom was feeling under the weather. He was tired of urinating blood, which often felt like tiny razor blades slicing through his urethra. Not one to lie around all day, he headed out of the cell.

"Hey assh-ole!" Tom was startled as he saw a maniacal inmate charging toward him.

"Ya' fuckin' liar, I know ya' was givin' away my pills."

Before Tom could say anything, he saw lumps of clenched muscle at the corner of his jaw and fire in his eyes. Then Dino crushed his chest with one of his brick-sized fists, bouncing Tom off the stairway door, almost tripping the alarm. Tom buckled, let out a tortured gasp and crashed to the floor.

Hearing the hubbub in the hallway, Iouri jackknifed off his bunk and bolted from the cell, finding Tom hunched over like a Slinky Toy. He zeroed in on Dino several yards downrange stomping away. Iouri sprinted at him, emitting a primal growl. He grabbed Dino's arm, pulled his index finger, while simultaneously pinching the median and radial nerves in his back. The intense pain traveled into the base of Dino's skull, his eyes bright with anger.

Gino gasped and moaned. "Let go, Pleesh le' go." Searing pain caused his black eyes to dilate and his face was turning a mottled plum color. He cried for mercy from the God he had so long ago denied. Still holding him in that stance, Iouri whispered in his ear.

"You leave him the fuck alone. And tell any of the boneheads you associate with that if they fuck with him, they are fucking with me. And you do not want to fuck with me."

"Okray, okray...le' go," Dino croaked through the excruciating pain. Iouri released him.

Dino stumbled over to help Tom up. "Sorry 'bout dat, dog. Don' know wat got inta me. I jus' thought ya' was reniggin' on ar' deal." Tom stood erect, his legs shaky underneath him. "It's cool," he assured Dino.

That evening, after lockdown, his chest wound still throbbing, Tom thanked Iouri for coming to his defense. Iouri nodded. Just protecting my investment. "There are no friends in prison," he added. "You will see Sabrina this week, yes?"

"Tuesday or Wednesday."

"And you will impart to her how her life will improve with the millions dollars and that there are more lucrative opportunities that you would be a fool not to partake of."

"Yes," Tom said, feeling the cell closing in on him. Iouri had succeeded in boxing him in.

"Very good, because time is of the essence. I will now give you a synopsis of the plan:" Iouri then sketched the escape plan, swiftly and succinctly. As he spoke, his face displayed the intoxicating thrill of a man about to commit an act of religious significance. "As you know, Petrov needs to get into position. I already have an Allen wrench." Iouri produced the tool, which he had hidden inside the aluminum leg of the countertop that supported the sink. "I already have three cells, including this one, where I have removed the black rubber caulking, so the windows may be readily removed and re-installed.

We will need cell phones. A line can be lowered and they can be brought in through the windows, making communication with you and my co-defendants easier. There is a list of tools that will be hauled up in several deliveries. Behind the mirrors, which are two feet by two and a half feet, and can be removed by a Phillips screwdriver, we will make holes, and score the inside of the outer wall facing the stairway, so they can be punctured quickly at the right time. For distraction, there will be scheduled disturbances on all three floors at the time of our departure."

Iouri stopped and glanced at Tom, noticing that he was increasingly engrossed in his words.

"Nikki will exit Nine, grab Petrov on Six. They will meet here, and we will go down to Three; for two reasons. One, there are cameras on Nine and Two, so we cannot go to Two. When Nikki enters the stairway on Nine, he will be just below the floor's camera angle. To be safe, I am having pictures taken of the hallway; they will be shrunk down and taped to that camera's face. So when Control flashes to that camera, they will always see the same thing."

Iouri beamed. "There are 126 cameras in the building and only 16 monitor screens in the Control room. Four of those are kept permanently tuned to the women's floor, Nine North, because of a rape case involving a C.O. And three are kept tuned to the visiting room. One thing I want you to do is pay attention in the next couple of weeks; how often and at what times do you hear the guards roving in this hallway.

As this point, Tom was enthralled.

"There are no exterior cameras on the North and South sides of MDC, which shows you how smart these people are," he said, rolling his eyes. "There is one camera on the Roybal Building, which is on the south side of MDC. So, ideally, we want the deliveries done at night, so vision will be hampered. There are 136 staff members on during the week, but only 31 on weekends. And five to ten of those do not show on holidays. A Saturday, Sunday, or holiday is ideal. The best time will be between 7:00 and lockdown at 9:30."

Tom was impressed with Iouri's thoroughness and especially curious at how he had learned all this. Everyone has a price, he assumed.

"On floors Five to Ten, MDC is constructed with these little windows."

Iouri pointed at the cell window which, he said, are 4 ft. by 4 ¾ ft. "Floors One through Four have 3ft. by 4ft. windows guarded by four hollow parallel bars. They are five inches apart and four inches in diameter; you have probably seen them in the visiting room."

Tom nodded. "How do you know all this?"

"I have blueprints," Iouri replied curtly. He did not like to be interrupted.

"On the third floor landing from this stairway, we can punch our way back in; that is where the storeroom is. Have you been to the third floor?

"I've been to the law library."

"Adjacent to the law library is the lieutenant's office which is usually empty at night and certainly empty on weekends and holidays. Across from the lieutenant's office is the storeroom. Once inside, I will cut the glass and, with a strong hydraulic pump, spread the bars eight to twelve inches so we can fit through. We will then rappel the eighteen feet to the ground. I want you to arrange for six motorcycles, with riders, of course, to pick us up, who will scatter in different directions. The three of us will meet at a place that is covered, like a parking garage. Once our exit is discovered, LAPD will respond first. Their helicopter response time is fifteen minutes, and they will be looking for people on foot, or ah, motorcycles. At the parking garage you will be there to drive us to a safe house that you will arrange for us. I have been over this a thousand times and I know it will work."

Amazing!

"I do have one concern that you or we need a contingency plan for?"

"What's that?"

"Are you certain that you will be released on December 16th?"

"I think so."

"I have no faith in your attorney because of what my attorney tells me.

So, I want you to meet my attorney on Monday. You will first meet his assistant, Reese Vanderwal, and then Victor, if he has time. I want a backup plan in the event your attorney does not do his job. Also I want to warn you that Victor Goldman is overbearing and arrogant, but he is the best."

The next morning, Sunday, Tom attended services down in the Chapel on the third floor. He noticed the entrance to the storeroom Iouri had discussed.

Under the circumstances, he thought a little prayer couldn't hurt. Besides, Father Don liked it when Tom showed up, because he was bilingual and would assist in the readings. Father also enjoyed the musical accompaniment; it gave Tom a chance to play the guitar.

"Where did you go?" Iouri wanted to know, when he returned to his cell.

"Chapel," Tom said.

Iouri tossed down his Architectural Digest.

"You Catholic?"

"I was raised Roman Catholic in Chicago." Iouri knew that. For Tom, the Church had been a relatively innocuous entity, primarily recording the benchmarks of his life—funerals, weddings, baptisms, and holidays.

"Remember how I said nothing is as it seems?"

"Sure."

"What if I told you the Catholic Church was just as evil as your government?"

"You're saying Jesus Christ was EVIL?"

"No, Jesus Christ was a good man, if he really existed, and Christianity has its good points. For the record December 25th is the ancient pagan holiday of Sol Invictus—Unconquered Sun— the Bible says Christ was really born in March. Also, Christianity's view or concept, if you will, of God as an old man with a beard comes from Zeus. Most people forget that all religions were created by man. And for thousands of years, they have argued and fought and killed with their 'My God is better than your God' attitude. Jupiter used to be the King of the Gods. Does anyone worship him now? Clarence Darrow said, 'I have always felt that doubt was the beginning of wisdom, and the fear of God is the end of wisdom'. I agree."

Tom was riveted.

"What I am saying is that the Roman Catholic Church, the organization, is evil. It is all about money. It even helped Hitler out in World War II because he gave them a lot of money."

"You're kidding?" Tom gasped. He found himself saying that a lot lately when listening to Iouri.

Iouri stood up. "In the 1940's the I.G. Farben Chemical Company employed a Polish salesman, Karol Wojtyla, who sold cyanide to the Germans for use in Auschwitz. The same salesman also worked as a chemist in the manufacturing of the poisonous gas. The same gas, along with Zyklon B and Malathion, was used to exterminate millions of Jews, as you probably know. Along with other groups their bodies were burned to ashes in the ovens. After the war the salesman feared for his life, joined the Catholic Church and was ordained a priest in 1946. The salesman was ordained Poland's youngest bishop in 1955. After a 30-day reign, his predecessor was assassinated, and the ex-cyanide salesman assumed the Papacy as Pope John Paul II."

Tom was stunned. Unbelievable!

"Malakov, Johnson, Barrazza, and Taylor - legal visits," the C.O. announced. It was Monday morning. Tom met up with the other three, was patted down and took the elevator to the first floor. There, he met Reese Vanderwal. Reese was tall, slender with a baby face and black hair. His demeanor was low-key, but all business when it came to the practice of law. His confidence was unmistakable; even more obvious was that he respected, revered, and somewhat feared his employer, Victor Goldman.

There was a commotion in the visiting room. Victor had swaggered in like royalty, unfazed by keeping his subjects waiting. He had an imposing, athletic presence for a sixty-two-year-old, and was forced to bend way over when he signed in at the registration desk. Hard to miss. He met with inmates. Barrazza and Johnson. while Iouri appeared to be socializing with Reese, then spoke briefly to Victor.

Tom was summoned. Victor bristled. In his grave, baritone voice and smiling like a shark, Victor said, flatly, "You are going to help my guy?"

"I'm thinking about it," Tom stammered, as Victor scribbled notes "What about my case?"

"Steve should be able to get you out; if not, I'll help. Now get straight with Iouri." It was a demand. Almost a threat.

Tom realized, now, that the Plan was big; larger and more complex than he'd imagined, involving Iouri's attorney. Iouri had proved he was a player at Grandmaster level. It was a brilliant stroke.

CHAPTER 31

Tom paid a visit to the law library. He wanted to know more before he reached the point of no return with Iouri. I'm probably already too late. He found US Code 18-752(a), aiding and abetting an escape. A maximum of five years and a $250,000 fine. That would definitely be no walk in the park. Aiding escapees who are murderers, even though I don't think they are murderers - they're not even convicted, an additional five years. If the Feds use their conspiracy claws and snatch Sabrina, theoretically we're both looking at ten years: A Pair-a-Dimes, as it's known inside.

Tom had learned that very few defendants received the statutory maximum, and that fines were based primarily on the ability to pay. With his accounting experience, he knew that it was relatively simple to perform a little window dressing to make himself look indigent, especially now that his house was sold, and his mother-in-law was in legal possession of his money.

He also knew that the judges were required to use the Federal Sentencing Guidelines. According to those, he was looking at 24 to 36 months, based on the crime and criminal history. Performing a cost/benefit analysis, he reckoned: A million dollars for three years; that's $330,000 a year. That's what I used to make in a good year in the car business. Fine, but this assumes that, even if the Feds did not charge Sabrina, she would not leave him. That's the real risk in all this.

He returned to his cell. Iouri greeted him by saying," You are going home soon, right?" He was concerned about Tom's disappearance, and a possible delay or significant matter that Tom may not have told him about.

"Supposedly; if you can believe the attorneys."

"Victor told you he will get you out if your dumptruck does not."

"Dumptruck?"

"Your attorney. A dumptruck is an ineffective attorney, one that does a bullshit job; basically he is shit."

Tom did not know if that was true, but he did not want to admit that he had chosen an incompetent attorney twice in a row, so he changed the subject.

"You told me you did time in Russia. Was it tougher than here?"

"I could tell you stories you would not believe. I spent five years pacing back and forth, like, how you say, a wind-up-toy. The worst was the interrogations I heard, and the battered bodies I saw. There was a Doctor Rosen; they called him 'Doctor Death'. He tried to get you to rat. To interrogate prisoners, he had some potions - chlorpromazine and haloperidol. He would shoot injections of three or four milligrams daily into the prisoners' asses. The effects would start with unrelenting drowsiness, then alternating with ferocious headaches. The men would become disoriented, then experience progressive memory loss. They would be aware but realize there was nothing they could do about it. Their mental functions would become slow and muddled, but their emotions would, at the same time, become more intense and volatile, with extreme paranoia.

He paused, reliving the experience. Tom thought he saw his eyes moisten. "Sometimes, they had crying fits and convulsive seizures. Tremors, constant dizziness, fainting and uncontrollable muscle spasms; sometimes the muscles would become rock hard. Their mouths would drool, they would have involuntary jaw and tongue movements that would go on for hours, making the weirdest noises. Tom, they sounded like aliens. Then they would lose total control of their faces. They would puff out their cheeks, grimace and yawn and hoot, barely aware they were doing it. Eventually they would begin to realize they were losing their minds. Those drugs could actually instill fear and stupidity. Doctor Death knew he was destroying the…ah, humanness of the prisoners, and he seemed to enjoy it. If he kept it up, the prisoners' skin would turn dirty gray. Painful nodes like gravel would appear on their muscles. The lenses of their eyes would fog over with little, star-shaped cataracts. Then they would be incontinent. They would no longer be human."

"I see why you think this is Disneyland," Tom said, shaking his head.

"Been waiting long?" Tom asked Sabrina, as he entered the visitors' area..

"You need some new lines, dear."

As they talked, Tyler crawled the length of the table, wriggling his little bottom like a happy puppy. Tom kept pulling him back, then he would slide and laugh.

"I saw Steve, and he's confident you'll be home for Christmas."

"God, I hope so. I don't want to be negative, but what happens if I'm not?"

"I don't know."

Silence. It was painful for both of them. Tyler looked at his father, concerned that no one was playing with him. Tom gazed at Sabrina, thinking how much he loved her.

"What are you going to do? I mean, more specifically, how're you doing for money? What if you run out?"

"You know I can't call Mom," she said, drawing a finger across her throat. The shit would hit the fan. In French.

"Honey," when we're close to people, and love them, we often exaggerate their flaws. I don't think it would hurt if you had to call her. I think she would understand."

"You really don't understand my mother, I can't tell her you're in jail and I won't."

Silence. Tom did not want a repeat of the last visit, but decided to approach the subject anyway. "When I told you about my new cellie, did you hear the amount?"

Sabrina stopped cold. "Are you stupid!?" she snapped. "I would never do anything that would separate me from our child."

Silent moments, as they both gazed at Tyler; his smile and laugh broke the mood. Tom slid toward him, kissed him, then handed him to Sabrina.

"I'm just curious if you heard the amount." He said, quietly.

"No, I really didn't pay attention," she admitted.

"I didn't think so."

"What was it?" she asked.

"A million dollars," Tom said.

Sabrina gave her nanny the day off to prepare for her college finals. The weather was warm, and she enjoyed pushing Tyler in his stroller around the pond in the park - throwing crackers at the ducks waddling about. Tyler laughed every time a duck would catch one in mid-air She knew the times she spent with him were priceless, but her mind kept returning to the visiting room: "A million dollars" kept echoing in her brain; but the thought of being separated from Tyler filled her with horror.

She enjoyed her new home in Aliso Viejo, although she missed the spaciousness of their estate; but the upkeep had been daunting. Besides, that home was Tom's dream, not hers. Money's getting low, she fretted, as she sat paying bills. But I can't tell Mom. If she knew Tom was in jail, she would ridicule me until the day I died; or she died. She remembered being 13-years-old and her mother wagging that finger, warning her, "Don't ever get fat, no man will ever want to fuck you." Thanks, Mom. The emotional scars still clung to her, like grime she never could wash off, no matter how hard she scrubbed.. No, I can't tell her. I won't tell her.

CHAPTER 32

In the middle of the night, Iouri threatened Tom openly. Tom was either in or out. He would not have him walking around knowing his plans. He claimed he did not want to hurt Tom. But he would hurt him, his wife and child if Tom was not 100% committed. Ironically, Tom understood, and did not entirely blame him. Iouri's life was on the line. And the escape was his only salvation.

Iouri told him that Nikki had suggested using a Claymore mine in a briefcase. One of the most deadly antipersonnel weapons ever invented. Shaped like a disk, it leaped in the air when detonated, then sent thousands of ball-bearings outward at waist height. A moving sheet of these missiles would slice through hundreds of human beings. After blowing a hole in the visiting room, Nikki thought the destruction would be fun to watch, like a scene at Normandy Beach from WWII. But a drastic exit would mean they could not stay around to complete the Big Score, so Iouri said no.

Tom fought his fear, but decided to take last night in stride, even though it resurrected his concerns about whether Iouri was a killer, which now seemed more obvious.

As the guard locked their door, Tom was on his bunk and Iouri leaped down from talking on the vent.

"What's with all the scrap paper? Tom asked, pointing at the toilet.

There was a mountainous mess accumulating in the bowl.

Iouri was surprised that Tom appeared so chipper after last night's encounter. Maybe this guy's not as spineless as I thought. He decided to engage him. "In all the boxes, there are two and three copies of many documents, so I am trying to get rid of some of them and make room. I saw you talking to Bandit and some other guy when I was taking my shower; what was that about?" he asked, with a hint of paranoia.

"Nothing much. Bandit thought Harold and I should play together at the talent contest they hold every year around the holidays."

"Ah." Iouri appeared relieved. "Do we have a deal?"

"I think so," Tom said, guardedly. He was convinced Iouri would follow through on his threat, but did not want to exacerbate the process by lying.

"Yes or no?"

"On Saturday, I will see Sabrina. She's thinking about it this week; but I know she won't be able to pass up the money." Tom hoped he was right. Sort of.

"Nikki and Victor have this crazy idea of filming the escape. I think it is stupid and dangerous, because, if we get caught, they will have all the evidence they will need. And who needs to be hauling around a camera when we are trying to get out of here?"

"How does that help Victor?"

"He has friends at CBS and thinks he can get 10-15 millions for it."

Wow! Tom realized the national and/or global implications of the deal.

"Victor wants to stick it to your government and thinks the B.O.P. would be the easiest way. He believes heads would roll from the top down. He also believes they would close this place and turn it into a parking lot. He knows how corrupt your government is and how they do not play fair. So it is his way of getting even."

Saturday morning, Tom visited with Sabrina. Surprisingly, she initiated the discussion, as if they were connected by some sort of universal consciousness.

"I want to see if this guy is for real." Her face was angelic, but her bearing was ferocious.

Tom felt a bizarre mix of relief, curiosity, and dread. Relief he no longer had to persuade her, curious as to why she had changed her mind and dread that he might be leading everyone down a ruinous path.

"Court is in two weeks. Let's pray you get out of here," she said, softly. "I'll see you Monday."

Returning to the cell, Tom was greeted by a grave-faced Iouri.

"We have a deal," Tom reported. Iouri nodded, distractedly. Tom expected a warmer reception. "What's wrong?"

"I've been trying to call London all morning and the line has been busy or there's no answer. My friggin' wife is playing games with me." He opened a folder and handed Tom a piece of paper. You made a smart choice. Give this to Sabrina; it is my contact in the Caymans. He will help her setup an offshore account."

"Just so we understand each other," Tom added, "we really don't have a deal until she has the money. We want fifty-grand good faith money."

Iouri looked like he would grind Tom into pumice. "Ah, alright," he said, harshly. "You will also need this." He wrote down some instructions on another piece of paper and handed it to Tom. It listed: Name of bank, address of bank, name on account A.B.A. #, S.W.I.F.T. CODE

"About ten days after I receive the account information, assuming I get through to Marina, the money will be wired from Barclays Bank in London. Ah, you have a computer, right?"

"Yes."

"Good, because your offshore account can be managed from it."

Tom nodded, focusing intently now.

"Here's a pad of paper. I am going to walk and talk, as I usually do. I want you to write down the list of tools we will need." Iouri appeared more settled now that Tom was committed. Amazing what a death threat can accomplish.

"This will be in no special order: An assortment of standard and Phillips screwdrivers. Make sure all the tools are the best quality. I do not want any cheap crap or anything that might break. In my experience, Craftsmen are the most durable; hacksaw blades, but cut in half, so they can be used by hand, drywall knives and saws, large bolt cutters, the hydraulic pump; it should withstand 10,000 lbs. of pressure, so it will probably have to be custom made."

Tom nodded as he scribbled.

"Also, I will need the highest quality diamond cutter you can find, a couple of pairs of construction gloves and a large tube of construction adhesive; also, tin snips, electrical tape, crescent wrenches, ½ inch and 3/8 inch box wrenches, a ratchet set, probably with a 3/8-inch drive and adjustable wrenches."

His look was pensive as he continued to pace. "I think that is it. No, wait. I almost forgot the most important thing: the cell phones. Get Nokias. They are best for global calling. Do not forget the chargers, and do not forget Victor's video camera," he said, rolling his eyes. "Of course, we will need some disguises. And do not forget you have to arrange for six bikes and riders. Also, I will need two guns; nine-millimeters."

"Guns!? What do you need guns for?" Tom's volume and pitch rose sharply, startling Iouri. He was not expecting such a reaction. Nor did he wish to be challenged. "In case we encounter guards in the stairway."

"There's a better way. If you encounter a guard, disable his radio, give him ten grand and tell him to sit tight. You can tie him up, but no shooting.

"It is my millions. Get me the guns."

"No guns or no deal," Tom said, his heart pounding.

"Ah, alright."

Tom was definitely in. He was on a course that would change his life forever. One way or another.

CHAPTER 33

On Wednesday, Sabrina arrived without Tyler. There was an inner excitement about her that day. He hugged her and slipped the account information into the back pocket of her jeans.

"That felt good," she cooed, as they sat down.

Tom smiled, aroused by her cleavage. Memories. She seems to be enjoying this cloak and dagger stuff.

"I don't want to put a damper on your good mood, but I want to make sure we have an understanding," he said, taking her hands.

"What understanding?"

"I went to the library, and if this goes south, I'm probably looking at two to three years, possibly more. But I won't do this if you're gonna leave."

"Leave what?"

"What do you mean? Leave me. Us."

"What have you been smoking in there? Don't you know me? I love you with all my heart. Of course, I'll never leave." She leaned forward, kissed him lovingly and brushed his cheek with hers.

There was a relief in her response, and he wanted to believe her; but he had learned that it does not take much to destroy a marriage, even one as solid as theirs.

"Sorry I took so long," Steve said, panting. Those damn metal detectors slow everyone up.

"We set for next week?" Tom asked.

"You've done enough time, you're sick, you're not getting the attention you need, and we have proof that Vickie was lying. I'm sure Judge Sunland will let you go."

"Sure?"

"You'll be home for Christmas."

"Man, I hope so."

"I've got to get to court," Steve said as he gathered his briefcase and shook Tom's hand.

While Tom was meeting with Steve, Iouri confirmed with Nikki and Petrov that they had their man - fresh meat. He also had called Marina and forewarned her about the wire transfer. He was aware that the calls were recorded, so they spoke in Assyrian, an ancient dialect rarely used and difficult to translate. Marina did not seem happy with the progress of his plan, and she was especially upset at the request for money.

Iouri conjectured about the many possible underhanded reasons that would explain her reluctance. But he quickly thrust the negative thoughts aside when Tom entered the cell. Nothing would cloud his chances for success.

"I finally reached Marina in London. She is aware of the transfer. I just need the account information as soon as you obtain it from Sabrina," he said, pacing.

"I want an agreement on the arrangement and timing of the money," Tom blurted out. "$500,000 before you leave and $500,000 once you're at the safe house."

Iouri stopped pacing. Tom's nerves vibrated like guitar strings, concerned that he had gone over the line. Iouri looked like he would jerk Tom off his bunk and stuff him down the toilet.

This Tom is not as stupid as I thought; I will have to pay closer attention.

"Alright," he said, calmly "We will agree on payments to be distributed after each delivery. Assuming your government lets you out."

Tom was relieved. "Do you really believe the government is evil?

"Are you having second thoughts?"

"No. I just find it hard to believe."

"I will tell you a story. Then, we'll see how you feel. Do you know what the universal satanic symbol is?"

"I think it is an, um…upside down pentagram."

"Correct. Would you like to guess the shape of the Congressional Medal of Honor?"

"Inverted pentagram?"

Iouri nodded.

"But why?"

"I do not know, but it is no accident. If you take the following streets in Washington D.C. starting with Connecticut Street up to DuPont Circle and Vermont Avenue up to Logan Circle, then take Massachooseets to Mount Vernon along 'K' Street, would you like to guess what shape this is?"

"An inverted pentagram?" Tom said, in disbelief.

"That is not the amazing part. Guess what building sits in the middle?"

"The Washington Monument?"

"No, but you are close. The White House."

"Wow. But why?"

"The Washington Monument is a Masonic obelisk. Masonic, as in Freemasons. The Freemasons were descendants of the Knights of Templar and were formed on June 24, 1717. The Knights of Templar, Freemasons, and the Jesuits formed the order of the 'Illuminati'. Do you know who they are?"

"I've heard of them."

"All but a few of the 56 signers of the Declaration of Independence were Freemasons. Now, I mentioned, obelisk. That is the technical name of one ray of pencil light emanating from the sun. The Washington Monument has a specific name for its shape. Do you know what it is?"

"It's a pyramidion."

"Very good. I have never asked anyone that knew the answer I believe that your government built the Washington Monument, which is one of the world's most famous phallic symbols, because it viewed power as the big dick that their God conveyed to them to use and have fun with. Bear with me; I am leading up to something."

"I'm not going anywhere."

"The Egyptian God of the sun was called Horus. His symbol evolved into the all-seeing eye. That became the symbol of the

Illuminati. Their motto is 'out of chaos comes order'. By that, it is meant war, revolution, and devastation. When the world is reduced to a state of chaos, whatever or whoever is left will have to submit to their Utopian, New World Order. Your beloved USA will commit these terrible and time-ending acts. Who do you really think attacked the World Trade Centers?

"Are you saying the U.S. Government did it?"

"There is a more practical example of what I am talking about: The cashless society that the U.S. is forcing on everyone under the guise of convenience is really all about control. Think about it. Cash is one of the few things the government cannot readily control. But total control is essential for the New World Order to take effect."

Iouri stopped pacing. "That all-seeing eye is under 'Novus Ordo Seclorum', which means New World Order; it is on the back of every American one dollar bill. It also is on the Great Seal of the United States.

"Incredible."

"Now, you may not believe in the evolution of a New World Order. But there are no coincidences, only patterns we do not see yet. Think about this: After two World Wars, the U.S. created the League of Nations and the United Nations. These were two huge steps in the advancement of the New World Order. They are just some of the methods your government uses in order to become the dominant and only world power. They are doing this in order to control everything and everyone on the planet. To me, that is the essence of evil.

CHAPTER 34

Tom saw Sabrina hustling through the milling crowd of visitors. Male eyes followed her as she crossed toward their assigned table. That hip-swaying walk of hers truly was a sight to behold.

"Hi, wifey."

"Hi, husbo," she said in her velvety tone.

As they released their embrace, she tucked the account information into his hand. They exchanged the lightest and sweetest of kisses. Tom felt pleasure stirring in his groin as they sat down.

"Cut that out."

"What?"

"Do you have a warrant for that strip search? You're staring at me like I was naked."

"If only."

She laughed. Then, her tone became serious. "Is this plan going to work?"

"Yes. I've learned everything about it and it will work. Actually, it's brilliant."

"Okay, if you're confident, then I'm confident."

"I don't want to be a stick-in-the-mud, but I want to be sure you're going to stay if this goes wrong."

"Didn't we cover this already?"

"If you have any doubts, say so now, before we take any money. After that, there's no turning back."

"Whatever you think," she murmured, transferring the ultimate decision to him.

"Now, remember, if say, 'I took the baby to the doctor and the baby's fine', that means I received the money. Let's just pray everything goes well on Friday.

Back on the floor, Tom took off his sock and handed Iouri the crumpled piece of paper containing the account information. During the strip search, Tom kept talking, knowing that when he engaged the C.O.s, they only performed cursory inspections. The paper in the sock made it through undetected.

"I will tell Reese on Monday to FedEx the information to Marina."

Tom smiled and Iouri seemed pleased. "After the Big Score, where we will take 80 millions from National Title in New York and 20 millions from U.S. Title in LA, I will go to Costa Rica. The government there is literally begging for anyone to go down there and set up an export business in coffee."

"Sounds nice, and very intriguing."

"I will make you another deal: If everything goes right and you want to come to Costa Rica, I will give you this house," Iouri said, handing him a magazine.

"What's this?"

"I did not know they were doing it, but that is my home on the water in Costa Rica. They featured it this month, along with a few other homes in the current issue of Conde Nast Travel."

"This is beautiful," Tom said, admiring the photos of Iouri's elegant estate. "Thank you. I just might take you up on it."

Later, returning from the rec room, Tom entered the cell as Iouri was on the vent, his voice loud, crackling like a whiplash. He was drenched in sweat.

"Something wrong?"

"Not now," he snapped, then ran off like he had to catch a plane. Later, he reappeared and said, "Sorry about before." He understood that Tom knew something was amiss. "I reached Marina in London and we had a big, ugly fight. But she did receive the package from Victor's office."

"Will she do the wire?"

"She will do what I say; but she did seem to be in a hurry. That pissed me off. She receives $25,000 wired to her on the 15th of each month from the Swiss account and I know how much she spends."

"Does she normally do what you ask?"

"Usually, yes; but I have asked her before to send money to other people, some whom have not performed yet, or took my money and left."

"You know I wouldn't do that."

"If I thought that, I would not do business with you."

"When should I tell Sabrina to expect money?"

"Seven to ten days."

Tom was guardedly optimistic. He acted as sentry against any inmate who might have barged in on Iouri while he was carving out the hole behind the mirror. Iouri had placed his green windbreaker over the cell door, which denoted he wanted privacy.

As C.O. MacGregor passed Tom, their eyes met in a conspiratorial glance. MacGregor was one of the two C.O.s on Iouri's payroll that Tom had encountered in their cell a few weeks ago. As he walked away, Tom heard the windbreaker sliding down the cell door, signaling that Iouri was finished excavating for the evening. That night, after lockdown, Iouri and Tom discussed plans for Saturday evening:

"Be here at 7:30 sharp," Iouri said, authoritatively, "and bring a flashlight.

I will flip the cell light three times if we are set. Then come back in one half-hour."

"Okay."

"Make sure the cell phones are packed tight and will fit through the cell window easily. Good luck in court tomorrow."

CHAPTER 35

The cattle call at 4:15 a.m. was the most inhumane aspect of being in custody. It was a full ten hours before Tom's scheduled court appearance. One advantage of being sent to Orange County, the Santa Ana marshals were more congenial. Handcuffed and shackled, Tom had butterflies the size of dinosaurs as he was escorted into court and seated next to his attorney. He genuinely liked Steve, but that day, his smile had overtones of insincerity.

"How are you doing?" Steve asked.

Noticing Sabrina with the baby, Cris and Bob Beem in the gallery, he replied, "Okay, I guess. The real question is are you ready?"

"Of course," Steve said with a chipper tone.

"I need to go home," Tom muttered. The stent really needed to be extracted. "In case I don't get out of here today, please tell Sabrina I talked to my brother and the package she is waiting for will be seven to ten days."

"Case number 0327089. U.S.A. vs. Thomas Taylor," the clerk announced.

"We are hearing the matter of a probation violation concerning Thomas Taylor," the judge announced. "Have parties come to any agreement?"

Steve immediately went on the offensive. "Your Honor, we have proof that Ms. Stanford lied on her detainer. Mr. Taylor did not resist arrest, or hide behind the bushes behind his office. For if he had; he would have fallen 200 feet possibly to his death." Steve handed the pictures to the marshal, who couriered them to the bench. Sabrina glared at Vickie. Tom's groin screamed with pain.

"Obviously, there must be a misunderstanding," the judge said, staring at Vickie Stanford. Up until now, Tom had a reserved respect for Judge Sunland. But she had slid her finger on the scale of justice, tilting it in the government's favor.

"That's a nice way of putting it," Steve muttered, but ventured on:

"Your Honor, we request time served and termination of Mr. Taylor's probation, in light of the fact that Ms. Stanford maliciously insisted on his incarceration. The termination is warranted due to what your Honor has referred to as a 'misunderstanding'; I'm sorry, your Honor, but I'm going to call it what it is - a lie, a blatant lie; an attempt to help a weak and overzealous prosecution."

"You have made your position abundantly clear," the judge stated. "Ms. Stanford and the Government - do you have a reply?"

"Your Honor, I will accept time served, but request that Mr. Taylor's probation be extended for another three years. This will still allow him to rejoin his family for the holidays," Vickie said, with an underlying smugness.

As unexpected as a lightning bolt, Sabrina blurted out, "Screw her. We're not dealing with her crap anymore! She'll just have him back here next month."

Tom's head snapped around, astounded at her outburst. Her voice had shattered the courtroom's stillness like a jackhammer. She shrank in her seat and felt the blood draining from her face.

There was an interminable silence, thick with tension. Everyone expected to hear the thunder of the judge's gavel. Her face was austere, and her lips pursed. Steve battled on:

"Your Honor, Mr. Taylor has a wife, a new child and gainful employment. He doesn't need or require further supervision, or invasion of his life by Ms. Stanford." Then, he whispered to Tom, "What do you want to do?"

Tom understood the immediate consequences of Sabrina's decision, but in his heart, knew she was right. "You heard the lady. No probation or no deal."

"But you won't be home for Christmas."

"We need to be free of her web."

Judge Sunland still did not speak. Her face was austere, her lips pursed.

"Your Honor, we accept time served, but we still stipulate as to the termination of probation. Mr. Taylor served half of his three years without incident, and this alleged violation is petty at best."

"Ms. Stanford?" the judge said.

Vickie Stanford rose, indignant.

"We still feel that Mr. Taylor requires supervision. The Secret Service has him under suspicion, and I need to be certain society is safe." Her tone was sharp and insistent.

"Well, it appears we are at an impasse. I'm going to trail this to another date to be announced. Let's see if you two can come to something amicable before we meet again." The judge swung her gavel.

"Court is adjourned," the clerk proclaimed.

As Tom was whisked away by the marshals, he ached when he saw the scarlet look on Sabrina's face.

CHAPTER 36

Tom was shepherded back to MDC, depressed and overcome with fatigue. He stumbled onto Five South and heard an inmate performing open-guitar surgery on James Taylor's *Fire and Rain*. It did not sound like the song was going to pull through. The unit was staged and illuminated for the Holiday Talent Contest, about which, he had forgotten. An anxious Harold was relieved. They played two songs, which were well-received.

Trudging back to his cell, Tom's depression returned when he realized he would be spending Tyler's first Christmas in jail. And he still had to tell Iouri he was not being released. He entered the cell.

"When are you being released?" Iouri asked.

"I'm not."

Silence. Iouri stared at him, hard and unforgiving. With all the energy he could muster, Tom recounted the details of his court appearance. When he finished, Iouri's expression improved to a slight scowl. "Suki! That means, what a bitch!" he exclaimed, pacing faster, blinking rapidly.

"What do we do now?"

"Is there anyone you could trust?"

Tom was pleased and relieved by Iouri's question, because, what he really wanted to know was if they were still partners.

"Let me think about it."

"I saw you play," Iouri said, in a lighter tone. "You have some talent."

He shot Tom a lopsided smile.

"Thank you."

Tom lay on his bunk, trying to think of who he knew, other than Sabrina, that he could trust. After a long time, he sat bolt upright. "Mike," he blurted out. He jumped down, ignoring the pain, hobbled to the phone and dialed his number.

Mike was the next brother in the lineage, two-and-a-half years older than Tom, born on Christmas Eve. An excellent welder and mechanic, a perfectionist at any task he undertook, he was uniquely unfazed by the usual struggles of daily life. Nothing bothered the man; he was insouciant, something Tom admired and that perplexed him. The last thing anyone was concerned with was Mike Taylor having a heart attack. At least not from stress. Unfortunately, a heart attack from an overdose was always a possibility. Mike took life in moderation, his vices, not so much.

Tom had always had a bone-deep liking of Mike, and accepted his brother in spite of his rampant drug use. Mike had tried rehab five or six times and failed miserably each time. He had been on probation for almost ten years, and had to take drug tests every other year, frequently resulting in short jail terms of thirty to ninety days. On each occasions, Tom accepted his collect calls, wrote him letters and sent him money. Ironically, this time, it was Mike accepting a collect call from Tom.

Tom waited for the monotonous voice to complete its mechanical pronouncement.

"Mike?"

"Are we having fun, yet?" Mike said, his signature greeting. He belched before continuing, "You still in, huh?"

"Yeah," Tom mumbled wearily.

"When are you out?"

"Don't know; not too much longer. But that's not why I called. Are you on layoff?"

"Yeah, why?" Mike replied in his low-voltage way. Another reason he was able to keep his job was that he was laid off two-to-four months a year. Mike considered it a vacation and that was typically when he would use.

"I have a partner who needs some welding done at his shop," Tom said, mindful that the call was recorded.

"Oh yeah? Will Sab let me come out?" he asked with real concern.

Tom used to invite Mike and his woman, Queenie, out to his house regularly, until two years ago, when he had come for a visit by himself. Mike had found a drug hook-up and stayed out all night in Sabrina's car. He had even sold some of her CDs to pay for the crack. Sabrina invited him to return when Hell froze over.

"I'll talk to her," Tom replied, reassuringly. He knew she wanted the money and if Mike was the only way, she would acquiesce. "Okay," Mike said.

"I'll keep you posted, but be ready when we call."

"California in the winter. Awesome." Mike said

CHAPTER 37

Tom informed Iouri that he had a solution to their problem. He explained Mike's background and that getting over on the law would be fun for him.

"If Mike is alright with you, then he is alright with me; family is usually best, anyways."

Tom appreciated Iouri's allegiance, and Iouri liked Mike's sentiments regarding the law. That evening, after lockdown, Iouri and Tom began constructing a detailed storybook of the plan. Tom marveled at Iouri's draftsman-like ability. Many of the diagrams of the tools, and the printing in general, looked machine-drawn. They created a virtual Escape Manual for MDC LA.

During their next social visit, Tom presented Sabrina with Mike as a solution. Surprisingly, she was fine with the idea. "Mike is perfect for the job." They agreed she would buy the cell phones and the video camera. She thought the camera idea a little loony, but a deal's a deal. She would have Mike purchase the tools when he arrived. He would not stay at the apartment; it was too small, but she would have no problem arranging for a hotel.

"Still no money from Iouri," she added.

"I believe Iouri's being straight with us," Tom said, "but something is going on with his wife in England.".

Sabrina was dangerously low on money, but opted not to tell him, because she did not want to alarm him.

Back on the floor, Iouri was ranting into the vent. His speech was more rapid than usual. He consistently uses the same words around my name, Tom realized, and his voice sounds darker when he's talking about me. He did not know if he was being paranoid, but grabbed a pad of paper and scribbled down as best as he could, phonetically spelling out a handful of words. He would do a little investigating to calm his nerves.

The next day Tom heard Iouri berating someone on the phone.

"What was that about?" Tom asked.

"What?" Iouri snarled.

Uh-oh, I've awoken the sleeping giant. "The phone. I saw you on the phone."

"That damn woman of mine," Iouri griped." She is playing with me. She is giving me all kinds of bullshit about the money." His face became florid with fury as he spoke.

"What's the real deal?" Tom wanted to know.

Iouri reiterated that on the 15th of each month she received $25,000 from the Bank of Zurich, but he knew that her expenses only totaled $8-9000 each month. The remainder was supposed to go for emergencies, or to Iouri upon his request. He suspected that she had been hoarding the difference in order to purchase the London home in her name. She probably bought it believing she would never see him again. It was also possible that she had also bought an apartment in Moscow for her mother. As a result, when Iouri asked for money to be transferred, he surmised that she was short because she was waiting for the 15th to roll around in order to complete the transaction. Worst case, she planned on eluding him and eventually refusing his phone calls. But as far as Iouri was concerned, there was no logical reason she had not already completed the wire transfer.

"So where does that leave us?"

"I have a back-up plan," Iouri remarked.

"I thought you might. What is it?"

"Victor. He has some of my money in his trust account. If you do not see money soon, I will talk to him."

Later that day, Sabrina called Mike, concerned that their conversation might be awkward; but it was fine. Mike was congenial. She explained that she was waiting for something, and when she received the package, she would send for him. He alerted her that he could not fly because he had lost his license, so it would have to be a bus or a train. Typical Mike, she thought, as she hung up.

The next morning Tom was called out for an unexpected legal visit. "Did you and Sabrina reconsider three years more probation?" Steve asked him.

"I was surprised at her reaction in court, "Tom admitted "But I agree with her. What's the longest they can keep me?"

"Ten months with two months good time - that should be the max. I'm setting a court date for February."

"So I'm here at least another month?"

"Looks that way, but I really want to get you out asap so you can get to the hospital."

Tom left the legal office and was greeted with a welcome surprise: Sabrina was waiting to be cleared to visit him. But as he looked closer, he saw she was crestfallen. She did not have Tyler with her. Did something happen to him?

"What's wrong?" Tom asked. As he reached across to hold her hands, tears ran down her cheeks.

"I'm down to my last twenty dollars," she said in a voice choked with emotion. Each word was like a hammer blow. He was dumbfounded, but relieved it was not Tyler. A wave of vertigo swept over him. He felt overwhelmed, like a man trying to outrun an avalanche. He fought all reflexes to scream, "What did you do with all the money?" According to his quick calculations, she still should have enough for another six months.

"And the money didn't come from Iouri. Is he legit?"

"Yeah," Tom said quietly. He was not going to delve into Marina's possible personal extortion situation. "Well you have two options," he said, calmly.

"You can sell some stuff; or you can call Mom and…".

"I would rather chew off both arms than tell her you're in jail; we'd never hear the end of it." Her voice went up an octave.

Tom was speechless.

"You know I've always been a good person and tried to do the right thing.

How did I get into this situation?"

Tom was frustrated. He had always been self-sufficient, and now he could not care for his family. His mother-in-law had his money, money he could use; but he was not going to argue with Sabrina. Tears rolled down her face. Trying to compose herself, she muttered, "For now, I'm going to pawn my ring." Tom wanted to say "don't do it," but he knew she had to do something.

CHAPTER 38

Walking with purposeful strides towards the rec deck, Tom motioned to Iouri, who was on the bench press. He followed him to their cell. Tom had to do some quick thinking. He did not want to appear desperate or vulnerable; he believed in negotiating from a position of strength. So he improvised.

"What is wrong?" Iouri panted

"I just had a visit with Sabrina."

Iouri cut in. "I thought you had a legal visit." Boy, he does pay attention. "Yes, I did; she showed up to surprise me. But she's pissed. She just sent Mike money for expenses to hold him over, so he would remain available and wouldn't go back to work. She's concerned that you don't have the money. She wants money immediately or the deal's off. I didn't tell her anything about Victor, and I especially didn't want to argue with her in the visiting room."

Fucking Marina. Iouri remained composed. "I'll see Victor tomorrow. How much?

"Ten grand."

"Alright; but I want those cell phones immediately, so I don't have to rely on Marina."

"Done."

Ta-Da! As if trumpets were proclaiming his arrival, Victor Goldman burst into the visiting room in his customary majestic manner. With a cavalier attitude and exaggerated hand gestures, he looked like a baron motioning to his peasants. The C.O. pointed him toward Room 12. Victor strutted his imposing frame toward Room 11.

Iouri entered and they shook hands. "I will get right to the point," Iouri said. "I need you to overnight $10,000 to Tom's wife immediately. Marina is not cooperating; if you do not, then the deal will fall apart."

Victor did not want that. "Is this Tom Taylor solid? Are you sure he'll do the job?"

"Yes, he will be fine. If he turns out to be a problem, I will handle it. But, right now, his wife does not believe I am, as you say, 'solid'. I have to prove that Iouri Malakov always fulfills his deals, that I am a man of my word. If not, we will have nothing."

"Are you still taping the event?"

"Yes."

Victor looked perturbed. "What's the real problem?" Iouri asked.

"No problem."

`"You are lying." Picking liars out of the soup of life was one of Iouri's many talents.

Victor grinned, like a kid caught with his hand in the cookie jar. "I need more money; my exes are killing me, and my fifth wife just took me back to court for more child support." Victor despised himself for begging.

"I have already paid you $500,000."

"I know," Victor said, uncomfortably.

"How much do you need?"

"$50,000. Right away."

"Alright," Iouri growled. "Take it out the trust, but make sure that money is sent to Sabrina today." Iouri was not really upset; actually, he enjoyed it when Victor groveled for money."

"I will call Olivia right away when I leave."

"Very good. Tell her I will call her for the tracking number."

Tom hobbled into the cell to use the toilet. Occupied. Iouri was standing on its plumbing, launching into the vent what sounded like orders. Tom sat patiently, but again was disturbed at hearing certain Russian words, in conjunction with "Tom." Again, Iouri started chopping his words when he realized Tom was in the cell. Tom had to find out something, so he went and signed up for the law library and promptly got to work. He pulled out his sheet of paper with his scribbled, phonetically spelled words used by Iouri:

M-o-z-h-e-t - maybe. Not important.

T-y-u-r-m-a - prison.

Vra - enemy. I'm not the enemy.

S-t-a-r-i-y-k - old man. I'm only two years older than Iouri; makes no sense.

P-s-y-k - psycho!. I'm not psycho; well, maybe for being involved in this.

P-r-e-d-a-t-e-l - traitor. I don't know what he means, but I'm not liking this.

P-a-d-l-a - scum. I've been called many things, but scum?

The next two findings disturbed Tom:

P-a-t-s-e-l-u-i---smeryt---Kiss of Death!?

Tom looked up, stunned. The next word he heard most often in conjunction with "Tom."

M-u-s-o-r - garbage. Why would he be calling me garbage? Unless he plans on throwing me away."

Tom's head felt like an engine revving on bad fuel. What he had not discovered was that "Musor" also was slang for "cop" or "rat," the worst epithet in the Russian criminal lexicon, reserved for those to be eliminated.

Is Iouri really thinking of betraying or double-crossing me? Anger started to drown his fear. As he hurried into the cell, looking at Iouri's boxes of discovery, he knew what he had to do; he had a plan. Hanging the green windbreaker over the door gave him twenty crucial minutes. He dug into Iouri's boxes for hidden treasures, and found them.

Ignoring his cramping groin, he ran to find Ochoa. The orderlies had access to the copier in the Counselor's office, and Ochoa gladly obliged him.

"Would you please ask the Counselor to arrange a call for me before Count?"

"Okay, but what's the reason?"

"It's an emergency."

He hustled back to the cell to replace the originals, then drafted a letter to his lifelong friend, Cliff Searcy. They had been friends forever. Cliff was a dapper Anglo-Saxon from a long line of well-bred Searcys in England. He was handsome, with sandy-brown hair, broad shoulders and a body tapered like that of a long distance runner. From the eighth grade through college, Tom and he were inseparable. During their high school years, Tom was a lifeguard at the local pool. One day Cliff was trying to do as many somersaults as he could. He became disoriented, tried to swim to the bottom of the pool, hit his head and floated to the surface unconscious. Tom pulled him out, administered CPR, and literally saved his life.

Since then, Cliff would do anything for Tom. No questions asked. Tom appreciated his loyalty, and attributed it more to their Chicago roots. But Cliff would correct him, "It has nothing to do with where we're from; you saved my life."

Currently Cliff lived in Indianapolis, working as a pharmaceutical salesman. Educated in marine biology, computers were his passion. Tom thought him to be the unknown Einstein of the computer world. That talent was the primary purpose of Tom's letter.

He called Steve's office, requesting that his attorney visit him tomorrow, explaining that it was urgent. A confused Ochoa passed him. "I thought you needed a phone call?" Ochoa whispered.

Tom hung up. "I do."

In the Counselor's office, Tom called Sabrina with some good news: the tracking number; money was on its way. Needless to say, she was pleased.

So was Tom. The phone call was not recorded. He went to the cell and packaged the finished Escape Manual to be mailed to her.

The next day, he saw Steve, who took both packages. Attorneys and inmates were not supposed to exchange materials during legal visits, but attorneys carried volumes of discovery and the C.O.s did not know which was which; nor did they seem to care.

Two days later Sabrina visited, and was happy. She had her ring back. Tom explained that $40,000 would be sent after Iouri had the cell phones, and $500,000 would be received after they left. He also relayed information about the Big Score and the ocean-front home in Costa Rica. When she left she was elated, almost giddy. Tom still had not told her that, under the new conspiracy laws, she could go to prison as readily as him.

CHAPTER 39

Iouri knew that all thinking boiled down to two procedures: rearranging the pieces and inventing new ones. He spoke into the vent with Petrov, trying to concoct a way to convince the inmate in 619 to move out. The man was being stubborn. Iouri was distracted when pandemonium erupted on the floor. Checking it out, he learned that inmates were being transferred to other floors. One of them was Tom. He was talking to a C.O. with manic hand gestures.

"Why do I have to move?" Tom asked.

"You go, or you go to the hole," the C.O said, gruffly.

Tom's mind was swimming. "Can I see the Counselor?"

"He's not available."

A wave of panic washed through Tom. Why am I moving? Why did I get singled out? Did I do something wrong?

Shouldering through the crowd, Iouri called to Tom. "It will be alright." Obviously, he knew something Tom did not. Tom's mind was clouded with disbelief. Then, suddenly, like a crowd dispersed by a single gunshot, the voices were silenced.

"Quiet!" Lt. Danko barked, as he strode onto the floor. "I'll answer any questions you have, one by one, over here." Tom was first in line.

"Why do I have to move?"

Lt. Danko explained: Tom was not being singled out. In order to keep racial harmony, primarily the among the blacks, whites and Mexicans, Lt. Danko maintained certain ratios on each floor. When the numbers were too skewed, he transferred inmates accordingly. The bottom line: Tom was moving to Six South.

Tom gathered his belongings, wrapped them in a blanket and bed sheet. Iouri reassured him that everything would still work. All the groundwork had been established and they could communicate through Petrov.

In light of his paranoia after his recent law library visit, Tom realized it might be better to be away from Iouri. He felt kind of a reprieve being cocooned on another floor.

A little bedraggled, he settled into a cell two doors down from Petrov.

He met his new cellie, Pablo Martin, a clean-cut, athletic Mexican with a boy-next-door face, who had been Indicted for running marijuana up from Mexico. Moments later, Tom met Petrov, who was standing outside his cell. He was nothing like Iouri. Thin, no muscle definition, long brown hair in a pony tail, beard and mustache; he was mild-mannered, and had a much thicker accent than Iouri, but more pleasant to converse with.

He told Tom to call him Peter; most Americans did. He invited Tom into his cell for a spot of tea. Tom was impressed by Petrov's makeshift contraption, made from sliced headphone wires attached to a socket in the lighting fixture above the sink.

"Here," Petrov said, handing Tom a mug. Unlike Iouri and Nikki, who were atheists, Petrov considered himself an apathist; he just did not give a damn. All he cared about was his wife and child, and computers. And of, course, getting out of prison. He explained that, unlike his partners, he was not militaristic.

Petrov's cellmate padded in. He was a former Olympic silver-medalist from Armenia who was detained while entering the country with $15,000 cash. Because he did not have proof of the source of the money, he was arrested and charged with money laundering. His case was currently pending a Habeas Corpus motion so he could be released. This further aggravated Petrov's opinion of the American justice system.

Later, Tom saw Petrov stroll out of cell 619; he had been talking on the vent to Iouri. Tom surmised it was the cell he needed to commandeer. "Is that the cell?" he asked.

"Yes. Iouri wants to know if your brother's on the way; he's getting anxious."

"I don't know. I'm going to call Sabrina in a little while."

"Be careful on those phones," Petrov cautioned him, "you know they're recorded."

"So what's with the cell? How come that guy doesn't want to move?"

"I don't know," Petrov said. "It's weird. I offered him money and everything I could think of, and still nothing. But he's being sentenced soon, and I get along with the floor orderly, so I can probably get in there when he's gone."

"Well, that's good news," Tom said. "I want you to know, I don't plan on leaving you behind. I'll wait until you get in that cell."

"Thank you," Petrov said. He appreciated Tom's steadfastness, a trait lacking in most Americans.

Squirming in his high chair, Tyler grinned while Sabrina fed him. The phone rang. "This is a collect call from Cook County Jail."

Mike! He's supposed to be packing to come out here. What the hell did he do now? "Mike, what happened?" Sabrina blurted out.

"I had a dirty," he groaned.

"You mean a bad urine test?"

"Yep."

"So now what?"

"$250.00 gets me bail and court is in two months. Um, can you handle it?"

Mike asked sheepishly. Thank God I got that ten grand. Mike explained that she could send it Western Union and gave her the instruction She hung up.

The phone rang again. "Hi Sabrina, this is C.J." Cliff Searcy referred to himself as C.J. - his middle name was Joseph. "I received a letter from Tom; he gave me the scoop. Don't worry, he'll be home soon and everything will be alright. Please tell him I took care of everything."

On Six South, Tom approached the bank of inmate phones and called Sabrina. "Hi honey," he said.

"Honkas," Sabrina replied in that soft tone that thrilled him.

"Well somebody's in a good mood."

"Every day you get closer to coming home."

Tom absence was difficult for her, but she knew it was tougher on him and forced herself to remain positive as often as possible for his benefit.

"Have you heard from Mike?"

"O-o-o yeah. Still a buffoon."

"What now?"

"He had one too many dirty tests and his P.O. threw him in County. But I wired the bail money and he should be on his way soon."

"But won't he have court?"

"Not for two months; so he might have to cut his visit short and come back if he's not done with the welding job. Also, Cliff called and said to tell you everything's handled."

"Perfecto."

CHAPTER 40

Sabrina knew Mike could care less where he stayed, so she chose one of the cheesy motels in the low-rent areas of Los Angeles. Her face was a mask of disapproval, when she showed up with Mike, all disheveled from his cross-country trek.

"How long?" the clerk asked listlessly.

"One month."

"That'll be $400.00."

Sabrina gave him the money and they went to find the room. The Garden Grove Beach Hotel was eight miles East of the Pacific Coast Highway on Beach Boulevard. It was strategically located between the apartment and MDC LA, so Mike was close, but not too close, and not too far from MDC, to minimize his chances of being late.

He threw down his duffel bag. The motel sign buzzed and flickered as they headed to the greasy spoon next door. They took a seat at one of the old Formica tables. She told him she would loan him her spare car, and warned him to be available anytime she called. Her mind kept slipping back two years to that sleepless night when Mike had the same car while on a crack binge. She called him on the carpet about hooking up with the local dealers, warned him to quit the drugs, but knew there was a greater possibility that Mother Teresa would become a hooker.

"I'm going to purchase the cell phones in the morning. I'll buy five. One for you, me, and Tom, and two for Iouri. Once you deliver Iouri his, you can call him directly." Mike just stared at her as he stuffed himself with an avalanche of calories. His eyes were in the early stages of glazing over.

"Mike! Pay attention."

He smiled and pitched her a look that said, "I'd rather have jock itch."

"Do not make any personal calls on the business cell phone. That's why I had you bring out a cell from Chicago with the 773 exchange, so you can call Queenie and your P.O. If Iouri's phone is discovered before they're out and you've made some personal calls; you'll be Iouri's next cellmate."

After ten minutes of this, his eyes had begun to fully glaze over. He continued baptizing his cheeseburger in a puddle of ketchup, reminding himself to never marry again. Totally disinterested, if she had said she was going to pick up some keys on Neptune, he would have nodded at that, too. He finished inhaling his soda with the typical slurping sound. The emptied cup was the size of a children's wading pool.

Back at the hotel, she handed him the 32 page Escape Manual. That did grab his attention.

"Wow, this is amazing," he said. "Didn't think I was here for a welding job."

"Study that. Soon, I will give you money to buy tools."

Mike was impressed with the exactness and the quality of the plan. He knew it had taken tremendous diligence; most importantly, he could tell that it could work. For him, this job was a crusade; it was not just about the money.

The money would help replace all he had lost in his divorce ten years ago; but it would help get even with the man for continually throwing him in jail So he did a little drugs now and then. Big whoop. He did not sell them. They were for his own recreational use. And if he wanted to screw up his own body, he should be allowed to. Ironically, with all the time he had done; failure on this project would bring him more time than all his visits combined. But he knew they would not fail. It was not an option.

He also believed that Tom would not have entered into something like this if he did not have a way to protect everyone. He didn't know what it was, but knew he would find out eventually. When they were kids playing Monopoly, Tom usually ended up with the "Get Out of Jail Free" card. He hoped Tom was still carrying it.

Sabrina went to several cell phone shops, until she found a specialty store that carried the particular Nokias Iouri requested. They were expensive and in short supply. She purchased two, three lesser models and instructed the clerk to charge Iouri's phones with several hundred dollars of pre-paid phone time.

Dropping off Mike's phone to him, she was impressed he was still at the motel, and had not gone gallivanting around. But Mike perpetually confirmed Newton's Third Law of Motion: Objects at rest, tend to stay at rest. He did enjoy his sleep.

That evening, she called Tom. Mike was in the living room, playing with Tyler. "Hi Honey. Guess who's here? He's playing with his nephew."

"You mean he's with you, at the apartment?"

"Uh-huh."

"So Hell actually froze over. How's it going?"

"As well as can be expected."

"Would you put him on?"

"Mike. Phone." she hollered.

"Is it my P.O.?"

"It's your brother, dummy?"

"Are we having fun yet?" Mike yawned into the phone.

"I don't know. You tell me."

"I'm playing with my new nephew. He's good-looking and funny."

"Gets it from his mother. Did you see the plans for the welding job?"

"Yeah," Mike said with almost obscene enthusiasm. "Cool, and a no brainer."

"Hey, glad you're here, man. We'll talk soon."

"Hey, Peter, Mike's in town," Tom said, standing in the doorway of Petrov's cell.

"Great. Iouri has been bugging me constantly about those cell phones."

"Better you than me." For once, Tom was glad he had been transferred to another floor.

"Iouri wants the first delivery on Saturday night between 7:00 and 7:30.

It's supposed to rain, which is good. Iouri takes credit for that, too."

"What do you mean?"

"He said he had an Indian on Five South do a rain dance for him."

"Why am I not surprised." They both smiled. "I'll see Sabrina tomorrow and set it up."

The next day, Sabrina visited without Tyler; he was being watched by Lisa.

"Saturday will be the first delivery," Tom told her. "After that, we will receive $40,000 in a wire."

"Sounds good." Her eyes brightened.

"Then I will receive instructions as to where you can pick up 50 grand. His name is Dmitri Djevdevich. He's been taking care of Iouri's cash reserves and Iouri is confident he's not being watched. He lives in Glendale. When you meet, him the password is 'Bordeaux'. When they are in Costa Rica, Iouri wants us to have an elaborate steak dinner and champagne with him to celebrate. Two of your favorite foods."

"We'll discuss it later, if and when we get to Costa Rica."

"Now, make sure Mike is on time Saturday, before 7:00, and that he's wearing a white cap. Tell him to go ten feet past the courtyard tree, which is two-thirds toward the back of the south side. That faces the Mobil Station on Alameda Avenue. If the coast is clear, he is to light a cigarette at 7:00 sharp. If Iouri is set, he will flip the cell light three times. Mike should walk away and come back exactly thirty minutes later. There should be a rope hanging; he's to attach the bag with cell phones and screwdrivers, tug on it lightly and walk away."

CHAPTER 41

Sabrina looked outside at the grey puddles. It had rained last night; it only happened fifty to sixty times a year in Southern California. She was fidgety. Glancing at Tyler, she wondered if it was all worth it. She was relieved that she did not have to call her mom; and the money and the Costa Rica home will be nice. But not at Tyler's expense. If she tried to stop everything now, Tom would be in extreme danger, the consequences probably fatal. There was no turning back.

Tom awoke, saw the dampness outside and smiled. Mother Nature was cooperating. He forced himself not to fret over the myriad of negative possibilities. The Russians' freedom was at stake and he had learned they played for keeps. They would succeed. They had to succeed.

Mike stirred when he heard a knock at the door.

"Maid service. You want?"

"Come back in a hour," Mike hollered in a gravelly voice; he was groggy and hungover. He'd had some liquid refreshment last night. Too much. Way too much. Hammers were swinging inside his temples. He struggled to sit up, slouched into the bathroom, looked in the mirror. "Oh. Geez," he moaned. His face looked like an battered old shoe, his hair like he'd been struck by lightning. He yanked on the roll of toilet paper, blew his nose like a bugler. Frrrrupp. He let out a six-second, four-note fart that sounded like a strangled cry for help.

Stumbling back into the room, he began thinking about the day's plans. His first notion was, cool - he was going to deliver some cell phones and tools to the Russian Mafia at a Federal Holding Facility. It did not faze him at all. No problem.

The visiting room was crowded and clamorous, like a belated Christmas party. It had stopped raining, but was still moist, creating the desired effect on the security cameras. A waning moon had cast a sliver of light over MDC.

Tom and Sabrina were volleying the conversational ball of small talk, as they sat across from each other, holding hands. But their minds were elsewhere. Tom saw an imposing figure saunter out of one of the legal offices.

"Hey look, it's Victor Goldman," he said, then nodded.

Sabrina looked around. "He's tall, and he looks cocky."

"He's a real ray of sunshine," Tom said.

A familiar face strolled his way. "It's Iouri," Tom whispered, "I'm surprised Victor's here on a Saturday night; there must be court on Monday."

There were hordes of attorneys. Most played the courts like an elaborate game of 'Let's Make a Deal'. The only thing that mattered was their record of acquittals. Not the Law. Not Justice. Not Innocence. Or Guilt.

Sabrina continued staring at Iouri as he approached the inmate's table. Looking straight ahead as he passed, Iouri murmured, "Bad C.O., no go!"

"What did he say?" Sabrina asked eagerly.

"Bad C.O., no go," Tom whispered, "Evidently, not a good night on the floor."

The C.O. called out a few names: "Johnson, Haynes, and Malakov." When Iouri's name was called, he looked unflinchingly Tom's way and mouthed, "Tomorrow."

Sunday night, Lisa was not available, and Sabrina was not about to loiter around MDC with a baby, so she followed Mike to the general area. God, I hope we're not late. Her palms were moist against the steering wheel.

At 6:50 p.m., they exited Los Angeles Street; she waved off Mike, said a silent prayer and turned back. Mike threaded his car among the customers pumping gas at the Mobil Station and parked around back. At a few minutes to 7:00 p.m., he crossed

Alameda Avenue. Approaching the designated spot, he had the presence of mind to notice there was a big man coming his way. Mike was not sure if he was a security guard. But it did not matter. The sidewalk he was on was a shortcut to Temple Street, where there was a large public parking lot. Mike's presence should not have raised suspicion.

He stopped, fished in his jacket for his cigarettes. The big man passed him, unconcerned. It was 7:00 p.m. Exactly. No one else was around. He lit his cigarette, felt the brim of his white hat and looked up. About thirty seconds elapsed. He got the signal. A cell light on the fifth floor flickered three times. Mike walked away.

Upstairs, Iouri hurried to remove the twenty-four screws, something he had rehearsed a hundred times; but this time was for all the marbles. Two inmates stood sentry outside the cell door. He used another inmate's cell, because it was closest to the target spot. Iouri's cell was too close to the front of the building and overlooked the entranceway's concrete steps.

The Mobil's Mini-Mart cashier nodded at Mike with no more interest than a stick of furniture. He bought a Coke and went to chill in the car. At 7:25p.m., he walked casually along the South side of MDC, this time with his backpack.

He spotted the rope. It dropped down and rested on the six-foot retaining wall situated fifteen feet from the building. He retrieved the bag from the backpack, attached it to the rope, tugged on it twice and turned to walk away.

Circling around, he glanced up and caught a glimpse of the contour of immense shoulders. Must be Iouri. He heard a thud, as the bag hit the wall; then a voice muttered softly, "Shit!" He was tempted to look back, but maintained his expression of innocence. He did not want to draw any ill-timed attention.

Air brakes from an eighteen-wheeler screeched. Mike hopped in his car, pressed the on button to his batphone, and sped away. Thirty minutes later, his phone rang.

Iouri jumped up to talk on the vent, gave Petrov and Nikki the good news, and dialed his cell phone. "Mike?"

Mike knew who it was. The Russian accent was unmistakable, even though the voice sounded neutral, almost artificial. Mike decided to be himself.

"Are we having fun yet?"

Iouri was caught off-guard, and reminded himself that Tom said his brother was crazy, but in a good way. Ignoring his remark Iouri said,

"Good job."

"I know."

Iouri looked outside the cell door; he thought he had heard someone. "When will you be ready for the next delivery?"

"Don't know. I think Tom's waiting for more money, but that's not my department. Work it out with him."

"How about next Saturday?"

"Fine by me."

"I'll call you on Wednesday and we will talk, so make sure your phone is on."

"Okay. Later, dude."

"Wait. You were on time this time; very good. But please do not be late. Punctuality is the courtesy of kings."

"Yea, sure, whatever." Mike hung up, shaking his head. Does this guy think he's a king? He called Sabrina and gave her the good news.

Petrov gestured thumbs up to Tom. They exchanged no words. It was 9:20 p.m. The phones went off at 9:30p.m.

Sabrina waited anxiously for the introductory recording to finish. "Honey?" she said.

"We're good."

"I know. By the way, Steve called; he's setting a court date for Monday, February 17th."

"I'll be there."

CHAPTER 42

Iouri spent the next week resurrecting old business contacts. Remarkably, many had known where he was and were unfazed that he was calling them from a cell phone in prison. They knew he would contact them eventually, prison or no prison.

Expectedly, Marina was not glad to hear from him. He suspected that she was moving on with her life. Instinctively he shoved aside any thoughts concerning her. He did not care that his marriage was in the rinse cycle, but was committed to providing for Natalya. He took comfort knowing she was healthy. He lowered Marina's monthly allowance from $25,000 to $10,000, which was plenty for Marina to support the baby. His banker in Zurich, Edgar Bonjour, an inoffensive gentleman, called Barclays Bank in London and arranged for the transfer to Tom and Sabrina's account. The money would be received within five to ten business days.

Sabrina sent Mike shopping. It was an eclectic shopping list: bolt cutters, hacksaws, tin snips, a diamond glass cutter, work gloves, construction adhesive, drywall knives and blades, and hammers. A few crescent wrenches completed the ensemble. Mike ordered the custom-built hydraulic pump that would spread the security bars, making the plan viable.

Sabrina purchased the video camera and the clothes that would be stenciled with three letters that should give the Russians legitimacy as they walked away from the jail: F.B.I.

Though she paid Lisa well, with her ingrained motherly protection she still hung around whenever Tyler was sick. Like a lioness and her cub, she was very doting. She loved Tom immensely, but Tyler was her whole world.

Iouri called on Wednesday, as scheduled.

"I got the tools and the jack is ordered," Mike told him. "Sabrina needs more money before I can continue."

"Tell her I talked to London; everything is arranged."

"Alright, but until she tells me, I can't make another drop. I don't need her pissed at me."

"Okay. Leave your phone on weekends so I can call you."

"No problem," Mike said, and hung up.

Mike spent the week getting high and sampling the local talent. Most importantly, he spent a great deal of time and effort wrapping and re-wrapping the tools in duct tape, in the manner specified by Iouri in the diagrams. They had to be arranged correctly or they would not fit through the cell window. The windows were 5 feet by only 5 inches wide. The width was the bottleneck.

After rearranging the package twenty times and exhausting two rolls of duct tape, he was satisfied.

It was the Tuesday before Valentine's Day. Sabrina had waited an excessive amount of time, as Tyler had a bad cold and was antsy and irritable. She was happy to see Tom, but exasperated because of the baby. Tom slid her a piece of paper he had received from Petrov, containing Dmitri's information. She asked to end the visit early, because Tyler was being so unruly. Tom was concerned as he watched Tyler rub his bloodshot eyes, while his nose ran. "Poor kid."

Iouri called Dmitri. They talked about old times, and Iouri revealed details of the escape plan. Dmitri was impressed. Iouri told him they did not have a target date yet, but it would be soon, that Sabrina would be calling shortly and that the password was 'Bordeaux'.

The days rolled on, a tense, numbing boredom. The project gave Tom things to occupy his mind, and with court on February 17th, he might even go home. The idea was too good to be true.

On February 13th, he called Sabrina. She told him she had gone to the doctor's and the baby was fine. He was relieved, but did not realize what she meant. The next day, Valentine's Day, they spoke again. Tom was very sentimental. He had sent her a card expressing his love for her, and she had sent him a card that he would cherish forever. They chit-chatted for awhile. "I went to the doctor's and the baby's fine," she said.

"I know. You told me that yesterday."

"No, dummy, I went to the doctor's office and the baby's *fine*," she reiterated slowly with emphasis.

"O-o-o-oh, okay. Well, that's good."

"No, that's real good; and if you come home Monday, all will be just fine."

"I haven't heard from Steve lately. Have you?" Tom asked.

"No, I'll give him a call."

"Good. There's the click; we have to go," he said. "Call you tomorrow."

Sabrina called Dmitri. She had wanted to meet him on Monday, but Tom had court; she needed to be there to support him, even though the sight of him handcuffed and manacled made her angry. Tom told her when it comes to collecting money, sooner's better than later.

She took the Tollway 73 North, passed the Glendale Galleria, turned on 6th Street then made an immediate left into the strip mall. Leave it to Iouri to arrange a wine rendezvous, she thought, as she spotted the Glendale Wine Shop. She went in, purchased a bottle of Zinfandel, sauntered out and approached the platinum-silver Jaguar XK.

Standing there was a suave, Latin-looking man, well dressed in a Hugo Boss suit. Eyeing his dark olive skin, square jawline and slicked back hair with sexy curls against the back of his neck, she was instantly aroused. Calm down girl. You're married. She was extremely faithful by nature, but this reaction was partially triggered by her recent dry spell. No Honkas for seven months; there had to be a law against that.

She sauntered up and said, "Do you have my Bordeaux?"

"Absolutely, young lady," replied Dmitri, in a smooth debonair tone.

He smiled and bared even white teeth that could have been in an ad for the dental association. He had the kind of smile that made sensible women do foolish things. His cologne was a clean, ice-like fragrance.

Dmitri was as comfortable around pretty women as Wynton Marsalis was around a horn. He also had an inflated opinion of himself. He often thought he should change his name to something American sounding, like Justin as in "Just Incredible". He was taken with Sabrina instantly. A natural beauty, he thought there was something Florentine about her. Olive skin, full figure, a certain vibrancy, hand cream with a scent of orange blossom.

There was an unspoken lure in their eyes that could have produced sparks. They exchanged packages. She glanced inside hers; saw the bottle of wine and several two-grand bundles of one-hundred dollar bills. She assumed it was all there, but was not about to count it outside, and was not worried, it was a great day.

Seemingly out of nowhere, two LA Sheriff's squad cars squealed into the parking lot and screeched to a halt, blocking both their cars.

The world came to a shrieking halt. Time stood still. As if rehearsed, Sabrina and Dmitri glanced at each other, but kept their composures. Sabrina immediately began concocting an alibi. Dmitri folded into his Jaguar. She strutted around the front of the Explorer her eyes, liquid and courageous, still riveted on the sheriffs but trying to look casual.

Curiously, they remained in their squad cars. She was not sure if she would have a heart-attack or throw up? Was she being set up? That made no sense. She could explain the bottle of wine but how could she justify the $50,000 in cash? "Think fast," she told herself, fighting to remain calm.

The officers exited their vehicles, ran toward her. She felt she'd been hit by a cyclone. Then, she heard one say, "You cover the back. I'll take the front. They were still running toward her. In the wink of an eye, fear changed to confusion as the officers sprinted past her toward the currency exchange. She let out a puffed cheek full of air, hopped in the Explorer, drove away sedately. For a moment, though, she thought about chugging the bottle of wine. The whole bottle. Later, she learned from the radio that there had been a robbery in progress, but the perpetrators had escaped.

CHAPTER 43

Tom woke up Monday as the C.O. was making rounds and unlocking the doors at 6:00 a.m. While dressing, he realized they did not wake him at 4:00 a.m. for court. Court was not scheduled until 3 p.m., so it was possible he could be pulled out at noon and still make it on time. One thing was certain, if the U.S. Marshals wanted him to be there, he would get there. Nevertheless he was concerned. If there was a chance to be released, he was not going to miss it.

He called Sabrina, who was already awake, feeding Tyler. She would page Steve. After several hours, Steve called back and said the clerk had not put Tom on the calendar; he would try and set another court date right away. Sabrina was suspicious; she had paid him in full. Tom had been warned that if you want an attorney to quit working for you, pay him in full before the job is done. Tom had asked her not to pay Steve before he was released, and she was beginning to believe he was right. Shades of Randal Hunt.

MDC was full of defendants whose attorneys were inattentive because the checks had been cashed and the accounts stamped, 'Paid in Full'; they were moving on to their next victim. Tom wondered who was the bigger criminal, the inmate or his attorney. He had become to believe that the Bar Association, the good ol' boys club, was a lying, racketeering ring.

The next day, Sabrina called José Ocevasquez and inquired about the motorcycles and their riders. He told Sabrina the riders each wanted $2000 now and $2000 upon delivery. Iouri was paying expenses but those were the numbers Tom was anticipating. He would stop by the local Taco Bell and pick up the $12,000.

After his workout, Iouri called Mike to set up the second delivery. Same place at 7:00 p.m. "Make sure you paint the bag beige, to match the building."

"I already did that," Mike lied; it still was blue. Mike did not want to look stupid but it would be done before Saturday. "The package is already wrapped to perfection," Mike reassured him. "But is the rope strong enough? The package is heavier that you realize."

"How much?" Iouri inquired.

"Forty to fifty pounds."

"It should be alright," Iouri said.

Mike did not like the sound of 'should be', but Iouri was not the type to be second-guessed.

"Do not be late."

"It's a date."

Mike left the motel for downtown LA. He was an extremely skilled driver, having raced sprint cars; and he even learned to drive Indy Cars at the Skip Barber Racing School down in Florida. He could turn a car on a dime. Always dancing along the precipice of life, a kamikaze in training, he had a hidden fantasy or sickness that he had never told anyone about - almost a Death Wish: Driving flat-out, the tachometer screaming 6500 rpm at one point, he was hell-bent on trying it just once. Whirling past street lights like pistols flares, he wanted to cross lanes and see how many people he could dodge before he hit someone, unconcerned that the chances of survival were close to zero.

Fortunately for him and LA, his plan was impede, when he was caught behind a Cal-Trans garbage truck.

"All the stupid luck," he griped, as he smacked the steering wheel. He reached for his cell phone.

"Yes?" Iouri whispered.

"You want me at 7:00 or 7:30?" Mike asked, trying to remember.

"Make it 7:30," Iouri replied.

"See ya' there," Mike said. "That's what I thought," unaware that Iouri had just switched the time.

"You are sure the package is wrapped tight?"

"Yeah. A bomb couldn't rip this puppy apart. See ya' soon."

Mike arrived at the Mobil station with body and automobile intact. Walking gingerly along the south side of MDC, his profile poked in and out of every lake and puddle of darkness. He could see the beige rope slipping down the building. It plopped over the retaining wall. Mike remembered how the last package, which was not heavy had hit the wall with a thud, so last minute Mike had wrapped the heavier package with a thin layer of Styrofoam to deaden any bumps.

Taking a few steps past the rope, he spun around, walked back, lifted the package over his left shoulder and attached it to the clip. He tugged the rope gently twice and headed back toward the car. Peripherally, he could see something was amiss. The package had hit the building with a subdued thud, but still with some force. The impact was barely audible above the traffic din. It was struggling to reach the fifth floor. Abruptly, there was a crash, like the sound of a large tree branch hitting the ground. He heard, "sonofabitch," softly in the harsh burr of Russian. Instinctively, he hopped over the retaining wall, grabbed the package, ran over and rested it on the wall. He hurdled the wall, secured the package in his backpack, and ambled, with deceptive casualness, back to the car.

His cell phone rang.

"And you were worried that the package was wrapped correctly," Mike remarked.

Iouri despised looking stupid, and he sure as hell did not want any condescending wisecracks from that knucklehead; but this was no time for an argument.

"Yes, I know," he conceded.

"That's alright." Mike's tone became more cooperative. "I'm going to go to a hardware store, I'll pick up a heavier gauge rope. Tomorrow you'll drop your line and I'll attach the heavier line and that'll solve the problem."

"Good thinking," Iouri said, impressed. Maybe this Mike is not such a doofus, after all. He was gaining respect for Mike's resourcefulness.

"I'll see you tomorrow, same 'bat' time, same 'bat' station."

"Bye," Iouri replied, bewilderment plastered on his face. He had never heard that expression before.

Sunday's delivery went off without a hitch. No broken ropes, no loud noises, no shadows; and there was a mist that should have clouded the security cameras.

Iouri spent the next couple of days safeguarding and camouflaging the tools in his cell - underneath the storage cabinet, in the legs of the countertop, in socks hanging from pipes behind the mirror. He used his ingenuity to ensure the contraband would not be discovered in a surprise assault. At times, unannounced, inmates were sequestered on the rec deck. The C.O.s then thoroughly inspected the cells. That was called a shakedown, and was Iouri's primary enemy right now. Then, there was Tom's attorney. When was that dumptruck going to get him released?

Iouri called Mike and set two more delivery dates for every other Saturday.

Mike would call Orange County Hydraulic to see if the pump was ready. He was still waiting for Sabrina to stencil the clothing.

"Did she find a safe house and buy the disguises?" Iouri inquired.

"I don't know, but I'll find out."

Petrov ambled over to Tom. "Iouri wants to talk to you." His tone was plain, almost doleful.

"You talk to him," Tom objected, "I'm not talking in the vent."

"No, in the toilet," Petrov explained

"The toilet?"

Since they were on floors vertically aligned, if the water bowl was drained, with a rolled-up magazine, inmates could carry on private conversations - the prison version of the string-and-cup method. It sounded like the inmate was talking in a long, partially-clogged tunnel.

Iouri was furious, cursing at Tom. Mind reeling, Tom was stunned, mortified and indignant all at the same time. He struggled to respond. Apparently, when Iouri was scoring the plasterboard behind the cell mirror, a screwdriver broke. It must have been one of the inexpensive ones Sabrina had purchased. Mike exclusively used Snap-On and Craftsmen tools, Black and Decker and Makita for power tools. Trying to calm Iouri down, Tom asked if the tools from the second delivery were of acceptable quality.

"Yes, it looks like it," Iouri mumbled.

"Well, then, chill out," Tom said, stridently.

Silence while Tom imagined Iouri exhaling, trying to relax.

"Any more fuck-ups, and you are a DEAD MAN!"

Tom took the magazine and threw it at Petrov. "I'm never talking to that asshole again," Tom snapped, as he stomped out of the cell.

Petrov said nothing. Later he tried to explain: "Iouri gets like that."

"But I'm on your side," Tom said, angrily. He has no call to talk to me like that. Who the hell does he think he is?"

The temper tantrum in the toilet gave Tom a real dose of reality, and sent him spiraling into kind of a depression. It was late so he headed out to the rec deck. What did he do? What had he done? How did he get there? Eight months ago he had nice life, a beautiful home, a gorgeous wife and a child and a new business. Now he was in federal custody helping the Russian Mob escape. He thought he would laugh if it were not true.

And for what? Money? Greed? The challenge? So his mother-in-law would not know he was in jail? Was it worth it? He felt like just another clown in the same old human circus of bravery and cowardice, selfishness and selflessness, mercy and heartlessness, cleverness and stupidity, charity and greed.

He was glad he still had his wife and child; but a ten-year sentence for each of them would undo that. Now, he was being threatened. Again. Was the threat serious? He needed to protect himself better than he had already. He saw his present life as vulnerable. He had always preached, "cover the downside; the upside will take care of itself." Now the downside might include DEATH. And they probably would not stop with him. Like Mike said, he needed a "Get Out of Jail" card. But this was not Monopoly. This was reality. What could he do?

CHAPTER 44

Tom did not get up for breakfast. He lay around ruminating about yesterday's events. Life, he reflected, was made up of equal parts idiocy, fear, irony and pain. He could sense the sounds of human life passing beneath his window, the ebb and flow of ordinary life, almost a distant memory.

He fine-tuned his plan, and considered other possible safeguards. Getting out was definitely not an option, unless he wanted to be a clerk at a Wal-Mart somewhere in Des Moines, sporting a strange name tag. They would probably find him anyway. He was angry at himself for being so naïve and greedy. He had risked his freedom and his family's freedom to help these guys, and himself, and now his life was once more being threatened. He could not and would not let that happen again.

Footsteps squeaked in the doorway. Petrov. "Pool?" he asked. A man of few words. Tom believed him to be a gentle soul; it was a mystery how he ever got entangled with a megalomaniac like Iouri.

Tom racked and broke, his stroke precise but almost gentle, as if he did not want to injure the balls.

"You okay?" Petrov asked him. Tom shrugged and took his shot.

"We still got a deal?" Petrov asked, concerned with Tom's non-answer.

He wanted to make sure he was going to see his wife and child again.

"Like I'm going to tell that idiot I want out," Tom remarked. "You might as well as beat me with that cue stick and save him the trouble."

Petrov laughed in his odd way.

"Don't worry about him; he's got, how you say, a fast fuse, but he calms down again. You never saw him real mad."

"Not like that," Tom muttered. Not at me, anyway. He remembered the time Iouri briefly tortured Dino. "I guess we were still in the honeymoon phase. Do you know how he is going to get the tape to Victor?" he asked.

"I don't know," Petrov said, "but I'll find out."

Iouri was in his cell. He had been shortening his workouts recently because of all the hidden items: in walls, in pipes, even under cabinets. The inmate lockers were bolted to the floors. He had unfastened the bolts and stored a layer of tools in the two-inch gap between the bottom shelf and the floor itself. "Quite ingenious," he boasted to himself.

"Damn voice mail," Mike mumbled. "Hey Iouri. Just called to let you know I picked up the pump. Call me back when you can."

Iouri called back later in the evening, acknowledged Mike's call and asked him to pick up a few more hacksaw blades. Also, he requested that Sabrina purchase more pre-paid phone time.

"Talk much?" Mike asked. His tone dripped sarcasm.

"I am conducting business," Iouri said in his usual tone of suppressed vehemence.

"I know," Mike said. "Relax, ya' Russian freak; you'll have a heart-attack before we can get you out of there."

They set the next delivery for Sunday at 7:30 p.m. to include the pump and a few miscellaneous tools. They switched to Sundays because they proved luckier. Downtown LA was usually quieter on Sunday evenings.

Mike relayed Iouri's message to Sabrina and gave her a general update. "After the delivery, in a few weeks, I need to get back to Chicago for court or I'll end up with warrants. Then, with a half-laugh, "Tom'll come out and I'll go in."

"No, we don't need that." Sabrina said emphatically.

"When will he be out? When's his next court date?"

"I haven't heard from Steve in awhile. He sweet-talked me into making his final payment, even though Tom warned me not to. Now, he seems to be ignoring us."

"Asshole," Mike muttered, "And they wonder why they have such a lousy rep."

"I have an idea," she said. "I'll go to San Diego to get the disguises. We'll disguise you and make you the renter. You'll be an out-of-town salesman from Chicago looking to relocate because you're getting divorced."

"What's my name?"

"I don't know yet, but I'll think of something. She knew he would not object. He was going to be the house sitter, or baby sitter as Tom said, for the Russians anyway. She had to call Tom's friend, Sherry, at the DMV, to get Mike a new license. She would use "Mike" as the first name to minimize any confusion; also, so Mike would not screw it up, and chose "Reynolds" as his last name.

She reflected on her last conversation with Mike; it was amicable, even enjoyable. Like Tom said, he was a nice guy when he wasn't using. But he definitely was not her Tom. And she did respect their unfaltering loyalty to each other - thick as thieves, she thought, with a grin.

She reminded herself that she had a lot to do. She had been playing with Tyler a great deal at the park lately, and sprucing up the apartment for Tom's eventual arrival. She especially enjoyed Aliso Viejo, hoped Tom would like the apartment.

She left another message for Steve. He called right back and said the judge was out for three weeks for surgery in March and the next available court date was April 17th.

"Tom's not going to like that."

"Nothing I can do.".

Another forty-five days in custody because the judge was unavailable did not seem fair. Tom would not be happy about it.

Sunday's delivery went off like a well-rehearsed play. "Wonder how many Federal laws I'm breaking?" Mike joked to himself. More humorous to him was, how many heads are going to roll when these guys find out, especially if Victor sells the videotape to 60 Minutes. The B.O.P. will crumble like a retaining wall hit by a crash dummy. Mike laughed at the thought.

He had been a good boy lately, so he decided to go prowling for a little fun, Mike Taylor-style. The phone rang, it was his Russian crony.

"Nice pump," Iouri said

"I knew you'd like it."

"Next Sunday?" Iouri asked.

"As long as Sabrina's ready. Hey, this almost too easy, no?"

"Maybe for you. You are out there; it is getting crowded in here."

"Hey, I've been in there," Mike replied, not to be outdone.

"But not for life. They want me dead. Your fucking country is evil."

"Hey, I'm not in charge. I just live here."

CHAPTER 45

Sabrina spent the day emptying boxes to make room for her pet project: stenciling the three, slate-blue jackets and caps with chrome yellow F.B.I. lettering. Lisa had taken Tyler to a friend of hers, who had a little girl Tyler's age. It was good for him to be around other children; it also was good that Lisa did not know what Sabrina was up to.

She showered and dressed, then went to see Mike. It was 2:00 p.m.. He was still sleeping. "Definitely not Tom," she mumbled, as he staggered up. They drove to check out a potential safe house, for rent in Huntington Beach. It was in the middle of the block and appeared to be everything Iouri had requested: an upper-middle class neighborhood, well-manicured, stylish, but not too conspicuous. And not situated in a cul-de-sac.

It was a two-story, French villa-looking place, but not too dissimilar from the neighboring cookie-cutter, custom-built residences. Sabrina thought Iouri would like its Parisian flair and Continental elegance. She called the agent to inquire about the amount; it was exactly the budget Iouri expected.

"My brother will be in town shortly," Sabrina told the agent. "I will have him give you a call."

She called Sherry at the DMV, asked about her husband and kids, gave her Mike Reynolds' name, the safe house address and they agreed she would stop in for coffee tomorrow. Next she called the La Jolla Playhouse Theater and inquired about a complete costume and make-up kit.

She had just put the phone down when it rang. "How is my Lil Bebe?" the voice asked, in her typical Franglais.

"Hi, Mom. "Sabrina sighed, then tried to elevate her tone.

"I'm coming to see my grandson," Renée said. "I need a Tyler fix. I miss him so."

"Oh Mom, we'd love to see you but…" Sabrina spent the next fifteen minutes in a diplomatic tussle. Artfully, she convinced Renée that summer would be better. Tom would have more time. She knew Renée wanted to visit, and felt offended when Tom did not have enough time to spend with her. She admired her son-in-law and his ambitious nature.

"Let's shoot for June or July, okay?"

"Love you Lil Bebe."

Mike called Iouri, and told him he had the jackets and rappelling gear. They set another time for Sunday. He informed Iouri that he would be renting the safe house soon, and Sabrina was getting the disguises in the next day or so, he thought.

"Sounds like we are getting close," Iouri said.

"Yeah, and Sabrina's picking up a new license for me, so I can rent the house. I'll be Mike Reynolds, relocating salesman, getting divorced.

"You are wearing a disguise?"

"Sure. Sabrina says she'll make me better looking. I told her that was impossible. Anyways, she don't like me much. But that's okay. She's Tom's problem."

"I will see you Sunday, Iouri said, brusquely."

Sunday was March 9th. It had to go well. Mike had to be in Chicago the following Wednesday for court. It would be tight, but should work out if he left Sunday night.

Tom called Sabrina to find out if she knew anything about his next court date. "How are you, darling?" he asked.

"Oh, I've been real busy."

"Doing all your wifely duties?"

"Something like that. Mom called, and I spent fifteen minutes convincing her to visit in the summer and not now."

"I'll bet that was fun."

"Oh yeah."

"Have you heard from Steve?" She was hoping he would not ask.

"Yes. The earliest he could get was Thursday, April 17th. Judge Sunland will be out starting next week for three weeks for surgery."

Tom exhaled a slow, silent breath. She knew how upset he must be.

"Hang in there, honey. I'll see you soon and give you lotsa mooches."

"Can't hardly wait."

Sabrina drove South on I-5 to La Jolla, a quaint village where the wealth been hoarded down through the generations. It was nestled in Southeast San Diego County. The horse stables, where she learned to ride, were her fondest memories of an idyllic childhood, shattered when her parents divorced.

She found the La Jolla Playhouse Theater with little trouble. The supply shop was modest, but surprisingly well stocked - a thousand-and-one masks and make-up kits. There was a package that would do the job perfectly; it was designed for high school and college drama clubs.

She strolled up to the counter, and was greeted by a blonde-haired co-ed with startling, china-blue eyes. She looked to be about nineteen, and her name tag read, "Tiffany."

"What school is this for?" Tiffany asked, politely. Her voice had a typical valley girl twang.

"No school," Sabrina said, calmly. She was a little embarrassed at the question.

"Oh," Tiffany said as she rang up the purchase. Sabrina could tell there was something on Valley Girl's mind.

"Can I ask you a strange question? If you are not with a school, what are you using all this for?"

Sabrina knew she didn't have to answer but felt compelled to oblige. "Well," she said, with a smirk. "My husband and I like to play dress-up."

"Wow, that is way cool," Tiffany gushed.

"You have no idea," Sabrina replied, batting her eyelashes.

CHAPTER 46

"Victor, line 113," Olivia announced.

"Who is it?" Victor barked.

"Wouldn't say."

"Victor Goldman," he said, with smoldering impatience.

"It's me," the husky voice said.

"I told you not to call me here. I'll call you back. Olivia, I'm going out."

"Remember court's at 1:00," she, reminded him.

"I know. I know. I've got plenty of time."

Outside, he dialed his cell phone. "Is that project still happening?" the husky voice asked.

"Yes."

"When?"

"I don't know exactly, but soon."

"You know it will be a rating bonanza. It will break all the records, even for 60 Minutes. You know, it may topple some of the higher ups in the government."

"That's the idea," Victor replied, with a smile.

"How are you going to get the tape, I mean, meeting with your client after he's, you know, 'out', would be dangerous."

"Yes I know. It's all arranged."

"How, or should I say whom?"

"I have a trusted associate who will pick up the tape at the right time. I have to go, I have court soon."

"Please keep me informed."

"I will," Victor said then hustled back into the office, remembering he had to call his latest ex-wife, who was trying to extort more child support. As he aged, he had degenerated into a miserable misogynist; if women didn't have vaginas, they'd be useless. Just shut up and do me, then go away, was his motto. He blamed his attitude on five failed marriages.

Victor wanted to embarrass the government and beat them at their own game. But he also he wanted the money. They were offering fifteen million. That would be enough to bribe each of his ex-wives into lump-sum settlements. Currently he shelled out over one-million dollars a year in alimony. If he offered each two-million to go away, he'd be able to retire and go somewhere tropical, while the Bureau of Prisons got what it deserved.

Sunday. The last delivery had to go off without a hitch. Mike had to catch a midnight bus to make his Wednesday court date. There could be no slip-ups. He awoke, packed his bags, and inspected the final parcel. All in all, everything had gone relatively well, including yesterday when Sabrina accompanied him to lease the safe house and purchase a vehicle. It was kind of fun - another chapter in his cloak and dagger smorgasbord. He wore a disguise and it reminded him of his drama club days in high school.

He re-inspected the final package. Putting on his cap and checking out of the motel, he plodded into the pastel sky of early evening. He would leave Sabrina's Chrysler Sebring at the bus station; she would pick it up tomorrow.

He arrived at the Mobil Station at 7:15 p.m.. Contrary to his reputation, he did not like cutting it so close, but the LA traffic was unpredictable. He snatched the bag from the back and headed for MDC. As he reached Alameda, one of the local hookers approached him, looking at his cap and said, "Hey, I'm special too."

Befuddled, Mike did not respond. He hustled across the street, wondering what the hell she was talking about. He moved casually along the South side of MDC. This time he carried the parcel in a large Wal-Mart bag - a shopper passing through. Converging on the target spot, he saw there was no rope. Shit. He was panicked, for there was no tomorrow or next week, unless he wanted two warrants. His cell phone rang.

"You there?" Iouri whispered.

"Yeah. What's up. You alright?"

"Just a late start. Need five minutes."

"Alright."

Winging it, Mike continued towards the parking lot on Temple Street.

Stopping suddenly, he wheeled around, walking back slowly, searching the ground as if he had lost something. Out of the blue, he bumped into a security guard. For a moment, time seemed suspended. Mike had the presence of mind to say nothing, even though he felt his throat constrict and something tighten in his stomach. Despite the silence there was a crackling atmosphere of tension.

"Can I help you find something?" the guard said, holding a flashlight. Mike paused and chose his words carefully.

"No, thank you. I'm looking for a receipt I think I dropped; bought some clothes for my son - you know, in case I have to exchange something," he said, clutching the bag so the guard could not see inside.

"Okay, well, good evening, Agent," he said as he plodded away. Agent? First, some hooker calls me "special," and this guy calls me "agent. "What the hell is going on? Is it a full moon?"

He watched the guard disappear. Moments later, he spotted the rope as it crept down the wall. He took the parcel from the bag, hooked it on the rope, tugged twice, and continued toward the Mobil Station.

Plopping down in the car, his knees cracked, announcing his arthritis was flaring up. He took off his cap. Tossing it on the passenger's seat. Something out of the corner of his eye snagged his attention; it made him laugh out loud. On the cap was: F.B.I. Special Agent. He recently had purchased a California Speedway 500 cap, the same color as the ones he just delivered. When he bundled the package he must inadvertently have made the switch. Boy, is Iouri's gonna be confused.

It was an unusually warm and muggy day in Chicago for early spring. as Mike traipsed into the court building.

"Taylor. You again!" Judge Flanagan said, peering down his bifocals.

Mike nodded, acknowledging the deserved rebuke.

"Let's see, a dirty test, and petty theft," the judge mumbled, glancing through Mike's file. "Aren't you tired of coming to see me, yet?"

Mike was tired, tired from his cross-country trip - a three day bus trip sitting straight up; and yes, he was tired of visiting Judge Flanagan. He had been in his court at least twelve times over the past twelve years, primarily for dirty urine tests.

Perusing Mike's file, the judge noticed that Mike had already served two weeks in County. That plus a fine should suffice. "Taylor, can you pay a fine?"

"Yes sir." Mike perked up. Sabrina had given him five thousand before he left, so Queenie would be happy, and it sounded like the judge would let him go home.

"Alright. Time served and a three-hundred dollar fine. Pay the clerk."

"Thank you, your Honor." Mike said, genuinely and turned to leave.

"Hey, Taylor. Stay out of trouble, you're getting too old for this.

"So am I," the judge mumbled to himself.

CHAPTER 47

"Hey, want some tea?" Petrov asked Tom, who was watching TV. "Anything to break the monotony."

"Iouri's getting real anxious with all that equipment in his cell. He has stuff everywhere - in walls, behind cabinets, in pipes, hanging from pipes. If the peegs ever found it, we'd never get out of here."

"Can we talk about something else?" Right about then, Tom could have cared less what Iouri was anxious about. Sometimes he wondered if it would be better if Iouri was caught with all the equipment. Then this nightmare would be over. Iouri would probably not rat out his source and Tom eventually would be released and free to go on with his life. But there was still the allure of the money. Petrov snapped his fingers lightly in front of Tom's face.

"Oh sorry, uh, I'm going to court soon; there's no reason to keep me any longer. My attorney tells me they can only keep me until May at the latest."

"Your government can do anything it wants," Petrov said, brusquely.

"I'm still wondering something," Tom said. "Did you find out from Iouri how he's going to get the camera to Victor?"

"Iouri told me his attorney would have someone there when we leave the building, Iouri's supposed to call when everything's a go. Why?"

"Just curious," Tom replied, nonchalantly, hoping Petrov believed him. Can't have too many "Get Out of Jail" cards.

The days lumbered one into the next in what felt like judicial perpetuity. What really got under Tom's skin was the mindless warehousing of otherwise capable, productive human beings. It seemed such a waste of time, money and human potential. There were incorrigibles that deserved harsh punishment, but they were the exceptions, not the rule.

The latest editorial he had read in the LA Times stated that 70% of the prison population was non-violent. The U.S. currently was spending four to five billion a year to deposit people in its correctional corrals. The majority of the offenders, referred to as "political prisoners," were drug users, and many were involved in victimless crimes. There was absolutely no emphasis on counseling and/or rehabilitation; not to mention the ripple effect when the primary wage earner was removed from a household, and the psychological damage done to the children left in its wake.

"Taylor," the C.O. whispered. "Court-line." April 17th, 4:15 a.m.

Please let this be my last court-line. He was ushered through processing on the fourth floor, handcuffed and shackled, then off to court.

He glanced at Sabrina in the back row. She shot him a nervous smile.

Her fingers were tented in the attitude of prayer as he was escorted through the side and seated next to Steve.

"How are we looking?" Tom whispered.

"I'm going for the jugular," Steve promised. "This bitch has been screwing with us too long. She's lying and she knows it. I've been trying to take the high road and not embarrass her in court, but today, all bets are off."

Court was called to order. Suspending protocol, Judge Sunland allowed Vickie Stanford to go first. Steve did not mind; he wanted to be last. Prattling on ad nauseam, she reiterated her reasons for Tom's violation, and insisting on his incarceration all these months. Her tone was one of quiet contempt.

Then it was Steve's turn. He looked very confident, almost smug. The first issue had been raised before, but Steve started there, presenting the judge with the photos of the drop behind Bob's house: "Your Honor, Tom Taylor did not hide behind any bushes; he would have fallen 200-300 feet and sustained serious, perhaps even fatal, injury. She accused Tom of not filing his probation reports on time, by the fifth of each month." Steve produced reports showing they were all entered on or before the fifth of each month. He was not without friends, even in the probation office.

Vickie kept trying to interrupt and break Steve's concentration. But he was on a roll and she knew it. She bounced up and shrieked, "How did he get those copies?"

"Sit down, Ms. Stanford," the judge ordered. "Continue, Mr. Reid."

"Thank you, your Honor. May I address Ms. Stanford directly?"

The judge nodded. Tom could see in action what he had come to believe: the court system was not about justice; it was about win or lose. Period.

"Ms. Stanford, in the third item on Mr. Taylor's detainer, you stated that, beside his late reports, Mr. Taylor refused to be drug tested. Why would he do that? Everyone who knows Mr. Taylor knows he doesn't drink, and has never taken an illicit drug in his life. Further, isn't it true that Mr. Taylor, in his 11.00 am phone conversation with you, asked you to move a drug test to a different day because of a 4.00 p.m. business appointment he had that day, but you insisted that he make it to you by 6:00 in the evening?

Vickie did not respond.

Steve held his stance in silence. He could see the vein in her temple. Her gaze grew pointed angry.

"Bitch." Sabrina murmured.

"Answer the question," the judge ordered. She suddenly seemed intrigued.

"Well, Item three is misunderstood," Vickie said, backpedaling.

"Misunderstood!?" Steve snapped back. "Call it what it is - a lie!"

"I didn't mean to lie," she whined, blinking as if she'd been slapped.

"Allow me to finish," Steve said, continuing to seize the moment. "Item 4 is about police contact. Mr. Taylor has never denied talking to the Secret Service; he has maintained his innocence in that matter and was never charged with a crime. Non-reporting of police contact is a minor infraction, a Class C violation in the Code and doesn't necessitate confinement. My client has been needlessly in custody for nine months, and for what - three lies and a minor infraction!?"

The judge was immersed in his words.

"After Ms. Stanford first visited Mr. Taylor's luxurious home, which since has been sold, she started acting in a suspicious manner toward him for no apparent reason, focusing on him and taking his case personally.

Vickie bolted up. "I did not!"

Steve kept plowing through, ignoring her. "She was actively looking for a way to get him, and she knew police contact wouldn't be enough for your Honor to issue a warrant, so she added three trumped-up charges."

"No I didn't!" Vickie interjected.

Judge Sunland motioned with her hand for Vickie to sit down. Each wave of the judge's hand felt like a mallet on Vickie's head. Her lips were taut. She flashed the judge a big, phony, prom-queen smile, seeking the judge's sympathy. There was none to be had.

Steve did not skip a beat. "Let me summarize:" His voice flowed like fine wine - strong, firm, reassuring and commanding. "Item one: My client hid behind bushes when the marshals came to see him. As I demonstrated at his last court appearance, along with photographic proof, if he had hidden behind them, he would have fallen 200 feet, two-thirds of a football field, possibly to his death. Lie number 2, I mean, Item number 2:"

Tom could see Vickie Stanford was ready to erupt.

"He filed late reports. I have seventeen documents that say differently."

Steve could see Vickie was flustered and did not know what to do.

"Item or lie number 3: He refused a drug test. She already admitted that was wrong. Item number 4: we plead no contest and remind the court it is a negligible infraction. For these reasons, and the apparent fact that Ms. Stanford lied not once, but three times…"

Vickie Stanford sprang up from her chair violently and screamed, "I AM NOT A LIAR!" It resounded like a gunshot blast. There was an eerie silence.

Trying not to show his shock, or laugh, Steve wondered how long it would take the Judge to react. Not long.

Judge Sunland, her face now hawkish, was incensed at Vickie's hissy-fit. As she spoke, Vickie slumped back into her chair, mortified.

"It is apparent that the probation department's pursuit of Mr. Taylor has been overly aggressive. I grant the defense's motion for time served and I order Mr. Taylor's probation terminated." She swung her gavel "Mr. Taylor, you are free to go."

Tom was ushered out, and smiled when he heard the judge order Vickie into chambers. His spirit was floating.

Sabrina jumped up, elated. Yes! Yes! Tom is coming home.

CHAPTER 48

"Free at last! Free at last!" The immortal sound bite from Martin Luther King Jr.'s timeless "I Have a Dream" speech echoed in Tom's mind as he walked out of MDC. It was April 18th, his fourth anniversary. His first sight of freedom was Tyler in Sabrina's arms, smiling. Priceless! Sabrina drove, and it felt strange to ride in a car; it had been nine months and three days. Everyone was happy, but the reality of what they were involved in overshadowed Tom's high spirits.

Life was full of ironies, of choices, of unintended consequences. Apprehension tightened his spine, his personal barometer of impending doom. Should he finish? Should he get out? Could he get out? He could run, but could he hide from these guys? Probably not. Iouri was too wealthy, his influence too far-reaching.

Then, there was the green goblin of greed resting on his shoulder whispering, *"Remember the money."* There was another $400,000 to be wired before the escape happened. And $500,000 and the Costa Mesa beach house after they arrived at the safe house. And if Cliff had been successful, all of that was moot also. There was also a piece of the Big Score. Tom was not counting on that money; it would be merely icing on the cake.

Easter Sunday was to be Escape Sunday. Iouri thought the timing perfect. "I will be having my own resurrection," he proclaimed. He viewed it as a significant slap in the face of the two institutions he despised - the U.S. Government and the Catholic Church. Tom had nine days to decide.

"How's he doing, doctor?" Sabrina asked.

"He's in recovery," Dr. Vo replied. "You should be able to see him soon.".

"How did it go?"

"I'll tell you, the lack of attention by the government did him no good and made my job very difficult. Removing a urinary stent is normally a fifteen to thirty minute procedure. But it took three hours, as you know. I wrote numerous letters to Dr. Sinavsky, the Chief Medical Officer at MDC, as well as the Warden, advising them the stent needed to be removed after three or four weeks, but never received a response.

"Doctor, he's awake now," the recovery nurse reported.

"Thank you. Well, just follow her," Dr. Vo said.

"Don't stay too long," the nurse whispered. "He's very weak and I have to give him more sedatives soon."

"Tom saw blurry, white forms when he awoke. He decided he was either in an asylum or in heaven. He smelled astringents and strange chemicals. Then he saw Sabrina, and knew where he was.

"Hi honey," she murmured, bending over to kiss him. "How are you feeling?"

"Top of the line."

She smiled, explained that she'd left Tyler with Lisa, then relayed what Dr. Vo had told her about the complications during surgery. His eyes opened in silent horror. They exchanged light talk for about half-an-hour; actually, Sabrina did most of the talking. She informed him that Dr. Vo wanted to hold him for a day or two while he convalesced. He would call her when Tom was ready to be released. Or paroled, as she put it.

"I'll see you soon," she said.

"I love you," Tom croaked.

"Love you more."

Petrov was upbeat when he told Iouri and Nikki that Tom had been released. "Tom said, 'He'll see us Easter Sunday'." The three Russians spent the next week squaring off the holes behind their cell mirrors and scoring the outer walls. They also tightened up the arrangements for their distractions on their respective floors. This was their one shot at freedom, so they were taking no chances. The plan was brilliant. As long as the execution equaled the design, they would be successful.

Marina and Iouri stopped communicating; she no longer answered the phone when it was him. He decided he would deal with her later. For now, he had bigger fish to fry. He had a 100 million dollar score to perpetrate; hoping to secure his future and retire, in fabulous Iouri style, to a vineyard in the South of France - his version of Mt. Olympus. Reminding himself to stay cool, he would not allow Marina's disloyalty to interfere with his dream.

Mike arrived back from Chicago, glad to be away from the humidity. Tom picked him up at the bus station; he had not seen his brother in almost three years.

"Hey, Dill." Tom flashed him a smile.

"Wassup?" Mike replied, happy to see him.

They hugged like two frat brothers. "Dill" was short for dill pickle, a term of endearment between the two, stemming back to their childhood, although, its exact origin was fuzzy. They caught up on old times and exchanged war stories about being incarcerated.

"Listen to us," Tom said, "We sound like members of the Gambino Family." Wouldn't Mom be proud?

Mike called Iouri. "Hey I'm back. Everything looks to be a go. I'm on the way to the safe house." Mike set his cell phone in his lap.

"You want to talk to Iouri?" he whispered to Tom. Tom waved him off. "I'd sooner wrestle an alligator." Tom still had not talked to Iouri since that fateful day when Iouri had threatened him - the tantrum in the toilet. Tom was going to hold firm and speak to him only when necessary.

When Mike hung up, Tom reminded him that they should only use their 'bat' phones to communicate until the Russians were gone. If Mike ever thought his phone was compromised he should lose it immediately. Tom also cautioned him to be vigilant with the Russians at the safe house. "I don't believe anything will happen, but these guys appear to be the real deal."

They pulled onto Via Amarilla and stopped in front of 1007, Mike's new home and the Russians' temporary headquarters. They went inside and looked around. A typical middle-to-upper-middle-class, four bedroom, two bath, Southern California house. But Tom thought it was perfect; no one would suspect a thing. Mike was astonished at the real estate prices.

"Now remember, after Sunday night, only call me sporadically; and if anyone's on to you, lose the phone. We can replace the phone; we can't replace you."

Tom was younger than Mike, but the more serious of the two. People often mistook him as the older one. They exchanged looks that said, "Good luck," but neither wanted to say the words, in case they jinxed it. They shook hands, lingered a little, then said their goodbyes.

Although he had been gone nine months, Tom felt as if he had just re-entered the earth's atmosphere after having traveled millions of miles to another universe, and found that things on earth had changed. Sabrina had done a great job of setting up the new apartment; but it was smaller, a lot smaller, than the estate he left behind in Fountain Valley.

He showered, thinking about the evening's plans. Doesn't everybody break out Russian mobsters on Easter? This is beyond nuts, but he knew there was no turning back.

"Honey?" Sabrina called. "Come and look." She beckoned sweetly from the other room. Tom walked in wearing his robe; and there was his fourteen-month-old in his Easter suit, beaming. He looked like he was decked out for his first prom - a little black suit with a white ruffle shirt, red suspenders, and a black bow tie.

"Too cute," he said, his throat tight with love.

They made the short trip to St. Bernard's Church in their old parish.

Though Tom was not the most committed Catholic, there was something reassuring about attending mass. He did believe there was something beyond what man experienced on earth, although he was not certain what it was. Spending a lot of time with and listening to Iouri, an ardent atheist, had created an unsettled feeling about everything Tom had felt was beyond reproach - his country and his church. Hoping he was not being too hypocritical, he said a silent prayer for being released and reunited with his family.

On the way home, Sabrina's cell phone rang.

"We good?" the voice asked.

"I'll get back to you," she replied, and disconnected.

"That was José," she told Tom. Our band of merry marauders awaits. Are we a 'go'?"

She knew Tom was having second thoughts; the indecision was in his eyes and etched on his face. Privately, she wished he would say no; but she knew that was impossible. Selfishly, she was glad he was home. And she would respect any decision he made.

He looked at her with the gravest grimace she had ever seen on his face. He tried to look elsewhere. Nothing in the world was more exhausting than fear. No race, no fight, no battle. Fear always ran faster, hit harder, fought longer.

"Babe?" she whispered. She never had seen him so torn. Tough decisions had always been his strength. Go or stop? Run or hide?

After an interminable, agonizing silence, Tom muttered, "It's a 'go'."

CHAPTER 49

Paulie Vitolo, dressed like an extra from the Sopranos, had left Henderson, Nevada a little delayed, due to the Easter Brunch with his wife and kids. Exiting I-15, he sailed down 10 West and looped the Hollywood Interchange onto the 101 Freeway, then slammed on his brakes. A parking lot of holiday hostility.

"Friggin' LA," he mumbled. The traffic was maddening, in a day that already felt achingly long. Victor said he had to be there by 7:45 p.m. He paid Paulie well, but held more than a few of Paulie's indiscretions and secrets as leverage. Paulie could not see what was going on; all he knew was to look for three Russians and six motorcycles outside of MDC LA. He was to wear a blue suit, stroll up to them and they would hand him a camera. No questions. No names.

Let the show begin! Iouri said to himself as he gathered his belongings. Today I might actually leave this dump. And make history in the process. That made his heart flutter. Not too many things did that. Iouri loved to do things in a spectacular way. With a little luck, they will tear this shithole down and turn it into a garbage dump.

He went about his normal routine - working out and reading, then confirmed with his colleagues that the planned disturbances were set. Everything would begin after chow.

Three cells on Nine South had toilets backing up like small geysers. Nikki fought back smiles as he watched angry inmates trudging around in water. The C.O. was frazzled, trying to enlist inmates to help with mops and buckets. The building was short-staffed in general. Serendipitously, there were no plumbers available; they were handling a plumbing problem on the women's floor. They were forever flushing hygiene products down the toilet that should have been thrown in the trash.

Iouri packed everything in a duffel bag, turned on the video camera, jumped up on the toilet plumbing and beckoned Nikki on Nine South: "It is time," he announced.

Tom picked up Mike at the safe house. They spoke not a word as they traveled downtown; only exchanging a few anxious glances. When Tom dropped Mike off at the Chevron, two blocks away from MDC, José was there with two other riders. Two were circling the area and another was down at the Mobil Station on Alameda

"Ready?" Tom asked, as he handed José an envelope, the remaining $12,000 for the bikers.

"We're good to go," José replied, nodding at the other bikers.

Tom then drove to the parking garage at Hacienda Heights Apartments. It was the closest covered parking garage structure to MDC not owned by the government. The coverage was needed to avert a possible helicopter pursuit.

Fifteen minutes later, as José was rounding up the rest of his bikers, a Jaguar XK rolled over to his Honda Valdyke Rune. The tinted window buzzed down revealing a stranger.

"You José?" the man said, with a slight Russian accent.

"Who wants to know?"

"Relax, I'm one of the good guys. Small change in plans." Dmitri held out a pair of keys. "Actually, an improvement in plans." José squatted down by the driver's door.

"There's a Rodeo Convention at the Forum, so we've provided a black Suburban, with a horse trailer attached. It's already at the rendezvous point. So if the cops are looking for a group of bikers, you'll be just another horse trailer on the road tonight. On the passenger seat are directions where to bring the Suburban and trailer. I even provided some refreshments for you and the boys. They are in the vehicle."

"Thanks" José said, took the keys and they shook hands.

"Good luck." Dmitri said in that suave tone of his, rolled up his window and drove into the night.

Nikki draped his green windbreaker over his door for the last time. Hopefully. With the plumbing mishaps, he should have plenty of time. But you can never be too careful. He removed the mirror and busted through the stairway wall. The plasterboard landed on the steps with a giant crash, much louder than anticipated. But so far, so good. He was not overly concerned, because the security camera in the stairway was masked with a photograph.

Before he climbed through, he knocked twice, then once again, on his cell door. That was the signal. His cellmate was standing sentinel right outside. All three Russians' cellmates, already handsomely compensated, would reinstall the mirrors and were prepared to go to the hole, if necessary.

Nikki hit the staircase four steps down from the landing and hustled down to the sixth floor, where Petrov was just worming his way through the wall. Back on Nine South, Nikki's cell mirror was already re-installed.

"Let's go," Petrov whispered. They heard an unexpected noise that reminded Nikki of the hollow popping of an AK-47. They froze, then realized it was Iouri coming through on the fifth floor.

"Smile for the camera," Nikki whispered to Petrov, aware that Iouri hated the idea and the encumbrance. Iouri shot him a look, then led the way, all of them conscious of the dark pulse of MDC throbbing beneath their feet.

Nikki held the camera while Iouri tunneled through the walls with the power of a locomotive, until he hit an obstruction: a metal storage cabinet.

"Shit," he whispered, his eyes narrowed in anger. "I was afraid of something this; it was not on the blueprints

"Now what?" Petrov asked, his face filled with tension. "What if it's bolted? Or what if it falls down when we move it?

"Keep it to yourself," Iouri snapped.

He squatted down and they scored the hole wider; the cabinet was only 14 inches wide. As long as it was not anchored, they'd be fine.

"Help me push." Iouri gripped a side at the top of the opening and Petrov grabbed the other side at the bottom.

"One, two, three…".

There was an eerie, screeching, scraping sound, then the cabinet moved. They shoved it out far enough, and Iouri could see it was only a foot taller than the opening; it was some sort of file cabinet. They continued pushing and spun it sideways to get clearance.

Startled by a noise, their gazes locked. To Nikki it sounded like the crack of a Smith and Wesson .22. Iouri put up five fingers, indicating, "fifth floor." He assumed Mike Cha, his cellie, was reinstalling the mirror.

He placed the duffel bag inside the hole and crawled through with the camera. The cool air from the stairway followed him. Petrov stayed a flight up and Nikki a flight down, both stationed as lookouts.

The acoustic tile was yellowed. A thin patina of dust laid over everything. Most of the room was sheathed in shadows. To Iouri's left was a row of 3' X 4' windows guarded by exterior railings, as shown on the blueprints. He removed the tools from the duffel bag, mounted the camera on a makeshift stand, then slipped on the work gloves and taped a rectangular area. He scored the perimeter with the diamond glass cutter, tapped it firmly all around. Slathering the gloves with construction adhesive, he placed his hands on the glass and yanked. The glass came away without extensive shattering. The outside air hit his face, inspiring him. He took a deep breath, smiled when he heard the traffic outside. They were close.

"Friggin' sixteenth-century elevator," C.O. "Red" Prakar groaned, as he stood in the foyer by the bank of elevators, trying to retrieve an inmate from the fifth floor for the visiting room. All inmates were escorted to and from social and legal visits by staff. There were four elevators: one used exclusively by executives, the other three took turns taking the day off. He did not know if the elevator was delayed or on permanent vacation. He felt sorry for the families that had to wait forever to see their loved ones. I think I'll take the stairway. He opened the stairway door, swore as he began his ascent.

Nikki heard the footsteps, motioned to Petrov to be ready. Nikki's Secret Forces training in the Russian Army had prepared him to handle unforeseen situations. He was poised like a boa constrictor.

Red was fixated on his black boots as he climbed the steps. Nikki was five steps up from him when he realized Red was still oblivious to his presence. His smile was like a light flashing on a blade. Red saw another set of feet. Startled, he began to look up. Before he could press the panic button on his radio, Nikki drove his right knee into his face. Bone and cartilage crunched and there was a crack of broken teeth. Then, Nikki chopped him with the stiffened blade of his right hand, a controlled blow, judged firmly to immobilize, not to kill. Catherine wheels of pain filled Red's head. His world drifted into a black delirium, then a permanent void; he was unconscious.

Nikki ripped open Red's shirt. All federal C.O.s had heart monitors attached to their radios, so that any prolonged heart increase would alert the control booth and the remaining staff. Nikki attached it to his own chest. Seventy. Perfect.

Then he attached the radio to his belt. Now they had better information; but their window of opportunity had decreased drastically. He and Petrov lugged the unconscious Red to the third floor landing.

Iouri grabbed the jack from the bag. He had not heard the disturbance in the hallway. Holding the jack, he grinned for the camera. This had better work. He had come to respect Mike's knowledge of tools and machinery, so he was not overly concerned. He maneuvered the pump between the two parallel, four-foot, hollow, steel pipes. It was a tight squeeze, but it did fit. Reaching for the tire iron and the nitrous oxide, he sprayed the enzymatic on the welding joints, inserted the rod and pumped his chiseled arm up and down, watching anxiously as the pipe began to bend upward. The welds creaked like old train wheels on a track, then separated. *Bang!* The bottom bar dropped to the ground with a long sharp sound like a rifle shot. Iouri looked out through the 18" gap. No one around. And just enough room.

Petrov crawled through the wall and grabbed the roll of duct tape, muttering, "We've got company."

"What?" Whatever it was, he would not let to stop them. Damn Tom for refusing to send up those guns. But they had come too far and were too close to be stopped by any- one or anything.

Petrov hustled back to the hole, reached through and dragged the officer in, with Nikki holding his legs and feet. Nikki then wrapped him in duct tape, covering Red's mouth. They found a musty tarpaulin discarded in the corner, tossed it over the unconscious C.O.

"Look what I've got," Nikki announced to Iouri, showing off Red's radio.

Iouri did not hear him.

"Is he dead?"

"No, unconscious," Nikki said, then mumbled, "I think. We got to go. Now!"

"I'm ready," Iouri said.

Petrov had already put on his F.B.I. jacket and rappelling gear. The other Two followed suit.

"You two first," Iouri ordered.

He punched his speed dial.

"Are we having fun yet?" Mike whispered.

"Go!" Iouri said.

Like acrobats, Petrov and Nikki rappelled down in less than thirty seconds. Iouri recorded the last footage, making certain to lift the tarp and capture Red's duct-taped body. He had developed a love-hate relationship with the camera.

"Take that, you assholes," he muttered, referring to the U.S. Government. Deciding, last minute, not to be strapped with the huge duffel bag, he left it behind. He felt as light as an eagle in flight as he rappelled down.

Mike, José, and the other three riders strolled up Alameda like a practiced

parade. Three of the riders jumped off and doubled up with them and the other rider. Petrov and Nikki hopped on the two vacant bikes. Iouri swaggered down the walkway, camera in hand, strutting like he had just pulled off the Crime of the Century.

Mike motioned to him. They shook hands and Mike explained the shift pattern to him, "One down and four up." Like dancing sitting down. Iouri passed it along to Nikki and Petrov. Iouri saddled in on the last bike, one chosen especially for him. He was about to give the signal when he looked around and a man in a blue suit, and blonde hair rolled up, walked past and held out his hand. Iouri handed him the camera. Nothing was said.

Iouri raised his arms and the riders dispersed through the streets of LA. Tom was relieved Mike had arrived at the same time as Iouri, so he could avert an awkward moment. They loaded into the Explorer while Iouri told them the story of the captured C.O.

"Better get going," Tom said.

"Absolutely," Mike agreed.

Petrov and Nikki arrived two minutes apart. Tom did not wait for José and company to retrieve their bikes; he assumed the black Suburban and horse trailer was for them. High-fives and smiles all around. The mood was electric; everyone was acutely aware of what they had just pulled off, but knew: they were not out of the woods yet. Nevertheless, the three Russians were savoring their first moments of freedom.

Headlights off, like a shark patrolling a moonlit bay, Dmitri spied from his Jaguar. The horse trailer and the black Suburban were waiting. José and the rest of the bikers arrived, saluting each other on their successful mission. José looked in the Suburban. "Hey, there's beer."

There was grunting and competitive belching while they hefted the motorcycles into the trailer. They piled into the Suburban with the satisfaction only criminals after a successful caper understood, almost like the afterglow of a sexual climax. Holding the directions to the drop-off, José started the vehicle and rolled out of the garage, tugging the horse trailer.

Fifty yards away, in his Jaguar, Dmitri detonated the C-4, creating an explosion like a noise heard around the world. When the vehicle erupted, it seemed to open sedately, like one of those time-lapsed movies. The metal of the stolen Suburban spread like grotesque black petals. A bright, white flame shot through it, glass blown away in a million glittering shards by the blast wave. The bodies were cinched and torched in a mass crematorium. The fearsome din shook the ground. It looked like a fireworks display gone awry. There were cries of anguish, fear and horror from nearby residents as the explosion rattled their teeth in their sockets.

Dust swimming in his headlights; Dmitri had slipped away long before human ashes started settling on the ground like snowflakes.

CHAPTER 50

Sgt. "El Fuerte" Herrera suited up as soon as he got the call. He was LAPD's elite tactical helicopter pilot. Hustling from the locker room, he was glad for the new squadron of helicopters - the old ones were as airworthy as a fleet of Buicks. His chopper hit the air and dove in between LA's hi-rises. His prey was six motorcyclists carrying three escaped fugitives.

Lost in self-congratulations, Iouri's antennae went up when he heard a radio squawk. Seated in the front seat next to Tom, who was driving, he spun around. "What was that!?"

"It's the radio," Nikki said, displaying it proudly. "I thought we could listen to what's going on. They still haven't found the cop."

"Are you crazy!?" Iouri raged.

Nikki thought he saw sparks in Iouri's eyes. Better you than me, Tom thought, fighting back a grin. "What do you mean?" replied Nikki.

"Get off at the next exit," Iouri ordered Tom. They were about a third of the way to the safe house.

"So what gives?" Nikki asked.

"G.P.S., you moron," Iouri spat out. "If those things have G.P.S. they will find us. We might as well call and tell them where we are."" Everyone understood. Tom pulled behind a McDonald's. Iouri grabbed the radio from Nikki, removed the battery and hurled the radio into the dumpster.

About three-quarters of the way to the safe house, sirens were heard.

"Think they figured it out?" Mike mumbled facetiously. Everyone looked back and watched the helicopters saturate the air, their blinding spotlights sweeping every inch of ground.

"10-4, I'll check it out," Sgt. Herrera responded to the report of an explosion near Dodger Stadium. Gloom settled on his face when he saw the destruction - the shrapnel and charred, scattered remains of six motorcyclists and their bikes.

Dead men cannot testify, Iouri reminded himself, as Tom pulled into the driveway of the safe house, Tom hit the door opener and they rolled into the garage. "Home sweet home, boys; at least for awhile," he announced.

They piled out, and went inside to check out the place. Iouri leaned against the Explorer with a look of total vindication on his face. *I did it.*

Tom did not leave the Explorer; Mike came out when Iouri had gone inside.

"Mike," Tom said, solemnly, "You know the rules." He was referring to the cell phone. "Also watch your back." Mike knew Tom was right, but had not given it much serious thought until that moment. He felt a chill as he walked inside.

Tom pulled away. When he thought about what he had done, he had the congested feeling in his chest that he had known all the way back to his childhood. He knew he had done something horrendously wrong. He was numb.

After making the fifteen minute trip home, he hauled himself out of the SUV and went inside.

Sabrina heard the front door. She was never so glad to see Tom as she was in that moment. He had never seen her so ashen and frightened. Choking on her breath she said, "It's all over the news - EVERY CHANNEL." Their eyes locked in a freeze frame of terror.

CHAPTER 51

"Hey, Bob, if you don't mind, I won't be in today; I'm going to hang with Sabrina and Tyler," Tom said. He never wanted to leave the apartment again. He was plagued with nightmares of being greeted by a S.W.A.T. team if he stepped outside.

"Will I see you tomorrow?"

"Sure thing," Tom said, halfheartedly. Bob had been very patient and supportive during Tom's government-sponsored sabbatical - lot more than most partners would have been. He desperately needed Tom's help, but understood there would be an adjustment period once Tom was released. Tom appreciated his understanding; internally, he was a nervous wreck. A basket case.

Sabrina and Tom made a pact not to talk about the situation unless absolutely necessary and definitely not in public. They would resume their normal lives, because as far as everyone was concerned, Tom had been gone awhile and that was it.

The media coverage was intense. It was the leading story on all the networks, endlessly broadcast on CNN and Fox, and the front page story in both the LA Times and the Orange County Register.

The Warden was suffering the raw tension connected with an accusatory, media-driven spectacle, while working to save his job. The reporters turned him into a piñata. Soon, the trumpets would sound in Congress, looking for people to blame and heads to axe.

The general consensus was that the fugitives were in Mexico, or en route to Mexico. The C.O.'s radio was found on Interstate 5 South. The I-5 South led directly into Tijuana. They reported that Petrov's wife and child had taken a flight to Moscow the night before. Iouri Malakov and Nikki Stolov had no family left in the U.S. Attempts were made to talk to Iouri's wife in London. She had no comment.

After reading the newspaper accounts, Tom was immersed in thought, oblivious to Sabrina's attempts to attract his attention. His focus was snagged when he heard, "Earth to Tom, come in Tom. I forgot to tell you that Cliff dropped off something last night," Sabrina said, pointing at a package on the coffee table. "He said he couldn't stay; he had to get back to Indy."

So he did get it, Tom mused. That should make things interesting.

"I didn't know he was part of the plan."

"He wasn't, originally; just a last minute detail."

"One more thing. Let's not get the rest of our money until the heat dies down."

"Smart girl." He stowed the package in his briefcase, spun the combination numbers. He would hide it in the office tomorrow.

The safe house was sparsely furnished, but adequately enough for the four of them. Iouri and Nikki were the early risers. Addicted to fitness, Iouri did an hour of calisthenics, push-ups, and crunches. They grinned at the radio reports that the Russians had left the country. Iouri was wary of possible misinformation, but he figured the probability was nil; that would be giving the U.S. government too much credit.

They prepared an overall game plan with an itemized itinerary and schedule. The first things they needed were food and cash. Nikki went to retrieve Petrov, and Iouri woke up Mike. He learned that Mike was lackadaisical in the mornings, so he made a mental note to wake Mike an hour before he needed him.

While Petrov and Mike wiped the sleep from their eyes; Iouri made a few phone calls. The first was to Dmitri, his man in the darkness. He alerted him that he and Mike and would fetch his remaining $300,000 in cash that Dmitri had been safeguarding.

"Is Sabrina coming with?" Dmitri inquired.

"No, why?" Apparently Sabrina had made an enduring impression on Dmitri. "Keep it in your pants," Iouri snapped, "Besides she's married, and if not for her husband, I would not be seeing you today."

"I know," Dmitri grumbled. They set a rendezvous place and time, then hung up.

Iouri roused his contact at the National Title Company on Wall Street.

Frank was stunned, but not totally surprised; if anyone could have pulled it off, it was Iouri Malakov. Iouri told him he would see him in a week or so.

While Mike became Mike Reynolds, Iouri created his disguise. Adding facial hair - beard and mustache, he was careful to cover the thin scar that skirted his jaw line, the result of plastic surgery he'd had when he came to California. It took awhile to adjust to his new look, but Iouri had no shortage of love for himself, so the transition was not that difficult. He finished his disguise with mock designer sunglasses, topping it off with Mike's California Speedway 500 cap. He laughed every time he remembered opening the last package and finding it.

Mike drove to McDonald's. While waiting for food, he eyed the Kiddie Playground. Oh to be that young again. He wanted to jump around the netted room with the multicolored balls. But he knew better. Must not keep the Russian Mafia waiting. He brought back several colossal cholesterol combos.

"Let's go," Iouri announced, while Mike was polishing off his Big Mac. "Nikki. Petrov. Do not leave this place!" Mouths full, both nodded. "Each of you make a list of the clothes you want, and Petrov, make a list of the computer equipment we will need."

Driving the 405 North, Mike was blown away by Iouri's indifference that the whole country was looking for him, and might shoot him on sight. He was a hard man, and had experienced a great deal in his thirty-nine years; to call him stoic would be an understatement.

They arrived at the Glendale Galleria on the third floor of the parking structure, by the J.C Penney entrance. A silver Jaguar appeared. That car looks familiar, Mike thought, but could not remember passing it the night of the escape. Dmitri got out and so did Iouri. Iouri's eyes constantly surveyed the surroundings.

He told Mike to leave the car running. Dmitri did a double-take. "Good disguise," he said, then handed Iouri a shopping bag.

"All there?"

"300 grand."

"Good. I do not mean to be short, but you know it is not safe for me," Iouri reminded him, heading toward the car.

"I know, but hold on. What's the game plan?"

Silence filled with suspicion. Iouri reminded himself to be careful. Dmitri was one of his most loyal and trusted allies, but caution was prudent at this point. He glared into Dmitri's eyes, to try to discern if Dmitri had accepted thirty pieces of silver from the Romans. "I'm going to New York to take care of some business, and renew some contacts." Dmitri knew what he meant.

"Is he going with?" Dmitri asked, nodding toward Mike.

"I cannot fly and I will not do all the driving myself."

"Then what?"

"I have a big score planned." It all made sense to Dmitri now; Iouri had not explained why they were still in the country. "Then we are gone like the wind."

"To where?"

Iouri began to feel interrogated. Internal alarms started clanging. "Do not worry. I will contact you."

CHAPTER 52

Victor chose to wait a few days to contact Paulie Vitolo, surprised by the explosive reaction from the media and uncertain if the Feds would hound him.

Miraculously, they only contacted him once. They requested he contact them if heard from his client. He informed them he was only required to advise his client to turn himself in if he did hear from him. He further informed them the likelihood he would hear from his client was non-existent and they might as well get the wrecking ball ready to tear down MDC. Downtown LA needed more parking space. The Feds should have known better than to expect any cooperation from Victor Goldman.

"Paulie, it's Victor. Did you get it?" Victor asked. He could tell Paulie was just stirring. It was 2:30 in the afternoon. In addition to the scams he ran up and down the Strip, he was burdened with a serious drinking problem and a weakness for wagering, Paulie was a car salesman, an exceptionally good one. Ironically, he was a sponsor in the local Chapter of AA.

"What?" Paulie muttered, not wanting to talk to Victor right then; or anyone, for that matter; but especially not Victor.

"Are you hung over? Where were you last night?" Victor barked

Who are you, my father? Paulie thought, then said, "The Strip. Where else? think my last stop was the Bella..." before Paulie could say 'Bellagio', Victor screamed, *"Did you get the goddamn tape!?"*

"Uh, no," Paulie moaned.

"No? What the hell happened?" Victor shouted in disbelief.

"Well, I hit some bad traffic, and when I got to the court building, around

8:30, 8:40, there were more cops and Feds than I'd never seen in my life, so I split. It looked like an escape or something. Where did you send me?"

What an idiot! Doesn't this guy read the paper or watch the news? "You're as useless as tits on a bull. I should have you arrested," Victor shrieked.

"For what?" Paulie asked, bewildered. He was awake now.

"I don't know, but I'll think of something." He was so flustered, he slammed the cell phone shut almost breaking it He saw his fifteen million fading away. The thought of paying his five ex-wives until he died made him physically sick. He wanted to kick a small, fuzzy animal. Damn cunts! They shouldn't call it alimony, it should be called vaginomy. He smirked at his own crudeness. Vaginomony; that's a good one. After a few minutes, he calmed down when he figured out that Iouri must still have the tape. So his plans were still intact, he would just wait a while before contacting him.

"Where's Mike going?" Nikki asked Iouri.

"I am sending him to South Coast Plaza; we might as well get some quality clothes."

Iouri had compiled a list of clothes, groceries and sundries. Mike despised clothes shopping. Iouri had instructed him to go to numerous designer stores: Versace, Prada, Armani, and Salvatore Ferragamo.

"Screw that," Mike said, when he arrived at the plaza. I'll get everything at Nordstrom's. And he did. "$20,000 in clothes, and half of it's Iouri's," he mumbled as he loaded the car He dropped off their new wardrobe, then went to the supermarket, where he filled up three grocery carts.

He spent the rest of the evening talking with Petrov; he was the most approachable. Petrov diagrammed the computer components Mike needed to purchase. The most secure systems were wireless with hi-tech firewalls; they were the best safeguard against intrusion. Petrov was on the lookout for the F.B.I. The media coverage seemed to die suddenly - too suddenly for his liking. Unlike Iouri, he believed it was part of their strategy, thinking that they would become comfortable and slip up.

Mike made the computer purchases, returned to the safe house, where Nikki and Petrov helped him unload, while Iouri was on the phone. The next day, disguises in place, Iouri and Mike left for New York City.

CHAPTER 53

Firewalls in place, Petrov settled in, staring at the huge computer monitor, thinking and planning, engines idling. His mind clicked and churned like the hard drive. In the sports world, they called it: "Getting in the Zone." He was known as Max-Attack and revered and respected in the hacker underground.

Away he went. His fingers blurred as he barreled along relentlessly, his speed increasing exponentially with every stroke. He could not and would not infiltrate the National Title Company on the East coast, with its $800 million dollar average daily balance. Iouri's primary plan was to have ten percent extracted by his inside man, and a nine-millimeter as Plan B. Petrov would go in the back way.

Petrov would practice on their second target, the U.S. Title Company.

Its account had only $200 million and was right there in Los Angeles. But there was always the possibility some white-hat hacker employed by the Feds would try and get a line on him. Failure was not an option.

Petrov was the best. He used a complex series of connections that only God might have had a chance of tracking. Nikki, an avid computer user, watched while Petrov worked his magic. His first target was the huge mainframe at UCLA; he had compromised that system awhile back, so he was like an old friend. Rapidly, he scanned through the catalogue of connected, trusted systems; it only took seconds to decode passwords and defeat security at each new target.

Max-Attack repeated his electronic assaults until he had a dozen computers globally woven into his web. At last, using the final system in his chain, he gently approached his end zone - the mainframe controlling the escrow accounts at the title company. This should lead him to the general fund, or he would manually bundle them and confiscate the target amount.

Ten percent of both funds was $100 million. It would not be detected for thirty to forty-five days when the accounts were reconciled. Petrov's share: ten million.

He proceeded prudently. He did not want to trigger an intrusion alarm. Gradually, the system gave up its secrets. He scrolled through the directory listing all the escrow accounts. One-by-one, he selected the twenty largest accounts by highlighting them on the screen. He opened another window and entered the wire transfer software program. Painstakingly, he copied and pasted the information into the new window. All that had to be done now was enter the amounts to be taken; but he would wait until Iouri returned. Both title companies had to be hit simultaneously. Then they would flee the country.

In New York, Iouri showed Mike some of the famous haunts of the Russian Mafia. Their headquarters were in restaurants and cabarets. Most notorious was the Odessa, named after the seaport on the Black Sea, a major seat of organized crime in Russia. Mike noticed most of the men Iouri met with were slick dressers and hard-looking. Very hard. One of them handed Iouri a package, and a case containing a Kalashnikov assault rifle. In a small package was a Browning nine-millimeter pistol affixed with a tubular-type silencer. Aware of Mike's reticence, Iouri smiled. "Do not worry; it is not for you."

Mike did not ask who it was for, and Iouri's remark did not make him feel better; it was a sober reminder of the nature of the man he was traveling with. Arriving at the National Title Company at precisely 12:00 Noon, they met Frank as he came out for lunch.

Like many men of influence and wealth, he had a bull neck and a solid jawline. Iouri lolled outside the vehicle while they chatted. Frank was glad to see Iouri, but distracted by the disguise. Mike saw beads of sweat forming on Frank's forehead. He did not know what they were discussing, but at one point he heard Frank say, "It'll take two to three weeks." Iouri nodded, then got back in the car.

"Good news?" Mike inquired.

"Good enough."

One more stop and they would rest up and get an early start in the morning. The combination of the heat, make-up, and mounting paranoia, was taking its toll. And the traffic did not help. It took about thirty minutes to go another two miles.

"Next time I go to NewYork, I'm taking a plane," Mike decided. He inspected his disguise; rivulets of sweat were wilting his facial hair. Sitting all day in the sun, encased in a metal and glass oven, he felt like a specimen in a Petri dish.

Iouri opened the car door, dabbing his perspiration, threw his briefcase in the back and tossed Mike a thick envelope. "Next month's pay."

Mike was paid $10,000 in cash a month and $100,000 for his help in the escape.

"Finito," Iouri proclaimed. "Time to relax."

"Where?"

"We are going to a five-star hotel, okay?"

"As long as they have beer."

Iouri smiled. Imagine that; he got the joke.

If they'd had had time, Iouri would have taken Mike to Trump's Taj Mahal in Atlantic City. It was the premier stomping grounds for the Russian Mob on the East coast; but they settled for Iouri's favorite hideaway - the Waldorf- Astoria. It was a sin for Iouri to stop in New York and not spend a night there.

The Waldorf people greeted Iouri like an old friend. He and Mike were quite the odd couple: Iouri was utterly at home in the lap of luxury. Scruffy Mike had never experienced such opulence; but vowed it would not be his last time.

The following morning they left for California.

CHAPTER 54

Tom was still recuperating, so Sabrina let him sleep. Coincidentally, Tyler also was asleep. That gave her an idea. Placing him in their bed, she snapped a picture of father and son. She knew Tom would love it.

Constantly fighting her fears regarding the escape, she decided to use the time to open mail and pay some bills. Snap out of it, and stay busy, she chided herself, then sat at the desk in Tyler's room. Speculating that she would spend most of her time in his room, she had the computer desk set up in there.

She did some online banking. After reconciling their primary checking account, she thought to check their offshore account. Next to Tom and coffee, it was her favorite stimulant. She entered the password. The screen displayed the balance; nonchalantly, she scribbled down the amount. Then she looked back at the screen. For sixty seconds. It felt like eons. Her eyes were riveted. She was speechless. Unable to say or do anything until the layers of disbelief peeled away, she mumbled, "*$10,464,350.53.*"

It had to be a mistake. She turned the computer off, rebooted it and started over. Making sure to put in the correct alias, exact twenty-digit account number and secret password, again she saw, "*$10,464,350.43.*" She was expecting $460,000 and change; but where did the extra ten million come from? There was only one person who knew.

"Honey?" Sabrina whispered to Tom, "I made you some tea."

"You spoil me," Tom mumbled, still half-asleep.

"That's okay, I never had a doll when I was a little girl," she replied. "Do you know anything about this?" she asked, then handed him the paper with the scribbled balance.

"Merry Christmas." he said, sheepishly.

"Oh my God," she whispered. "What, I mean…?"

"I told you Cliff was helping me with a surprise. Listen, There's a couple of things I didn't tell you while I was at MDC, because I didn't want to scare you. I had a sneaky suspicion Iouri might hurt me, inside or when I was released, and I wanted to get even with him. He actually threatened me. Twice."

"You should have told me. I had a right to know."

"I'm sorry. Anyway, money is the only thing that matters to Iouri, beside his daughter. And I don't think she's a close second. If anything happened to me, I wanted you and Tyler to be alright.

"You stole it from him?!"

Even if he noticed it gone, I mean, he has thirteen banks around the world with multiple millions in each account."

Her heart fluttered with concern for their well-being. Fear rose up inside her. In her mind's eye, she saw three tombstones, each one engraved with one of their names.

"Even if he notices it's gone, it will be virtually impossible to connect the dots to us. Cliff is a computer genius," he reassured her.

"Okay," she said, softly, her nerves strung tighter than piano wire. She started to leave then slowed.

"Jose's girlfriend, Gigi, called, have you heard from him?"

"No."

"She hasn't seen him since he went out for a ride on his motorcycle."

"Sounds like he 'turned rabbit'."

"What?"

"That's what the Feds call skipping bail."

Sabrina left the room, not knowing what to say; but it was not okay with her. She respected Tom's desire to provide for them, but that did not make the situation right. The road to Hell is paved with good intentions. What a mess. I've just found out I'm a multi-millionaire and I'm furious about it. Tears trickled over her lashes and down her face. "God, how much trouble are we in?"

CHAPTER 55

"Safe house, sweet safe house," Mike exclaimed, as he and Iouri arrived back.

"You are a weird one," Iouri said.

"Look who's talking."

Iouri laughed as they grabbed their luggage and went inside. After four days of constant driving, both needed to take off their disguises and shower.

Greeting his two partners in crime, Iouri was especially interested in Petrov's progress. Petrov informed him he had made a practice attack on U.S. Title via UCLA and was successful. "Just say the word and I'm ready."

Iouri informed him that it would be two to three weeks before Frank at U.S. Title Company was ready, and reiterated that both jobs need to be done simultaneously.

Victor assumed it was safe now. The media attention had subsided, even though the number of Iouri sightings rivaled those of Elvis. Sightings were what the F.B.I. called eyewitness accounts from people claiming to have seen Iouri, Petrov, or Nikki. They ranged from Venice Beach to the psych ward at Bellevue Hospital in NYC, to South Africa, not to mention the space-probe landing near Sedona, Arizona. No day went by without sightings being reported somewhere.

Victor was getting pressure from his contact in New York. "Iouri, it's Victor," he said, quietly, as he paced outside his office.

"Think it is safe to call me?" Iouri asked, suspicious of Victor's motives.

"I had to." He did not have to; he merely wanted to placate his anxieties.

"Can I have the tape," Victor continued.

"I do not have the tape."

"What do you mean you do not have the tape?" Victor shrieked, then caught himself, peering around, making certain no one had heard him.

"I do not have the tape," Iouri repeated, emphatically. He did not know what Victor was up to, but was rapidly enjoying the conversation less and less.

"This is no time to be joking," Victor yelled, afraid he was about to have a heart attack.

"I do not joke!" Iouri hollered.

He has a point. Iouri was not known for his sense of humor.

"Then who has the tape?" Victor whined, envisioning himself writing checks to his ex-wives until he croaked.

"How should I know?" Iouri yelled. He was upset and almost disconnected the call.

"Who'd you give it to?" Victor asked, his voice raw, almost a whisper, as if unseen hands were choking him.

"I gave it to a guy in a blue suit with blond hair. Was that not your man?"

"Well, it was supposed to be," Victor muttered, perplexed. "It sounds like him." He was dumbfounded. "What was his name?" Victor asked; he felt as if his stomach was being clawed by the manicured nails of his five ex-wives.

"No names; that is one of the rules. Call your guy and find out what is going on," he snapped.

Ferociously, Victor interrogated Paulie Vitolo on the phone for fifteen minutes, until he was convinced Paulie did not have the tape, and still had not figured it out. Victor warned him if the tape showed up anywhere because of him, the repercussions to Paulie would be horrendous. Possibly fatal. No one double-crosses Victor Goldman.

Having missed too many days since his release, Tom decided he should work on his birthday. Late that day, he went home, saw Sabrina in the shower, preparing to go out. He had gone too long without a close encounter of the Honkas kind. He popped his head in and surprised her with a kiss. That was definitely a sight he had missed at MDC. Even after bearing Tyler, she looked stunning. They were going to his favorite Italian restaurant.

He breezed past the TV, when a news flash caught his eye: A Re/Max estate agent in her mid-fifties, who lived alone, was found in her home, murdered. Murders were not uncommon, unfortunately; but in upper-class Woodland Hills, execution-style with a nine-millimeter to the back of the head, that was uncommon.

She was identified as Melinda Schroeder. "Melinda Schroeder," Tom repeated. Apprehension flooded through his body. That was Iouri's real estate agent. He'd said he would seek revenge. Tom stared blankly at the TV screen. Boy, he didn't waste any time.

He began arguing with himself again - optimist vs. pessimist: It is possible she ripped someone else off. He knew that was just wishful thinking. His intuition told him Iouri had done it himself. Probably not. Iouri would not have ventured out of the safe house alone. Or would he?

"Honey, you ready?" Sabrina asked, interrupting his fixation. She wore a little black dress that renewed his faith in little black dresses. Parading a lustful amount of cleavage, she looked like an ebony-wrapped Aphrodite. Tom's heart skipped a beat. She was more alluring than when they had met six years ago.

"What're you watching?" she asked.

"The news." He thought he would tell her on the drive over; just not then. Maybe not at all. They said their goodbyes to Lisa and Tyler then went to celebrate Tom's birthday over dinner.

The next morning, Tom went for a run on the paved trail that encircled a small lake. His cell phone kept vibrating. After ignoring it for a quarter-mile, he stopped to check; he thought it might be Sabrina.

It was Mike. "I need to see you," he whispered.

"You know it's not safe."

Mike was obviously nervous or upset, very uncharacteristic of him.

"Are you alright?" Tom asked.

"I think so, but I'm not sure. I've got to see you." Tom knew it was not wise, but Mike was his brother and wouldn't ask unless it was absolutely necessary.

"Okay, where?"

"Um, how 'bout the McDonald's in Huntington Beach? It's close."

"I've got a better idea - more open and public - behind Ruby's on the Pier."

"What time?"

Tom glanced at his watch. "Eleven," he said, firmly.

"See ya' there."

Tom hurried in and informed Sabrina Mike had insisted on meeting him. Her face turned sour but she understood. Black despair joined hands with fear, but fear was way out in front.

"If you don't see me by 3:00, call the police," Tom told her as he left.

CHAPTER 56

Tom waited on the West side of Ruby's on the Pier. Mike scurried up from behind and startled him.

"Don't do that!" Tom said, reflexively. He did not recognize Mike through his disguise, although his eyes and voice were unmistakable. The disguise with its foam sponges altered the shape of his cheeks and nose, making him look heavier and fifteen years older.

"What's up?" Tom asked.

"I'm not sure."

Tom's eyes skimmed the Pier in sustained surveillance, in search of prying human eyes.

"A couple of days after we got back from New York, well, since then, the three of them have gotten cold. They don't talk to me anymore and their conversations are all in Russian. Not to mention, Iouri picked up a nine-millimeter in New York, with a silencer."

The connection to Melinda Schroeder was just made more certain. "You know his real estate agent was just found murdered, shot with a nine-millimeter to the back of the head. She had cheated Iouri out of $250,000 from the sale of his house," Tom told him. This was not making Mike feel any more comfortable.

"Damn him. I told Iouri, no guns, that you and I would have no part of any guns," Tom said.

"Yesterday they were pointing at the TV, talking in Russian. And the other night, I thought I heard one of them leave. I got up and looked around; it looked like everyone was still there."

"Are you sure Iouri was still there?"

"It looked like it. I mean, he looked like a cadaver under a morgue sheet."

Tom knew Iouri did sleep extremely still and quietly, with almost indiscernible breathing. He would even cover his face at times.

"Did you go close up to the bed?"

"Are you crazy?. He would wake up, shoot first and ask questions later."

"You're probably right."

Tom had to ask a question he thought he would never have to ask of any of his three brothers: "Do you think they're going to hurt you?" He just could not utter the word 'kill.'

"I don't know," Mike said, almost inaudibly.

That was not the answer Tom wanted. "What do you want to do?"

"It's only two or three weeks, tops, before they finish their job and go. If I leave now and go back to Chicago, they'll come after you, Sabrina, and the baby thinking we've jumped sides."

"You're probably right," Tom agreed. "So you'll hang?"

"I think I have to." Mike knew he was stuck between the proverbial rock and a hard place. "Things were much easier when we were younger," he mused, a troubled yearning in his voice.

"Don't get all sentimental on me now. Nostalgia is mostly just forgetting all the things that sucked."

They agreed that Mike would scrub the place, and not add any new fingerprints, be prepared to leave at a moment's notice and leave nothing behind. Most importantly, he would always leave his cell phone on, and they would check in with each other once a day.

On his way home, Tom decided he would play one of his cards. He drove to a pay phone in the Taco Bell parking lot near his apartment complex and dialed a number.

Victor looked at the caller ID: "Unknown." "God I hate answering this when I don't know who it is," he groaned.

"Victor Goldman."

"I have your tape," Tom said, matter-of-factly. There was a smug undertone to his voice.

"Who is this?"

"Relax," Tom said. "You'll recognize my voice in a moment"

Victor was desperately trying to decipher who it was; he prayed it was not a prank. He did not need a premature coronary.

"Your client came back from New York with a gun. Make sure nothing happens to my brother or me or my family and you'll get your tape. Besides, I want to watch it on T.V. myself."

As soon as Tom said "New York," and "brother," Victor knew who it was.

"Tom? How did you…"

"Never mind; it's not important."

"What do you want?"

"Nothing. As in nothing happens to my family or me. You'll get your precious tape when the Russians leave the country. So I suggest you have a talk with your client.

CHAPTER 57

"What are you doing?" Iouri asked Mike.

"A little housework."

"You? Why?" Mike did not strike him as neat or tidy.

"Listen," Mike said in a huff. "When you guys leave the country in a few weeks, I'll still be here; and if anything goes wrong, my prints are in the system. Red flags would fly everywhere and I'd be gone for a long time while you're drinking your wine on your yacht in the south of France.

Obviously, Tom told him some of my plans. Satisfied with Mike's answer, Iouri sauntered away. Mike was peeved at the tension since returning from New York. He did not do tension well to start with. He felt his every move was being scrutinized and that he had done nothing to warrant it. House-sitting the Russian Mafia had lost its luster. Mike was disenchanted and couldn't wait for them to leave.

The four of them had grown restless, for there was not much to do until Frank at National Title was ready. In a holding pattern, they felt like planes backed up in a snowstorm.

Characteristically the most disciplined, Iouri was downright miserable. He loved the Southern California weather and loathed being cooped with so little to do. Even at MDC he had a weight set to pass the time. Against the vehement warnings of his partners, he decided to go for a walk. They could not stop him. Changing Iouri's mind on almost anything was a formidable task. Unwittingly, even the cleverest criminals can make the most elementary mistakes. With his facial mask and sunglasses, Iouri set out for a stroll. Shaking his head as he left, Petrov mumbled, "a brilliant man with a dangerous ego."

Iouri was amused by the sameness of the cookie-cutter homes in the nondescript, upper-middle class neighborhood. The uniformity was mind-numbing. Nonetheless, it was a splendid day and he was glad to be out - out of MDC, and soon to be out of the country. Strolling along, he was reminded of another reason he loved Southern California: gorgeous women. Gorgeous, blonde women. He was overcome with a thirst like he experienced when he first saw Marina at the Parisian fashion show.

Poised conspicuously in front of her home, thumbing through her mail, a golden goddess stopped him cold. Debbie Cody was taking a break from tanning, her daily routine after her husband went to work. John Cody was a successful entrepreneur; he owned Luke's, an exclusive restaurant down by the Huntington Beach Pier. Tourists came from all around to dine there.

Iouri was mesmerized. She was the epitome of female sexuality, perfection of line and form, the dream made real. Exquisitely sculpted face, tanned, bare legs and taut thighs. Statuesque, a tight T-shirt clinging to her full breasts. He could see her nipples through the thin cotton.

Iouri slid his sunglasses down his nose to soak in the sight. Debbie was used to being gawked at and was happily married; but something about this man she found fascinating.

She convinced herself it wouldn't hurt to say "hi". Toting a handful of mail and her cell phone, she strutted down the driveway.

"New in town?' she asked, demurely, a smile in her sparkling green eyes.

"No, just visiting a friend down the street who might be making a move here," Iouri replied.

"My name's Debbie," she said, then reached to shake Iouri's hand, taken aback at her own bravado.

"John," Iouri said, trying to disguise his Russian accent. On a good day, he could almost sound British.

"John, that's my husband's name."

Their eyes locked. Absolutely stunning erotic picture of beauty, Iouri thought. He's so handsome, Debbie thought; but that's not it. It was his eyes. They were tunnels of pure, laser-like energy. The way he stared at her made her feel naked.

"He must be a good guy," Iouri said.

"Who?"

"John. Your husband."

"Oh yes, I'm sorry, I was distracted."

That is what they usually say. His ego was in full bloom on that spring day. Her cell phone rang, snagging her attention. She scanned the caller ID. "Excuse me, John; I'm going to take this." For reasons she could not acknowledge, she felt disturbed, spooked, entranced by Iouri's eyes.

"Good day," Iouri said in his best British, then sauntered away.

"Good to meet you, John."

"Debbie?" the tearful phone voice cried.

"Hi Lucy," Debbie said, sighing.

Debbie's friend, Lucy Winnefeld, recently discovered that her husband had been unfaithful; she was trying to decide whether to divorce or attempt marriage counseling. She called Debbie every day after John went to work. Debbie's heart went out to Lucy for her hurt, but the daily whimpering had become annoyingly monotonous, so she changed the subject.

"I want to tell you something," Debbie said, in a titillating tone. "I was checking the mail and this awesome-looking guy came along. And I said 'hi'."

"You're not thinking of...?"

"No, no. Never. It's not like, about that," she said pinpointing her thoughts. "He had these eyes." She was struggling with describing the experience. He had this look, I mean, I felt like I was in a Superman movie and he was looking right through me.

"Wow. Was it exciting or spooky?"

"I'm not sure; but I'll never forget that look."

CHAPTER 58

Linda Steelburg was fifty-one, looked seventy, but her kind demeanor gave her a homely quality. "Oh my God," she said, horrified, as she watched TV. Five bodies were found yesterday in Yosemite National Park. One of them was identified as Fedor Andreev, CEO of Radio International, her former employer. She had been his executive assistant for five years. After he disappeared, the company was sold; six months later, they let her go. She had lost a good job and a good friend.

The primary suspects were the Russian fugitives who escaped from MDC LA on Easter Sunday. The news was on every network, radio station, and cable channel. Pictures of Iouri Malakov, Petrov Kuvayev, and Nikki Stolov were broadcast worldwide. Unflattering portraits were pasted at record speed throughout America's post offices.

It was Saturday morning, and Linda was getting ready to visit her husband, Earl, at MDC. She visited him as often as possible, alternating weekends. She was certain the report would be the gossip circulating through MDC.

"You can do it. You can do it." Tom rallied himself, finally getting his wind back after being confined, and unable to run because of the stent. "Five miles! Yes! I haven't been able to do that for at least a year, he reminded himself, unaware it might have been his last run. Opening the apartment door, he saw Sabrina sitting at the kitchen table, her face drained of all color.

"I've been waiting for you to get back." Fear hung like a fog around her words.

"What's up?"

"They found five bodies in a lake or reservoir or something, in Yellowstone, Um, not Yellowstone, Yosemite National Park

"Yikes," Tom responded, still not comprehending the consequences or the connection.

"They think it's the guys," Sabrina said sadly.

"What guys?"

"The Russians! Pictures of Iouri, Petrov and Nikki are everywhere."

The truth was sinking in. Tom felt like he'd been struck by a cement truck. He turned white. He felt his spirits fail in the face of such monumental madness, as though his insides had been hollowed out.

"So they are killers."

Shame and anguish, a venomous, crippling mix, rose up in him, coursing through his veins. He had taken everyone down the Yellow Brick Road and straight to Hell.

"I'm scared. I'm really, really scared. Tom, we're not safe, what're we going to do?" Tears flowed as she became increasingly hysterical.

It took a while to calm her down to the point that he could talk to her. He explained that the package Cliff dropped off was the video of the escape, that he had intercepted it, knowing how bad Victor needed it; also knowing Iouri's respect for Victor and that Victor was probably disloyal enough to disclose the safe house. Tom felt he had enough leverage to keep everyone safe until they were gone.

Sabrina quieted down, but still was trembling. Tom's news was little solace.

She had always admired his resourcefulness, but this predicament, she felt, was way beyond him.

"How the hell did they find those bodies?" Iouri roared. "Who told them? No one knew where they were? Even Alejandra did not know. Did she?" Iouri considered himself iron-willed in a crisis, but his plans were crumbling. The whole world was looking for them. This time, they would not stop until they were found. The only place they would be safe would be in Russia. They had to make a break for Belize via Mexico and charter a jet. Fast.

CHAPTER 59

Saturday evenings, Debbie and John usually took in a movie or a play. But tonight, John was staying late at Luke's. Debbie was bored so she turned on the TV. and a voice announced, "America's Most Wanted." Uninterested, she gazed at the screen with unseeing eyes, reliving her last conversation with Lucy; the whining made her shudder. The TV flashed the pictures of the three Russians alleged to have murdered the five, whose bodies were found in Yosemite National Park. When they displayed Iouri's picture, Debbie was mesmerized. It riveted her. Flustered, she gasped, "those eyes; I mean, that look. It's him!"

Unexpectedly, Lucy had padded in. "Who are you talking to, and what look?" she asked. Iouri's picture filled the 84" big screen. He looked magisterial, bigger than life, even in an enlarged mug shot. In the photo, he had no facial hair, but she knew he was the man she had flirted with in front of her house.

"That's him!" Debbie said again.

"Who's him?" Lucy asked, still baffled by Debbie's insistence. Debbie grabbed the phone and dialed 1-800-CRIME-TV, the AMW hotline. Finally it sank in and Lucy asked, "Are you sure it's him?"

"Positive."

"Deb, I'm home," John called as he entered. A dark-haired, rather handsome man, with a deep forehead; when he slicked his hair back, he looked like a dashing daytime soap opera doctor.

"Hey, John, did Debbie tell you she's been flirting with a killer in the neighborhood?" Lucy announced. Debbie shot her a look.

"You didn't tell me you had company," John said.

"It was nothing. I was checking the mail and he was walking by," Debbie told him. She said nothing about calling America's Most Wanted.

"Where did he come from?"

"He's staying with a friend down at 1007 or 1014."

"But a killer in this neighborhood? Isn't that a little far-fetched?"

"You're probably right," the women said in tandem, but both knew Debbie was certain Iouri was the man she had met.

"You two talk," John suggested, "It's been a long day. I'm going for my walk."

It was not out of the ordinary for John to go for a stroll after work; but it was unusual for him to feel jealous. He felt himself being drawn down the street towards this mystery man, the stranger with the "look."

CHAPTER 60

Tom was looping his tie when he noticed his cell phone crawling across the dresser. Sabrina and he had decided to take in dinner and a movie to alleviate their preoccupation with the news. He answered the phone without checking the caller ID. "*You need to come now,*" the angry voice commanded. It was Iouri, the last person Tom expected.

"You know it is not safe, we must leave."

Stunned, Tom stammered, "Let me talk to Sabrina. We've got plans."

"You want your money or not!?" Iouri snarled.

"Of course," Tom said feebly. He now knew they were killers, and if he refused to pick up his money, Iouri would be suspicious. Then they certainly would liquidate Mike. Tom trembled with other fears: Had he discovered the ten million missing? Did he think it was him? Would he come after Sabrina and Tyler? The room began to spin.

"You have fifteen minutes," then the call was disconnected.

Tom sat down onto the bed; fighting to maintain his equilibrium. He explained to Sabrina what had happened.

"We have to go to the police," she insisted.

"We can't. The police aren't entirely stupid; it would be impossible to go to them without incriminating me and Mike; and who's to say it wouldn't create a deadly hostage situation."

"But what about you?" she cried. Her tone ripped at his heart.

"I won't be responsible for my brother's murder."

He dialed Victor. Sabrina continued to weep. "But what about you?" she cried, in barely-controlled hysteria.

Victor had had plans to go to the opera, but had said, "I'll meet you on the moon for that tape."

Tom tried to convince and console Sabrina that, as long as he had the tape, they were safe. Regardless, he was not going to let them kill his brother without trying to help. Her heart palpitated erratically.

"I'll change the reservation and we'll go later. When I come back," Tom said as he left.

"If you come back."

As the door closed behind him, the only sound was her sobbing, full-throated and ragged, as she whimpered, "Goodbye, my darling."

CHAPTER 61

Angry that he would not be able to retire in sybaritic fashion, as planned, Iouri tried to pacify himself by paying homage to the money he still had. Checking his global accounts via the Internet, he found ten million missing. The only person who had access to that information was Tom. But how the fuck did he do it? Iouri was flabbergasted. I don't care how he did it. "Now I will absolutely kill him!" Iouri snarled, hot with rage. The only thing that genuinely infuriated him was being ripped-off. "No one gets over on Iouri Malakov."

Victor consulted the internet to find the best route to the safe house in Huntington Beach. It was a forty-five minute drive. He bolted from his house, an enormous grin glued to his face, as if he had just found out that one of his ex-wives had croaked. "I'm going to get my tape. I'm going to get my tape," he sang, as he jumped into his Mercedes-Benz and raced off.

John Cody strolled up the block. He felt silly for wanting to check out this mystery man, this alleged killer. Foolish with a capital 'F', he thought, as he walked. 1014 Via Amarilla had no lights on, but, at 1007, he could see from an oblique angle that it appeared to have a light on in the kitchen.

He stopped. Stared. Thought better of it and kept walking.

Iouri paced near the tiled center island with its colored stove top. He halted. The decision was final. Regardless of the missing money; Tom and Mike were liabilities and needed to be dealt with. They knew way too much. They even knew the escape route through Belize.

The others do not need to know, he thought. Nikki would not care, but Petrov might. No, he will care. He likes people and is not a killer. Iouri resumed pacing. This way, I will be able to keep Tom's half-millions. He reminded himself.

Going 75 mph, Tom swooped down a steep grade, anxiously punching redial to reach Mike. Still no answer. He kept thinking Mike was dead. Part of him felt naked, walking into a lion's lair. If he had been thinking straight, he would have stopped and turned around. Maybe Sabrina was right. But, inexplicably, driving faster and faster, he felt drawn to the safe house.

Flashing red lights suddenly flooded his rear view mirror. Cold-blooded lights of catastrophe. "Shit, this is all I need," he said out loud.

He pulled over to the shoulder, waiting for the officer to appear. Continuing to study his mirror, he noticed the squad car was unmarked and the officer still had not exited his vehicle. He tried to reach Mike. Still no answer. That did not help. He tried to quell his nerves, so he would appear calm when the officer came to his window.

A second squad car pulled up behind the first. "This is not good," Tom mumbled. His mind ran rampant with a myriad of horrible possibilities. Did Sabrina call the cops? Am I wanted for questioning because I was Iouri's cellie? What could it be? What? He was goading himself into a frenzy.

The second squad, also unmarked, drove away. The first officer ambled up to the window and Tom handed him his license and registration. He was angry with himself because that section of Tollway through Newport Beach was a known speed trap.

"C.H.P.," Tom observed, "Well, at least it's not the F.B.I."

Refreshingly the officer was pleasant, and apologized for keeping Tom waiting. The force was busy and shorthanded that day; his supervisor had asked him to work a double-shift, so his partner had brought him a sandwich. Tom smiled at the explanation. Not desiring a ticket, he laid on the charm with a shovel, telling the officer he was on his way to the Huntington

Beach Memorial, that his brother had been in an accident. He prayed God would not strike him dead for lying. It worked. Feeling sympathetic, the officer let him go with a warning.

"Must be the tie," Tom said, trying to lighten up. As he drove, he kept dialing Mike's phone, but still no answer. He prayed that the story he told the officer would not prove to be prophetic. He tried Victor's phone, to inform him he was running late. No answer there either. The emotional momentum was sweeping him along like a riptide. This does not feel right.

John Cody decided to extend his walk. As he sauntered, his mind was suffused with amorous thoughts. His walk had invigorated him, so he decided that tonight would be a good night to make love to his wife. It would also quell the green-eyed monster inside him.

His pace quickened. Entering his street, he approached the 1007 residence and noticed that the light was still on in the kitchen. His judgment still overwhelmed by curiosity and jealousy, he headed up the driveway; he wanted to meet this mystery man with the entrancing look. Oddly enough, for all his eloquence, he did not have a clue what he was going to say if he did meet him. But he kept walking, mysteriously drawn to the backyard. There he found a waterfall with a mesmerizing purl flowing into the pool, something he had been planning to build at his own place.

Seeing a shadow move in the kitchen, he decided to ask the owner who put this in. Standing erect, he brushed off his slacks and scanned the back door. The shadow seemed to see him, then disappeared straight down, as if it had squatted. A red pin light flitted across the screen. Strange. But he still was drawn toward the back door.

Victor's Mercedes crept down Via Amarilla. "Here it is. 1007. French-villa looking; touch of Paris. I bet Iouri liked that." He glanced at his Rolex surprised he had arrived before Tom. Should be any moment. He sat for a few minutes, ruminating about the video, how the tension had already mounted at the B.O.P. and how he soon will end his hemorrhaging cash situation.

Where is he? He glanced at his watch again. I think I'll go inside and say farewell to Iouri. From the angle he had parked, he could see someone walking around back. Probably Mike. Those three know better than to be hanging around outside. He took two steps, then eyed an Explorer racing towards him. Must be Tom. He stopped and waited. It passed him as he headed for the house.

Since time was tight, Iouri decided to dispense with any formalities when Tom arrived. Besides, he did not care to hear Tom pleading for his life or his brother's life. How pitiful that would be. He should know that when you play with fire you might get burned.

Petrov was occupied with some new software Mike had purchased, and Nikki was engulfed in a soft porn program on cable TV. A surprise attack was the simplest, so Iouri had crouched down behind the island in the kitchen. The Browning nine-millimeter with its Teflon finish, felt cool in his hand. He caressed it like a lover. It was the key to his kingdom: his continued freedom. The bullets were soft slugs, used by the Secret Service to do maximum damage to the victim, and minimize the damage of exiting and harming innocent bystanders. If he had enlisted Nikki for this job he probably would have used the Kalashnikov, massacring a few neighbors in the process. The more dead bodies, the merrier.

Iouri had a peculiar sense of wielding absolute power, the power of death Itself; but in reality it was just business. So nothing personal, Tom. Looking at the clock, he calculated Tom should arrive shortly. Crouched and rigidly poised, he felt like he was back in Russia in a military exercise.

Turning off the light, his steely blue eyes glowed with murderous intention.

Looping the 405 Freeway exit ramp onto Beach Blvd. Tom was riddled with anxiety, as he kept tried to reach Mike. He was terrified. Infesting his mind was the vision of Mike, shot dead by a nine-millimeter; and it would be entirely his fault. He did not even consider that he might be next. He could not think straight. He tried talking to his Mom to calm his nerves.

"Listen, Mom, if you have any connections up there, please let Mikey be okay," he said as he closed in on his destination.

"Boy, that's hot," Mike said, as Leeza handed him the pizza and his change.

Pizza D' Oro's was a local gourmet Italian food joint.

"You look nice," Leeza said. "I usually only see your brother in a suit."

Mike beamed. It was not every day he was complimented on his appearance.

"What's the occasion?"

"Belated birthday for Tom," was all he could think of.

Iouri had told Mike that Tom was coming over, so Mike thought he would surprise Tom with his favorite pizza. Tom and Mike LOVED pizza. Anytime. Anyplace. Afterward, he intended for them to go out and celebrate that their escapade was over. Mike drove away from Pizza D'Oro, inhaling the scrumptious smells, unaware that he might never get to eat that pizza.

CHAPTER 62

Approaching the back door, there was an eerie calm. He stopped, thinking he heard other footsteps. Nothing. He swung open the back door and padded in two steps. It was dark. Before he could say anything, Iouri leapt up. His shots were perfect, as if he was walking a combat shoot with jump-up cardboard targets. The ejected brass cartridges went tink-clink-tink across the tiled floor.

The body was thrown violently backwards into the screen door, as if hit by a speeding train; a tie went flying like a dead bird. The head took the full blast of the first shot and burst open. After the second shot, the body fell in a loose tangle of limbs and was completely still.

Iouri flipped on the light. The head, or what was left of it, looked like an aborted fetus. The blood was squelched on the floor. For a moment, Iouri still did not know who it was; then the realization set in.

Hearing the scuffle; Nikki and Petrov dashed in and bumped into each other in the kitchen doorway. Dumbstruck, they peered at each other.

Why did he kill Mike? Petrov wondered.

Why did he kill Tom? Nikki thought. And why didn't he let me do it?

For Nikki, murder was an almost religious experience.

Tom jerked the wheel severely left onto Via Amarilla, stopping abruptly just short of the yellow tape. He squinted to read the black lettering, even though he knew what it said: "Police Line. Do Not Cross." The whole block was cordoned off, in a melee of flashing lights. He saw a black Mercedes and a black SUV across from the safe house, parked down about fifty yards. There was a proliferation of police vehicles, a veritable alphabet soup of law enforcement agencies.

His heart began to heave. The safe house was still. But the area surrounding it looked like a scene from a Hollywood action movie. The media was there in full force. The motorized clicks of a hundred cameras sounded like crickets.

He focused on one particular vehicle; it was red and white, an ambulance, the word "Mortuary" on the door. Two grim-looking paramedics were transporting a stretcher down the driveway a sheet draped over the body. A crowd of onlookers appeared to be consoling a gorgeous blonde, who was hysterical.

The true horror of the scene drained the color from Tom's face. Grief-stricken, his face fell into his hands and he wept uncontrollably. "What have I done!?" He was having trouble breathing. Mike was dead. "I can never face my family again. Mom, I'm so sorry." He let out a bloodcurdling scream, in a fit of rage and despair. Pounding the dashboard, he left knuckle impressions with each smashing blow. He began rocking to and fro, like a little boy who just discovered his dog had been run over. The punishing pounding noise persisted. Was it his heart? No, the sound was too loud. Looking through his window, he knew he had gone crazy. He was seeing things. A mirage. A ghost. It was Mike, hammering on the glass. Tom gawked at him, as if he'd returned from the dead. In shock, he rolled down his window, never happier to see his brother.

He tried to speak. "Spit it out!" Mike said.

"Where the Hell were you?" Tom sputtered.

"Went to get pizza. Want some?"

"Where's your cell phone!?" Tom snapped.

"Right here," Mike said, displaying a cell phone that was turned off. "Oops, um, I guess it was off."

"Asshole!"

"Did you see...?"

"Yeah, I saw the ambulance when I pulled up behind you."

"Who was that?" Tom asked.

Just then, the three Russians, Iouri, Petrov, and Nikki were marshaled out by F.B.I. agents, handcuffed and shackled. Nikki let out a roar of rage that sounded inhuman. Petrov looked like he was going to cry. At first glance, Iouri's demeanor seemed undaunted. But a closer look showed a man who had sailed through life in first class, only to find out the cruise had gone nowhere. Another pack of field agents encircled them, armed with machine guns. S.W.A.T. team sharpshooters were positioned throughout the street and on rooftops. They were not getting away this time.

EPILOGUE

Two months later, the Dreamseeker sailed out of the Port of Monaco. Cruising past the crowd of onlookers, the palatial yacht steamed out into the Mediterranean.

Cliff Searcy was explaining some of the more pertinent details to Sabrina: "So when I was securing your future and Tyler's, as Tom likes to call it…"

"You mean, as you were stealing Iouri's money," Sabrina suggested. She was still wrestling with their having this newly acquired wealth.

"Well, can you really purloin stolen money?" Cliff replied. "Anyway, as I was sitting at the computer, I stumbled across the title information at the Bank of Cyprus, they're the guys who underwrote the purchase. I almost switched it the first time. But after they were arrested, I went back and put Tom's name on the title."

"Thanks, Cliff, but even for someone with my goals, this is all too much," Tom interjected.

"Well, Iouri's never going to use it again, that's for sure. Besides, Myn and I can use it when we'd like, right?" Cliff said with a smirk.

"So, the real reason comes out," Tom replied, thumping him. "Of course you can."

The Dreamseeker was the epitome of quality and extravagance. 139 feet with five staterooms, exquisite oil paintings, lush fabrics, and custom lighting. Among those on board were Tom's father, his stepmother, Mike and his girlfriend, Queenie, his sister Sherry, his brother, Gene, and his wife Sylvia. Of course Tommy and Samantha were there, too.

Tom was compelled to invite Sabrina's best friend, his nemesis, Joy Cafferty. Joy looked Tom's way. Their gazes collided with the force of trains crashing head-on.

"So what happened when the F.B.I. called you in?" Tom's brother, Gene, inquired.

"They interrogated me for four hours, which felt like four days, but I told them I didn't know anything." Gene rolled his eyes. He did not know anything, but had his suspicions. "Before they let me go, they said they'd be watching me. I think what really saved me was they seemed ecstatic that Iouri had shot his own attorney. I guess the Feds and Victor had been at odds for years."

"You were very lucky, little brother; you dodged a big bullet," Gene said as he ambled away.

Tom turned around and surveyed the vast Mediterranean Sea, trying to shake off this eerie feeling. Privately, he was feeling very smug about his new-found wealth and what he had pulled off. Life was good again. He was master of his own universe now. Invincible. He already had forgotten that many people, including him and his wife and child could have been killed. And he was blithely unaware of the ones that were dead. He continued gazing. The more he soaked up the blue water and golden sunshine, the more he felt bigger than Life. Steel-coated. Untouchable.

"*What's that?*" he said to himself spotting something peculiar in the water.

Strange. It looks like a body. He wiped his face to make sure it was not an illusion. It was still there. Floating face down, it had on a torn suit wrapped with a tattered rope around the waist, as if it had been weighted down. Mesmerized, his eyes were riveted to it, when a sudden wave flipped the body over. Gasping, Tom put his hand over his chest; he thought his heart had stopped. It was thumping like a steam engine. He let out a silent shriek. His eyes burned red from not blinking. Frozen.

The body, vision, illusion, mirage, whatever it was; looked like: Tom! He broke out in a cold sweat. Suddenly, the water began to bubble, as though an underwater volcano had erupted. Then a voice gurgled, "Who are you? What are you? What have you become? Then, the body flipped over and faded away, as it sank into the murky depths of the Mediterranean Sea.

In his prison cell, Iouri works on a detailed blueprint of the prison, all the exit points and routes clearly marked. A Corrections Officer stops by. Iouri hands him an envelope full of cash. They smile.